SPY STORY

James Burke

St. Martin's Press • New York

Design by Holly Block

Library of Congress Cataloging-in-Publication Data

Burke, James.
    Spy story / James Burke.
      p.   cm.
    "A Thomas Dunne book."
    ISBN 0-312-02985-3
    I. Title.
PS3552.U72325S6   1989   89-4179
813'.54—dc19   CIP

First Edition

10 9 8 7 6 5 4 3 2 1

This book is dedicated to my wife, Alvina, whose unflagging support and loyalty make it all possible.

PROLOGUE

It was 7:13 P.M. It had been 7:09 and over a mile away when the two Zhigulis had first pulled out of the anonymity of traffic and casually tried to box him in. He had evaded, and now all pretense was finished. Four minutes down, two to go. The frequency will not be monitored until 7:15. Of course he could automatically activate *their* automatic system, but too many things could go wrong, and this final time he couldn't chance it.

Borodin smiled grimly. They knew who he was, those hoods in the Zhigulis, but maybe, just maybe, they did not understand the importance of 7:15. They hadn't made a serious effort to box him again, seeming content to stay fifty or sixty meters behind and let him run. Maybe they didn't realize that his objective was the American Chancery. He *had* actually been heading away from it when they tried to take him. His earlier, spirit-sapping conclusion that they must know his goal, and had alerted the guard posts and the rest of the newly revamped security system in the area, now gave way to a glimmer of hope.

He made a wide left turn at a large intersection, hit his brakes hard in midturn, sluing the car's back end around, and then came down hard on the accelerator, hurtling back at his pursuers with frightening speed and noise. He passed their startled faces before they could maneuver into their practiced roadblock positions. Thank God for the paucity of vehicles on the street this rainy evening! A miserable night for his last one on earth. "Crummy," as his American friend Johnson would say. Fitting, thought Borodin to himself.

Seven-fourteen and still four blocks away. By now the Zhigulis had to know his destination; what he didn't know was what they would or could do about it. He'd gained space but lost time with that U-turn. He took a left, one block, then another, pleased to see that the Zhigulis were still behind him, gaining but not yet dangerously close. At least they hadn't cut away to head for the Chancery. It was exactly 7:15 as he approached the guard post, starting to slow down as the guard watched casually from under the sheltered post. He saw the guard start as he looked beyond his car toward the noisy, speeding Zhigulis, and at that instant Borodin's car crashed the fragile cross bar and then pulled to a stop in line with the right side of the Chancery building.

The eye on the front of Borodin's small transmitter glowed red as he pushed the Send button. The burst lasted three seconds, the light went out, and he immediately pushed the auto-erase. As he put the L pill in his mouth and bit down hard, he pushed the destruct button on the transmitter and dropped the tiny "box" onto the floor of the backseat. The Zhigulis had already screeched to a stop, and men erupted from the open doors and raced toward his car. The muffled explosion as the transmitter blew up slowed them only for an instant, but it was already too late: Borodin felt the sharp pains as the poison spread quickly through his system. In a few seconds he would be beyond the reach of Globitsyn's torturers forever. The screaming men were beating at the car's windows with gun butts as Borodin died. It was 7:16 P.M., Moscow time.

SPY STORY

ONE

NEW DELHI, INDIA

Telchoff wiped his brow but it was a losing proposition. It was the hottest day of the late summer, and the groaning air conditioner was no match for the heat that even in late afternoon shimmered in waves from the sky to the streets with breath-stopping intensity. Besides, the signal he'd just read was in no way conducive to staying cool. Not unexpected, to be sure, but nevertheless unnerving. It was just as Ivanova had told him: a low-key recall for "consultation." Even the timing, on the face of it very short, was tempered by the moderating words "if possible." All in all, certainly not an alarming communication; that is, if one didn't know what kind of man Globitsyn is.

His intercom buzzed. Telchoff picked it up. "Comrade Mahotin wishes to see you."

He grunted assent, and almost before he could replace the instrument, the door opened and Arkadiy Mahotin's pudgy form burst in. Telchoff watched, amused, as the man moved quickly and effortlessly across the carpeted floor and slipped gracefully into the large leather chair facing the desk. Telchoff mused: remarkable how a person so gross could move so fluidly, so lightly on his feet, his very small feet. He still looks like a fatter, younger Georgiy Malenkov. Maybe that was it. Perhaps he was Malenkov's bastard. That could be why he's so high so young. That, and of course his constant and sycophantic pursuit of Globitsyn's favor.

"Comrade! I understand you are returning home for consultation." Mahotin closed his tiny eyes in affected rapture. "How I envy you—getting out of this damned heat into the Moscow fall. When will you leave?"

Telchoff answered without hesitation. "I plan to take the Monday flight, Comrade. I won't get much sleep but I'll be in the General's office as requested, Tuesday morning."

Mahotin's tone showed no surprise, but his eyes belied the casualness of his answer. "Oh, I thought you might go tomorrow." He hesitated, apparently realizing that he might be coming on a bit anxiously, and then his face relaxed into what became a conspiratorial leer, lacking only the wink. "I mean, the weekend in Moscow, you know, real women—white, with meat on their bones—and not this stinking, dirty, oven of a place."

Telchoff smiled knowingly, then let himself look a little sad. "Yes, Comrade, I know. It would be delightful; but I have this hunting trip planned—business, of course—and, not that I couldn't get out of it, but you know. . . ." He let his voice trail off.

Mahotin sat unmoving, his pig eyes fixed unwaveringly on Telchoff's face.

"Oh, business? I see. Of course, Comrade, that must come first, still . . ."

Telchoff winked. "I should know better than to attempt to fool you, Comrade. It is my good friend the Indian signals colonel, Ghasavi. I hope to put the clamp on him this weekend." He smiled. "To land the fish while we hunt, so to speak."

The fat face nodded and returned Telchoff's smile. "Aha, my friend, now I do see! It would be nice to arrive in Moscow with such a triumph in hand. Yes, of course, the recruitment of a new and important agent would be a fine present for the General. Very good." He did leer this time, complete with the wink. "Your attention to duty is indeed admirable, Comrade, as is your prudence. Is the good colonel ready to take the bait? I'm sorry, Comrade, of course he is, or you wouldn't be offering it."

Telchoff answered with a straight, serious face. "Thank you for the compliment, Comrade. I *think* he's ready, but one never knows, does one? Anyway, I believe it's worth a try, and so I had set up this hunt to get him alone—giving me a whole weekend to select, as the Indians say, the most auspicious moment, for my proposal."

"You are leaving when?"

"Very shortly. That is, I'll be leaving here very shortly. I'll set out for Chandigar sometime after dark." He sighed. "There are times, Comrade, when I envy the capitalists their air-conditioned cars."

"How true. And you will return when?"

"Probably late Sunday evening or early Monday morning. I will be in to the office Monday and leave from here for the airport."

"Very good. Anything I can do to assist your preparations, please do not hesitate to ask."

"Thank you, Comrade, but everything is in good order. I'll just be packing for a week or so. I'm sure the General and his people do not have the time to be consulting with me for too long."

They both laughed, then Mahotin's tiny eyes became even craftier-looking. "Yes, yes, Comrade. I'm sure it's the same old routine. They feel we must see them—and of course, they us— every so often to make sure we're all the same persons who sign the signals back and forth." He laughed loudly, then stood up and offered Telchoff his hand. "I'll be most anxious to hear the news of your hunting trip. Give me a ring when you return."

"But of course, Comrade."

Mahotin left the room as quickly and smoothly as he had entered. Telchoff sat, drumming his fingers slowly on the almost bare desktop. The fat bastard of Malenkov certainly didn't waste any time. Oh well, the signal was routine "personnel classified," as it should have been, so it would have made the daily reading board; not that that would have been a bar to Mahotin anyway—he'd have seen it regardless. He had the communications people scared and cooperative. Damn! Telchoff didn't have time to sit around worrying about Mahotin. He had to plan.

He had known for years that sooner or later Globitsyn would have him on an eastbound cattle car out of Moscow, if not in one of those unmarked graves out in the dark forests along the Saminka. He had always made a point of keeping as much space as possible between them, but he'd known the man's arm, and his memory, were too long. Now at last it was a fact. Globitsyn was ready to repay all the defeats, the real and imagined slights, and then later, insubordinations, and most of all, of course, the matter of 'Talia Voroskaya, now Globitsyn's wife, and once, very long ago, Telchoff's mistress.

Telchoff's orderly mind and nervous hands began to make an asset and liability list on a scratch pad. Asset: it was apparent that Globitsyn did not know that Ivanova had warned him. If he had, there would be no signal, just a goon squad. It was possible, but not probable that Globitsyn did not know about him and Ivanova. . . . No, not even practical. Of course Globitsyn knew! More likely that Globitsyn just wrote it off, as everyone else did. It had been a long time ago, and Ivanova had been married to the pilot—happily—for three years now. Besides, Globitsyn didn't (or *most probably* didn't) know about Ivanova's insatiable curiosity and her many informers, including his own personal and confidential assistant. He'd have chopped that long ago had he even suspected.

Another asset: time and distance. It was Friday afternoon in Delhi and Globitsyn expected him in Dzerzhinsky Tuesday morning. This, coupled with Globitsyn's ego, might just add up to a big asset. Telchoff reasoned that Globitsyn would be so sure he'd deceived him with that routine, unexciting consultation request that he hadn't considered the goon squad, alerted the Ambassador, or used any of the other usual and available safeguards. Correction, he thought, there is *as yet no indication* that he had! Anyway, no need to panic on the time factor. He had maneuvering time as well as room.

Asset: preparation. This was the touchy one. Even though he'd been concerned with it for months, Telchoff had still not admitted to himself exactly what he was preparing for or why. He just couldn't bring himself to say the word. Anyway, he had been considering his options and taking steps accordingly ever since Ivanova's first ripple of warning. . . . Ivanova! He smiled to himself, thinking, At least I handled that business right. He'd been more surprised than hurt when Ivanova had told him she was marrying the pilot. Their own, once torrid, romance had pretty well run its course by then, although they still lived together whenever he was in Moscow. But he had assumed the "older brother" role, even assisting with the wedding preparations, and Ivanova—funny, she'd never let him call her by her given name, Mariya; thought it was "too intimate." Anyway, she and her moonstruck pilot, a cosmonaut as of six months ago, really seemed to appreciate it. Telchoff had assumed at the time that Ivanova had feared he'd be sticky about the breakup and the marriage, and was grateful.

So when he was about to leave for New Delhi (the pilot had been out somewhere on maneuvers), it had seemed natural that she'd slipped back into his apartment and bed for that last weekend; and natural again that, knowing both her proclivities and capabilities, he'd asked her to keep him posted on Globitsyn's maneuverings. Ivanova, tearful with emotion (she'd confided her disappointment with the pilot, who flew aircraft much better than he made love), had promised solemnly and agreed. They had chosen a simple coded correspondence, and then she had managed it by means of an extra figure sheet on the Residentura monthly audit that came over her desk as a matter of course. Ivanova, as his American friends would say, was "something else."

The best part was that Ivanova and Globitsyn's assistant worked on the same floor, came from the same area, near Kiev, and were natural friends. Ivanova pumped that girl dry about twice a month, and if Globitsyn had had an odd bowel movement the girl not only knew about it, but would describe it in detail. Of course Ivanova was a loyal Soviet citizen and had agreed only to report on material pertinent to Telchoff's safety, but that inevitably expanded to include the whole spectrum of news from Globitsyn's office.

Telchoff leaned back in his chair, smiling. Back to the asset business. Yes, we were on the matter of timing. He began to question himself. Why is the timing important? Why did you dream up that hunting trip with Ghasavi? Why don't you face the facts? You've known for months that you were never going back to Moscow, to Mother Russia, to Globitsyn's long knife. Never! Still can't say that word, can you? Try it. Uh, 'defection'! That's it. You said it. You said it. Say it again—'defection'! Right, That's it. You said it. Say it again—'defection'! Right, that's why you dreamed up the Ghasavi trip, isn't it? Right, to give you that sixty-hour head start!

He smiled again. His excuse for delaying was true, but not entirely. He really had been ready to "pitch" Ghasavi. He'd been setting the man up for recruitment for six months. He had introduced him to the finer things of life—foreign booze, women, food, handcrafted guns, and such—all things that Ghasavi's army pay, even as a senior officer, would never support. Ghasavi was smart—Telchoff wouldn't have courted him if he were not—and he knew that his position in charge of signals for the whole northwest military area was very attractive to Telchoff, whom he had long ago assumed to be KGB. Anyway, they *both* had accepted the bottom line that Ghasavi was going to spy for pay and Telchoff was going to pay him. It was strictly a matter of formalizing the relationship; and best of all, if Mahotin looked at the file this would be borne out. Well, so much for the timing. He could count on that head start . . . or could he?

Telchoff continued his listing. Asset: Mahotin's newness to India. He was an intelligent and ruthless man, but he *was* a novice here. He did not know the Indian people. He did not know the Indian military nor their routines. He could not imagine the kinds of things one could get done in India for the outlay of just a modest amount of hard Western currency. And while Telchoff must be careful not to underestimate the capability of the man Globitsyn had sent to replace him, he was confident that Mahotin had no suspicion that he would even consider defection, much less that he'd moved along so far so quickly in his planning.

Yes, Telchoff thought, the planning! That West German passport with the valid visa and the Bombay entry stamp, those U.S. dollars he'd saved so carefully over the years, the talks with Jack Glover, the airline arrangements. Even the scenario that he and Glover had worked out on a contingency basis— over too many vodkas last Christmas. He laughed to himself. Why had he been so reluctant to use the word "defection"? He'd had it in the back of his mind ever since Globitsyn got the appointment as chief.

He resumed his listing. Liability: Ghasavi was actually on maneuvers until Saturday evening, so a simple check would put the lie to the hunting trip–recruitment story. But Mahotin didn't know how to do this, and the procedures had been carefully omitted from the file. Not a real threat. Liability: Globitsyn could suspect that he might defect rather than return to Moscow, and he just might be sure *if* and *when* Mahotin told him Telchoff was not leaving till Monday and why. But still Mahotin just might not tell Globitsyn; there were a couple good reasons for him not to do so.

Another liability, maybe a big one: the Americans. Although he'd discussed such possibilities with Glover, he'd never raised the subject with Glover's successor, Bonney. There wasn't time now; he'd just have to assume that Glover had briefed Bonney on the matter. What he didn't know was whether or not the Americans could lay on the arrangements fast enough to beat the KGB counternets. Anyway, Glover was in Washington, and once he got into the act things would hum! Telchoff could only hope that the wheels would start to turn as soon as he gave Bonney the key phrase.

Back to the list. Liability: Delhi is a small town socially. No way could he leave securely from Palam Airport on the West German passport. Too many people knew him, and once the counternet was alerted, not even the Americans could get him out of Europe alive. He shivered as an icy finger traced a path from neck to tailbone down his sweaty back. Yes, indeed, Globitsyn would pull out all the stops! He could not let old Pete get in front of a microphone anywhere in the West. As far as top-level Moscow was concerned Telchoff was coming home in disgrace to pay for his costly foul-up of operation Delta, which damn near lost the Indian subcontinent forever. No matter that he had opposed it (it was Globitsyn's—and his toady, Megov's—idea) from the start. The Moscow records would show otherwise—Ivanova had confirmed it. Yes, very cute, indeed: with Delta as a cover, no one would suspect all of Globitsyn's *real* reasons for silencing Telchoff forever. So like dear Yuri!

He picked up the phone and pressed the intercom button. "Natasha?"

"Yes, Comrade."

"I must give you my schedule for the next few days. Ah, let's see . . . yes, tonight—late—I will depart Delhi, driving to Chandigar. I will be meeting Colonel Ghasavi and will accompany him on a hunt. We will be in the Sundaranagar area east of the big dam, and will check in with army signals twice daily, six and six. But as usual, don't contact me unless it's truly vital, as we do not wish to emphasize the fact that I'm with Colonel Ghasavi. Right? Got all that?"

"Yes, Comrade. And your return?"

"Probably late Sunday evening, or possibly early Monday. In any event, I will be in the office Monday morning. Please confirm my reservation, Palam to Moscow on the Monday flight.

Have them hold the tickets at the field. Oh yes, the necessary vouchers and all that, have them for me on Monday."

"Very good, Comade. It will be done as you require."

"And, Natasha . . ."

"Yes, Comrade."

"Anything you wish me to bring you from home"—he laughed—"within reason, of course, I would be pleased to do so."

"Oh thank you, Comrade, I do have a small list. I will have it ready on Monday."

Interesting, he thought as he replaced the phone. Either she doesn't suspect anything or she's one hell of an actress. Or, he thought with a shiver, Mahotin had her well prepared. She certainly gave the impression that she accepted his "routine consultation" trip as such and expected him to return. Maybe she wasn't a plant of Globitsyn's; but he'd continue to treat her as if she were—it was most certainly safer that way.

Telchoff got up from his desk. Time was becoming essential. He had to be ready to move when darkness settled in not too many hours hence, and he had many things to do first. He sighed, the sad sigh of a person who had made up his mind to accept the inevitable, but didn't really like it. Then he moved to a stubby, formidable-looking safe, bent over, and began twisting dials. Once it was open, he reached in and removed a bulky manila envelope and a second smaller one, then reclosed the door and whirled the dial. He put the envelopes in his briefcase and, carrying his jacket over his arm—the Ambassador, who was new in India, insisted that all embassy officers arrive, leave, and greet visitors in full business attire—exited the office door.

"Natasha, I must leave now. I will be stopping to phone Colonel Ghasavi from the hotel as usual, then home for an early supper and a little rest before setting out for Chandigar. You may, of course, disturb me for anything you or Comrade Mahotin believe is important; I shall start driving probably about nine-thirty or ten P.M., possibly a bit later."

"Understood, Comrade. I wish you good luck."

"Thank you. See you on Monday morning."

As the door shut behind Telchoff the woman lifted her phone and began dialing, paused, then, "Comrade, he has left."

"Carrying anything?"

"Only the usual briefcase."

"All right. Proceed as planned: ring him every hour beginning twenty-one hundred, and let me know immediately if he does not answer!"

"Yes, Comrade, it will be done."

Telchoff drove the faded blue Hindustan to the nearby hotel, left the car in the rear parking area, and proceeded to the pay phones off the lobby. He chose the one farthest from the operator's enclosure and dialed a local number. He asked the woman who answered if he could speak to Mr. Bonney, identifying himself with a common Indian name. When Bonney came on the line Telchoff said, "This is Pythias. I have a problem. Damon told me you would help."

Telchoff's heart almost stopped during the few seconds' silence until Bonney said, without emotion, "Yes, Pythias, Damon told me you might call. I am ready to help. Now here's what I'd like you to do. . . ."

Like any other Indian highway, the trunk road north to Ambala was a nightmare by day and utter suicide by night. The trucks, many of them using only parking lights but flicking low and high beams off and on, came hurtling out of the night like wailing banshees, often one-eyed, and always crowding toward the center of the too narrow road. Telchoff drove carefully with his left wheels riding on what passed for a shoulder, but was in reality a sloping, sun-baked strip of once graveled earth with the contours of a huge washboard, which extended no more than a meter out from the road and was spotted with deep, murderous potholes at irregular intervals.

After a few dozen kilometers the wagon, bicycle, and pedestrian traffic largely disappeared, and then in a few more kilometers the trucks thinned, so Telchoff was able to make better time. Still, it was an agonizing drive, and he was grateful for the respite offered by passing through towns where even the onrushing and overtaking trucks were forced to slow down to almost reasonable speeds.

It was as he was leaving the tie-up of Ambala that he was able to confirm for the first time that he was being followed. The car, another dark-colored Hindustan, had first captured his attention by staying the same relative distance behind for the last ten kilometers or so. Now it was bolder; either the driver was not skilled in surveillance or he simply didn't give a damn anymore. Of course this did not change Telchoff's plans particularly since the whole charade was aimed at determining whether or not Mahotin had accepted the hunting trip story. Now that it was apparent he had not done so, Telchoff was prepared. There was no question as to the assignment of the goons in the trailing car, just as there was no question as to the action he must take to survive.

There was a small village off the east side of the road about fifteen kilometers north of Ambala, and well before one was apt to hit the first military checkpoint around Chandigar (they were constantly switching these around), and Telchoff remembered well the desolate area just north and east of the village, where he had once hunted with Ghasavi and some other Indian officers. A hidden turnoff led to some high, but rocky and barren ground on which, unlike most of India, one was unlikely to raise a crowd of peasants simply by being there.

He recognized the turnoff as he went by, continuing on through a curve, up a small incline, until he could see on the horizon the lights of the first roadblock. He stopped the car quickly when there was for a moment no oncoming traffic, made a U-turn, and headed back the way he'd come. He flicked his lights in accepted Indian fashion as a car approached. Unless somebody had come out of a side road, an unlikely event in this area at this time of night, the car had to be the goons'. It was, and he was able to confirm his earlier impression that there were two of them. In a moment he could see their brake lights come on in his mirror, then he was at the turnoff. Hopefully the incline behind him shielded his own turn as he used the hand brake to slow, shut off his driving lights, and edged slowly along the parallel ruts in utter darkness. He went in about two hundred meters and parked in a copse of scrubby trees, still in darkness with even the interior light buttons of the car taped shut. He moved up a small hillock for twenty meters or so, settling down in an area near the top, which was protected by three large boulders, two of which blocked access from the downhill sides. Fitting the small silencer on his automatic, he held it loosely in his hand and waited. At his feet he placed a loaded sawed-off shotgun.

A car went past slowly on the trunk road, but didn't stop. It looked like a Hindustan, but then most of them either were or did. Nothing happened for ten minutes while he watched carefully to the unprotected south, his night vision improving with time. The silence was almost eerie, only broken from time to time by distant animal sounds and the muffled roar of a speeding truck; but the utter blackness was relieved occasionally by stretches of moonlight from the mostly cloud-covered sky. Suddenly Telchoff heard a sound that was out of place, a kind of metallic scraping, very quick and very light, but very definite. It was behind and off to the east, and not far away. He nodded to himself. The goons were right on schedule. One would be where the sound came from; the other doing a pincer from the west; both were avoiding the more open southern approach to the hillock, the latter being the logical place for the quarry to hide, as Telchoff had known and counted on. Their objective: to flush him from the sides, forcing him to move south and down, where they'd have him pinned between them.

No longer did Telchoff have any illusions as to what their orders were. Globitsyn and Mahotin had been one step ahead all the time. Obviously they didn't care where and how he died, as long as he was dead and there was no big flap. He could almost hear that arrogant ass telling Mahotin, "Just make sure you kill him!"

Telchoff waited thirty seconds, then picked up a small rock and tossed it easily off to his right. The pebble made a soft thud and then a clink as it hit a boulder. It sounded amazingly like someone had stumbled and kicked a small stone against a larger one. Almost immediately a shaded torch played its light in the direction of the sound, and Telchoff, who had indeed been looking in the right direction, took aim and loosed three quick "plops" at a point fifty centimeters behind and several above the profile of the torch. As the last "plop" sounded, he dropped quickly to the ground and rolled to his left, away from the boulder, coming up on his elbows, body and gun pointing straight ahead to what had been his left. The second goon was fast! He'd zeroed in on the muzzle fire and Telchoff had barely dropped out of the path before the slugs buzzed by. Telchoff returned the compliment as he loosed three quick shots at the point of the goon's muzzle fire, again rolling, this time forward, as he squeezed off the final shot. He lay quietly, not moving, hoping the moon would stay in for thirty more seconds. It did. Still no sound. Could he have been so lucky as to catch them both with semiblind calculated shots?

There was a weak moan and a sound of movement off to his right. The first goon? Trap? Telchoff chanced an almost silent slithering move to a cleft between the two large boulders, arriving just as the moon popped out again. He looked right and could see the outlines of what appeared to be a body lying spread-eagled on its face only about fifteen meters away. This body didn't appear to be capable of any kind of sound. It looked very dead. Then out of the corner of his eye he saw a movement off to the left, reflexively turning and firing in one motion just as his face and shoulder were peppered by rock splinters generated by the slap of slugs into the boulder beside him. This time there was an audible reaction, an almost animal yelp as the second goon, erect and clearly visible in the moon-light, seemed to fold in the middle, dropped to his knees, and then ever so slowly pitched forward in front of him as the moon went back into hiding.

Telchoff lay silently, his senses tuned more to the right, to the first man. Five minutes passed before the moon came out again. He protected his night vision with sunglasses until it went back in; putting the automatic back in its holster he stood up in the shelter of the boulder, holding the shotgun, and proceeded in a slow crouch, moving toward the second man, the one on his left. He stopped every few seconds to look back toward the first man. He could not be sure, but there appeared to be no movement. He reached the second man and, shotgun a few centimeters from his head, kicked him viciously. No reaction. He proceeded to roll the man over with his foot and saw why: there was a neat dark hole in the middle of the fellow's forehead. Telchoff wondered how the man had gotten the sound out, as he must have died instantly.

Telchoff turned and moved cautiously in an arc that took him back up to the boulders toward the first man, shotgun at the ready. As he came within a couple paces the goon made his move, rolling quickly to his right, downhill, and at the same time raising the gun that had been hidden under his body. He was quick and good, but Telchoff held all the cards; the shotgun obliterated his face before he could get his pistol off the ground.

It took Telchoff another half hour to find their car, bring it back, put the bodies into it, and drive it as far as he could into the gully farther off to the northeast, hiding it in a patch of scrubby trees and boulders. He retrieved his own car and headed quickly and carefully back to Delhi; this time to Palam Airport. Leaving his car in the guarded parking area, he walked around to the main entrance carrying his small bag, and got a taxi to the Ashoka Hotel in town. Dawn was still hours away. This hotel was dangerous territory, being so close to the embassy, but he needed to sow a little confusion. He waited a few minutes, then got another cab to the Intercontinental. Here he went into the deserted men's room off the lobby where he shaved his Stalinesque mustache and applied "instant tan" lotion to the newly bared lighter area of his face. Then he did some things with tiny foam rubber pads and an eyebrow pencil, and when he left there his face matched perfectly the picture in his West German passport.

Telchoff waited until the desk clerk was occupied with the phone before walking quickly through an "exit only" door at the side of the lobby and out into the parking area. The lights of a dark-colored, nondescript Hindustan blinked. He moved carefully toward it, his fingers lightly touching the handle of the automatic in its holster. The passenger door of the car was open. He got in. The car drove quietly out of the lot and, turning left, picked up speed as it disappeared into the still, dark night.

TWO

MOSCOW, U.S.S.R.

Gen. Yuri Aleksandrovich Globitsyn sat thoughtfully, drumming his long slender fingers on the stack of brown file folders that sat on the right wing of his huge desk. The Chairman of the KGB was a man of "medium" appearance in almost every way: height, weight, coloring, features, dress. A very ordinary-looking person—until one encountered his eyes. They were surprisingly dark for his Great Russian complexion, more of the deep blue—almost black—of the cold northern Atlantic. It was indeed the eyes that were the true measure of the man. His, at this moment, were almost closed, then suddenly they opened, and his whole body seemed to become alert, as if he'd heard a suspect sound and were reacting to it. He picked the phone off its cradle, hit a button on the large console, spoke a few words, hung up, sat back, and resumed his drumming. Thirty seconds later the door to his office opened and a man of about thirty-five, tall, slender, handsome in a way that was almost too classical, too perfect, came in and stood at military attention in front of the desk. The General nodded.

"Sit down, Comrade."

"Thank you, sir." The man even *sat* at attention.

The dark blue eyes blazed. "Sergei Mikhailovich, we must have some action. We can*not* let that traitorous snake, Telchoff, go free and unpunished. The Motherland cries out for revenge. We must act!"

The younger man nodded assent, but said nothing. Globitsyn went on. "He is a very dangerous man, this Telchoff. He is clever, ruthless, and merciless. He killed in cold blood the two unarmed escorts we sent to India. He has thumbed his nose at our glorious traditions. He has given our secrets to the CIA, and he deserves to die. I want this bastard dead, Comrade. I want his fucking head on a plate covered with fucking maggots." The dark eyes glinted. The younger man still awaited orders silently.

Then Globitsyn's face relaxed into a smile. "Yes, Sergei Mikhailovich, we will have action, action indeed. I have decided what it will be. You remember our discussion regarding Colonel Sadimoff?"

The younger man nodded.

"Well, I am giving the colonel a job. To rid the world of this snake, Telchoff, I will give him carte blanche—well, almost. He will have our full resources at his command."

Globitsyn motioned the younger man to move closer, then lowering his voice almost to a whisper he said, "And of course, Comrade, there is the even more important task of protecting our agent Kotch. I am giving this job also to Sadimoff. As you know, there is a chance that Telchoff may have discovered something somehow concerning Kotch. We cannot know, but we will act on the assumption that he must be silenced as soon as possible."

The younger man spoke. "Is this man Sadimoff that good, Comrade Chairman? Can you give him this much responsibility?"

"If it were not you asking those questions, Sergei Mikhailovich, it would be insolence; but I understand. Yes, Sadimoff is that good. And since he has been in the Middle East for ten years, including the time of Telchoff's last Moscow assignment, I am sure they have never met. Sadimoff is *very* good, and *very* loyal, and *very* ruthless—even more so than Telchoff! Now, draft me a 'hand-carry' to Beirut explaining exactly how we want Sadimoff to handle things. Make it 'eyes only' for that man, the French speaker, your friend, uh?"

"Grigoriev."

"Yes, Grigoriev, and send a signal to that bonehead, Valinskiy, that the dispatch is coming, and warning him that if he puts his nose into it, I'll cut it off. This will be Grigoriev's case and his alone. But tell Valinskiy to signal Sadimoff through Paris or Nicosia—you find out where he is at the moment—and set up a meeting somewhere safe. I guess it should be in Lebanon, if there is any such thing as a safe place anymore. Understand?"

"Yes, sir. I will have the draft for your approval as soon as possible."

THREE

JOUNIEH, LEBANON

Alexei Grigoriev looked nothing like the protocol-polished second secretary he was as he moved quickly along the dimly lit street leading to the harbor. He was careful; even in the moonless night he stayed in the deeper shadows alongside the ramshackle buildings that lined the narrow thoroughfare. He did not want to run into any official or unofficial patrols. Not that his dress, papers, or cover story were not impeccably middle-class Arab, as was his idiomatic Lebanese Arabic; but one never knew just what some crazy soldiers might do.

There was an occasional silent male Arab on the street, and even an occasional car, and the numbers of both were increasing each night following these days of relative quiet. There were still the intermittent percussion booms to the south in Beirut, but even these had fallen off in number as well as intensity. It had been an entire week since the clack of rapid-fire weapons had been near enough to the embassy for distinct recognition; and Jounieh, being deeper into the Christian zone, was even more insulated and quiet.

Still Alexei was careful. Meeting the KGB's most secret agent in the Middle East to brief him on his role in their most secret current operation had to be the acme of sensitivity. In fact, his chief, Comrade Colonel Valinskiy, was probably shitting his silken underpants at this moment, worrying about it. The Center's hand-carried letter of instructions, signed by Globitsyn himself, had scared old Valinskiy enough. And then the fact that he, Grigoriev, a relatively junior officer, was personally designated by Globitsyn to make the contact and handle the brief was an additional source of discomfort for the old fart, who would much rather have had his toady deputy, Artimov, do the honors. But the final straw was that the briefing paper was in a separate sealed envelope "For Grigoriev's Eyes Only." That was almost too much; but Valinskiy and Artimov were, if nothing else, organization men, and when Moscow spoke they bowed to the north and obeyed. Globitsyn, the arrogant bastard, had not even bothered to explain to them that he, Grigoriev, not only had fluent French (the language in which this prima donna agent, Hummous, insisted on conducting all meetings with his KGB masters) but had in addition met and conversed with Hummous a year before, giving him not only rapport, but instant credentials. How typically Globitsyn was the message: "Just *do* it!"

As he neared the harbor—small but busy, especially since Kaldeh Airport was closed more than it was open these days, and many arrivals to Lebanon came by way of Cyprus to Jounieh by boat—Grigoriev drew deeper into the buildings' shadows. Still walking casually, although not so slowly as to look furtive or so quickly as to appear hurried, he heard the voices and the engine downshifting only seconds before the jeep's headlights came out of the narrow side street, cornered, straightened, then came toward him. Damn! Too late to run, and no recessed doorways to hide in. He'd have to brave it out. It was difficult, but he maintained his pace and open demeanor. The jeep did not slow, and its four uniformed occupants never gave him a second look.

He passed the old Souk area, then came to the marked Harbormaster's Building. After a moment's search he found the doorway described in Moscow's letter. It had a long scimitarlike scratch from knob to ground on the right side.

Grigoriev opened the door, entered, and then quickly closed it behind him, even though the hallway in which he found himself was totally dark. He stood waiting (as the instructions had directed) and after ten seconds a door about halfway down the hallway opened and a shadowy figure stepped out and beckoned him to approach. When he reached the open door he went in and found himself in a sparsely furnished but clean office. At the desk against the far wall, a hooded light behind him providing the only illumination in the room, sat a man dressed in undistinguished shirt and slacks looking like any of the numerous Arabs who were around the harbor area by day.

Alexei recognized the man immediately. One did not forget Hummous. He was about six feet tall, slender, but like a steel cable is slender—strong and sinewy. He had coal black, straight hair, worn stylishly long and well groomed. His full black mustache drooped at the ends, accenting a smooth, dark tan complexion, a long, narrow, aristocratic nose, surprisingly full lips, and a strong bony chin and jaw.

The man spoke in excellent French. "My young friend. It is good to see you again. Much better circumstances than the last time, eh? Yes, that Jewish gunboat trying to shoot us . . . not what you might call great fun, eh?"

Alexei nodded, remembering his instructions to let Hummous set the pace, and not to force the briefing. (Moscow had spent a whole page of that letter telling him how to handle their prima donna, whom he, Alexei, suspected was not a prima donna at all.) The Arab went on. "I am sorry, uh, Alexei, if I may"—Grigoriev nodded—"that I cannot offer you some Arab hospitality, but. . . ." He rolled those dark eyes and gestured at the bleakness of the office. "However, I do have a small cognac that we might share." He opened a desk drawer and brought forth a small cut-glass decanter and two small brandy glasses. He poured, and then got up and brought one of the glasses over to Alexei. He sat on the desk and raised his glass. "Your health, Alexei."

Alexei spoke for the first time. "And yours, my brave friend."

Hummous liked that. (Moscow's letter had said he would.) But Alexei had meant it. This man had proved his courage often—even daily—in the last decade, and Alexei had witnessed one of these incidents personally. Hummous's voice brought him back to the present. "And so, since our time is limited, it is best we get to the briefing, no? My, uh, contact said this operation was most sensitive."

"Your contact was right. What should I call you? You gave me no name that other time."

"Why not use my given name, Pierre?"

They both laughed. "All right, M. Pierre. Yes, your contact was indeed right. *The most* sensitive. I was to tell you, quote, all messages of substance will be hand carried throughout the course of the operation—no electronic messages, end quote."

Hummous looked amused. "The Amis have some new wonder machine at Fort Meade, eh?"

"That I don't know, Pierre, but I think perhaps that our people are more worried about future publicity than present security."

"Like that? I see. And does this, uh, most sensitive operation have a name—one of your funny little names?"

"Indeed. The code word is Ninotchka. It is also an anagram for the name of the illegal, who is the subject of my briefing."

"Oh yes, Kotch. I remember. Go on."

Alexei could not prevent the flash of surprise from showing on his face, although he tried. He plunged on. "Simply stated, Pierre, Kotch is in trouble and the Center wants to help him out of it. They believe you're the best chance to do so."

Hummous shrugged, obviously pleased with the flattery. "And why do they think I could do the job? Do I have some unique qualification?"

"Yes, Pierre, you do. Obviously, I might say. They want

you to do, as Comrade Globitsyn puts it, 'whatever is necessary.'"

"I see. Good. And am I to decide what is necessary?" He
laughed and Alexei, after hesitating just an instant, joined him.

"I'm sure your suggestions will have great weight, Pierre, but
no, you do not have the carte blanche. Not even you."

Hummous chuckled. "Well put, my friend. I might say your
diplomatic cover fits you well! Now tell me, are our masters in
Moscow ready to sacrifice Pierre to save this Kotch?"

Alexei was dead serious. "While I'm sure that is not their
intent, I am just as sure that they realize it is one of the possibilities; and, yes, I think that the preservation of the Kotch
operation is paramount. They expected such a question, in fact,
and told me to assure you that in the event your cover is blown
they will make every effort to get you out, and then if such is
your desire, you will work in a different area of the globe as a
different person—after an appropriate interval."

Hummous raised one of his thick black eyebrows. "I see.
And so this Kotch is worth all the marbles, eh? A man for
whom our masters are willing to sacrifice me—with all due
modesty—their best Arab action agent in the Middle East?"

"You are much too modest, Pierre; I believe from all I've
heard that you are their best action agent, period! Which of
course is why they are giving you this assignment. Kotch himself is good, very good, but it is Kotch's potential that Moscow
wishes to protect at all costs. Now let me tell you why, and
how you will be expected to save him."

Forty-five minutes later Alexei Grigoriev was in his non-
diplomatic and very dirty Volks leaving the hotel parking area
and turning toward Beirut. He had left a quietly thoughtful
Hummous in that waterfront office and had retraced his steps
quickly but carefully to the hotel. He saw no patrols.

As he drove slowly south along the badly potted road his
mind went back over the meeting with Hummous—no, make
that Pierre. The man was not disturbed, in fact not even very
concerned, that his life, or at least his life as Hummous, might

be drawing to a close. He was quite a man. As he neared the embassy compound, Alexei turned his mind to his upcoming report—undoutedly Valinskiy and Artimov were waiting to be briefed. He must tell them neither too little or too much.

KGB Col. Nadim Sadimoff, known for the last ten years of his life as Salim Naheri, aka Hummous, the most widely feared but least known member of the radical and outlawed Palestinian terrorist group L'Ange Cinq, sat quietly in that dark office in Jounieh long after Grigoriev had left. His contact in Nice, Feodor Menin, had told him this was to be a very important operation. He did not know if Menin knew what it was all about. He doubted it. Menin could not have kept it to himself if he did; his nature and his ego would have required otherwise. Anyway, the comrades in the Center were taking off the gloves on this one. What they wanted, and what they were willing to risk for it, went far beyond anything he'd experienced, and he was both flattered and excited that they had chosen him. There was no way they could chance having this operation fail, and they were telling him: Do it right, Nadim (hell, he'd almost forgotten his own first name after all these years), or die there as Hummous with the blame on your Palestinian back!

Sadimoff looked at the radium dial of his gold Rolex. Time to go. Half an hour later he was asleep in the cabin of a small boat in Jounieh harbor as its two-man crew prepared to set course for Cyprus.

FOUR

WASHINGTON, D.C.

The man known as Fuad Maksud looked down on the frenetic noonday action in front of the building. His apartment/office was the top front of an old, three-storied brick row house on a short street not far from Dupont Circle, and day and night there was a constant stream of pedestrians and cars. He mused. It had been easy to get "lost" in Washington—almost as easy as getting there, he thought.

Maksud's Egyptian passport was real, as was the photo in it; the name was not. But it had sufficed, in fact served him well, even in these days of close scrutiny of Arab passports. And once he'd arrived in Washington as a brown-skinned human who spoke English with an accent, he assumed membership in a very large minority group!

The trip from Jounieh to Larnaca was uneventful, as were his twenty-four-hour stopover and identity change. His stored wardrobe was getting a bit seedy, but it was adequate to dress him appropriately and give him a small suitcase full of acceptable changes, so that he looked the part of a middle-level Saudi government official for his onward flight to London. Two days in London saw a greatly revamped wardrobe, some minor alterations in appearance, and a total change of identity. It was an obviously successful—and well-documented—Egyptian businessman who boarded the British Airways flight to New York from Heathrow.

He had been in Washington before, not often, but several times, and so after a quick refresher course with maps and taxi trips he had become sufficiently familiar with the layout of the city to get around quite well. The apartment was handy, adequate, and anonymous; and no one—not the landlord nor the young Kuwaiti couple who had been "sitting" the place for the last year nor anyone else—had an idea who the ultimate lessee was.

It was just what he needed for the next couple months. He closed the window, more for quiet than temperature, and sat down at the desk with a lined yellow pad. As he began to write, the phone rang. He answered, "Yes."

A man's voice, very accented English, came on. "Is the, uh, man there? Uh, Meester Sabaki? Yes?"

"No. He has moved away. I do not know where."

"Aha. He is leaving number for the phone, no?"

"No. He left no number. I don't know where he is, but he will not be back here."

"Aha. I see. So Sabaki is no there, no here in Deecee?"

"I told you, I don't know. Sorry. I just don't know."

"Aha okay. I am sorry to have bother you, sir."

"That's all right. Good-bye."

The Egyptian businessman was frowning as he continued writing on the yellow pad. The phone rang again. A look of disgust started to cloud his face as he picked the instrument up expecting to hear Sabaki's friend again. It faded as the voice came on. "Ah, Mr. Maksud, this is Aribi here. How are you today, sir?"

"I'm fine, Aribi. And you?"

"Just very fine, sir, very fine. I am calling to say my client is ready to sign the contract for the cotton."

"That is good news, Aribi, good news indeed. And when will he sign it?"

"Tonight, I am sure, sir. It is our plan, sir, to, uh, sign tonight. Yes."

"Very good, I'll be waiting to hear from you, Aribi; so call me when it is signed. And the other client? How is he?"

"He is fine, yes, fine, sir. But he is being a bit harder to sell. It seems there are other persons, uh, partners, you would say, who are involved. We have not yet, uh, satisfied all of them. But it will be soon, sir. The deal is looking good."

"Fine, Aribi. You are doing well, my friend. I shall remember it. Now call me tonight after the signing."

"Yes, sir, thank you. I will call. It will be good, sir. I am sure."

"Fine, Aribi. Thank you. Good-bye."

The Egyptian was smiling as he resumed writing. He stopped to muse. Well, that was that! War would be declared tonight, but hopefully the CIA wouldn't even know it. Number one was ready; number two in the wings; and the rest were in his sights. The Center said, "Go for it" and that was exactly what he was going to do. He raised his eyes to the ceiling and muttered, "Insha' Allah!"

FIVE

FAIRFAX COUNTY, VIRGINIA

Glover was tired as he drove north on the two-lane highway, and the lights of the truck behind didn't help at all. It had been a long day—and night—but one hell of a productive one. Pete is quite a guy, he thought. A phenomenal memory! Once he loosened up, it was like a stream of consciousness deluge, and the more he talked the more he remembered.

Glover smiled, remembering the moment, a few hours ago, when Pete asked—totally out of the blue—if he'd be interested in an illegal operation into the U.S. government in Washington. My God, a sure enough mole, and he asked if he'd be interested! Of course, the information is dated, he'd said, but there's no indication the operation is over. It could be assumed it's still on. And begun by the Chairman of the KGB! Glover laughed to himself. This will turn some of the heads who've been belittling old Pete—even saying he's probably a plant. Glover could hardly keep from grabbing him and shaking it all out, but knew he had to let Pete travel at his own pace. They had to stop—both too tired—before Pete finished the story. Lights from a car coming up behind filled Glover's car. He talked to himself: damn that bastard and his lights. Dumb asshole! Just pass, don't sit on my tail shining your fucking lights into my mirror.

*   *   *

The Fairfax County troopers were close enough to hear the crash, but they had to cut through on a smaller road to get to the scene. They hit the siren to alert traffic as they came onto the main road, but were blocked by the far end of the curve from seeing the hit-and-run truck speeding away. Their spotlight, arcing from side to side, picked up the tangled mess that was Glover's car. The driver let his partner out to examine the wreck as he drove on for a hundred yards, and then reversed the procedure, looking for a second car. Satisfied there was none, he returned and set up flares, having already radioed the emergency call to headquarters. It looked like a routine "missed curve accident."

The first trooper had already determined there were no live bodies in or outside the mangled car. A number of file folders and papers had apparently spilled out of a lock-sprung briefcase when the front door, passenger side, burst open on impact. The folders were all marked TOP SECRET, Property of the Central Intelligence Agency. The troopers were always cognizant of the proximity of the Agency, a few miles away inside the Beltway, when doing their patrols, and had standing instructions as to whom to call and how to guard the secret materials. They went by the book.

There was obviously nothing they could do for the driver, whose license proclaimed him to be one John E. Glover, and whose pockets contained a CIA ID badge. They began a closer inspection of the automobile and its immediate area. The front third of the car was telescoped, almost unrecognizable; but the rear two-thirds were clean and appeared well cared for—except for the door panels on the driver's side. These had several long and deep gouges lengthwise, with flakes and smears of a dark paint on them. All this was duly noted in the accident report they wrote after the emergency vehicles had come and gone with their grim loads. A few minutes earlier the CIA security officer, a pleasant and very serious young man, had arrived, presented his credentials, and taken charge of all the papers. He was very interested when the troopers showed him the possible evidence of another vehicle being involved in the accident. He had instructed an aide with a large flashlight to search the area for further scattered papers.

The director of security of the Agency phoned the night security officer of the Interagency Coordination Group (ICG) shortly after 2:00 A.M. to inform him of the accident. Since the establishment of ICG this was a routinely immediate procedure in any case involving a defector. The ICG officer, also routinely and immediately, determined that this was a matter of sufficient seriousness to warrant waking Gen. Neil Ashley. The General listened carefully, thanked him, and said he'd handle the matter from this point.

Neil Rogers Ashley, a three-star general at age forty-seven, had led his class at West Point and had begun his career with a real bang, earning the Congressional Medal of Honor as a company commander in Vietnam. He had led a daring rescue of a trapped platoon, most of which action occurred after he had suffered a near-debilitating shoulder wound.

In the ensuing years Ashley had risen rapidly through various foreign and domestic staff jobs of the army, always being careful to avoid the slightest tinge of partisan politics. Then, in line for a top job and his fourth star, the General turned his back on his career to accept the command of the newly formed ICG simply because his commander-in-chief had asked him to do so.

ICG was a brainchild born of the fragile union of congressional masterminds and executive branch wunderkind. It was to be the ultimate solution to the problems generated in the intelligence community by the National Defense Act of 1947 and exacerbated by the forty-plus years of bickering among the affected parties, who never accepted either the letter or the spirit of the act. The "Overlord concept" of the Director of Central Intelligence as envisioned under the act was an anachronism whose time had never come. The establishment of ICG indicated only that its creators believed that moment had finally arrived. To mold these disparate and disputatious factions into one U.S. team was the thankless task handed to General Ashley by the President.

There was no question that Ashley was uniquely qualified. He had no questionable areas in his background or career, and he seemed to be universally respected and admired. There was widespread agreement—even in the Intelligence Community— that the President had made a wise choice.

One of ICG's prime responsibilities was the handling, debriefing, and rehabilitation of "intelligence defectors." It could call on, or coopt, experts from the various agencies and services as it wished, but the control, responsibility, and—if necessary—the blame were centered in and on ICG. The General, as always, took his responsibilities very seriously, but he and ICG were still in the process of personnel staffing, so he had been delighted to obtain Jack Glover to work with Telchoff. Now Jack was gone, just when the Telchoff debriefing was getting most interesting, touching on a subject of prime and current interest. Furthermore, there were unanswered questions about Glover's death, which added a bizarre note to the overall situation. It was probably a coincidence, but Ashley instinctively distrusted coincidences. By late that evening he had decided to call in (or try to call in, as the man was no longer in government) his best operative.

SIX

FLORIDA

Patrick Morley loved the ocean.

He loved swimming in it, sitting by it, walking along its shore, even just looking at it. He also loved Angela Mornay, who in turn loved him and the ocean; and in both cases the intensity of her emotion matched his. Thus it was with great reluctance that she watched Patrick set out alone for what was usually *their* morning walk and swim. But she had an appointment—hard to get and unthinkable to miss—with the best hair cutter on the island, a person of indeterminate age and gender, who answered only to the neuter name of Lolly. Besides, tonight was to be a big night, a celebration with old friends, and she wanted to look her best.

The phone rang. "Angela, this is Neil Ashley in Washington. How are you?"

"Fine, General. And you?" She tried, but her lack of enthusiasm seeped through. She liked the General, beginning with the fact that he placed his own calls and identified himself by name rather than title; not to mention that he had been very nice to her and Patrick over the years. It was just that his calls only came when there was a problem and that meant when he needed Patrick, sometimes just for a conversation, sometimes for something more.

"I'm very well, Angela. You had a good summer down there, I understand."

"Delightful, sir, warm, and nice, and busy."

"Good. Glad to hear it. Umm, is Patrick available?"

She was tempted to say, "For what?" but she resisted. "No, but he should be back within the next hour or so."

"Would you have him call me, please?"

"Of course. I'm going out but I'll leave a note on the fridge. He'll be sure to see it there."

The General chuckled. "He hasn't changed, eh? Well, that's our Patrick. Thanks, Angela. I must get down there to Singer Island one of these days and see what its hold over you two is."

She wanted to say, "*Our* Patrick, my ass, he's *my* Patrick, and don't ever forget it," but she answered politely instead. "Do that, General. You're always welcome." She laughed. "You may never want to go back to that Potomac swamp again."

"That's what I'm afraid of. Well, nice talking to you as always, Angela. Stay well."

Angela hung up the phone, turned her pouting face toward the mirror, and said, "Oh shit!" Then she began to laugh at herself, at her little girl look and attitude. Hell, she'd known what Patrick was all about long before they'd become involved.

Angela was twenty-nine, very smart, very chic, and very beautiful in a strikingly smooth, brunette way. She was also a pleasant, likable person. Strangers and little kids talked to her freely; animals who ignored or bit other people curried her favor. Most women sought her friendship, and men were entranced. Angela was a transplanted Californian who had retained much of the outdoorsy free spirit of that state, a successful career woman, and in every way a fully realized person in her own right.

She had met Patrick at a low point in her career, when she was bogged down in a no-future job, and had accepted an adventurous but temporary task offered by an adventurous and temporary man friend.

He had soon become her whole life, and although they had discussed marriage and both wanted it eventually, she had—so far—not been ready to commit herself. Their life had evolved into a rather fast-paced social and fun existence, with lots of daytime water activity and nighttime variety. Patrick had plenty of money as a result of the adventure during which she met him, and although they were running through it at a pro-digious rate, neither of them was very concerned.

Angela had to admit that she resented Patrick's participation in these adventures more from envy than loneliness or fear; nev-ertheless, she dreaded them in a very real way and in moments of self-examination wondered if this fear was the real reason for her reluctance to marry him. She had succeeded in deterring him from a number of proposals by a globe-trotting private eye friend in Miami, but she knew that when Neil Ashley called, Patrick would feel he had to answer affirmatively. This time she resolved just to grin and bear it.

Morley read the note on the fridge and called the General's number. Ashley answered himself. "Patrick. Good to hear from you. Can you meet me at Homestead at one P.M. today?"

"Yes, sir."

"Good. You know where the C.O.'s quarters are. Park in the back out of sight, please. And your name at the gate . . . umm . . . Robert Brown, okay? The guard will have you down, just sign in. See you shortly."

He hung up. Morley, still cradling the phone, smiled. The General never had been one for small talk. He showered, dressed, left a note for Angela, and set out for Homestead Air Force Base, some thirty miles south of Miami.

The General was waiting at the back door of the command-ing officer's residence when Morley pulled into the hidden parking area next to the garage. Two minutes later they were seated in the study of the otherwise deserted house, with a cold buffet on a server. Even in his sport shirt and slacks, Neil R. Ashley looked like a general. He took a sip of iced tea, then pushed his glass off to the side. "As I'm sure you've concluded, Patrick, we've got a problem." His face became very serious. "I have the permission of the President and the Director of Central Intelligence to brief you. It has the highest security classification of our government."

Morley nodded and the General continued. "On the basis of very solid evidence, we believe there is a Soviet agent, a mole, within the government. One who has access to top policy-level information." Morley sat quietly, unmoving and concentrating as he listened.

"The problem surfaced four weeks ago when the CIA received a report from an agent in Moscow—John Milford of the Agency will brief you on this later—stating that there was such a mole. The report was limited in distribution to twelve government addressees, starting with the President. As you know, Patrick, nothing is held tighter than a counterintelligence report of this nature.

"However, two weeks later the Agency received a second report. It was really a blockbuster, because the Moscow agent had died to get it to us. He died, Patrick, *because the mole had seen that first intelligence report and told the KGB about it!* The Moscow agent said that within a week of his sending it the KGB boys were zeroing in on him, so that they had to have been told. They were cautious and slow, but inexorable, and were evidently seeking to arrest him when he sent the final report."

The General raised his eyebrows and grinned. "Like it so far?"

"Very interesting. Is that where we stand now?"

"Not quite. There's one more angle, I guess you could call it a complication, or maybe even a lucky break. About the same time—no, a bit before, actually—as the first Moscow agent report, the KGB chief in India defected and was brought to Washington. As you know, we, ICG, have primary responsibility in this kind of case, but since we're still in the process of staffing up we were delighted to get the services of a CIA officer to handle the initial debriefing. This officer, Jack Glover . . ." He hesitated and Morley came in on cue.

"Yes, I know Jack, good man."

"Uh huh, I know you do." His expression was odd, but Morley couldn't figure why. "Anyway, Jack not only knew the defector well but had set up his defection a year or so before, when he was stationed in New Delhi. So the defector liked him, Jack was a first-class debriefer, and all was well until the night before last when Jack was killed in a hit-and-run accident while returning to the Agency from a debriefing session."

Morley looked sad. "We lost a top-notch officer in Jack."

"Well, that's bad, Patrick, but it gets worse. Jack's notes and the tape from that last night indicate that the defector, whose name is Ivan P. Telchoff, had just begun to tell him about a KGB mole operation in Washington twenty years ago, which was being run or overseen, I guess, by no less than the current KGB Chairman, Yuri Globitsyn, who was at that time boss in the Washington Residentura. Telchoff had just started to open up, as I said, but now he doesn't want to talk about *any* KGB operations! Says he's scared—KGB 'sent him a message' by killing Glover, and he is next. You know the drill." Morley nodded silently.

"So that's about where we stand, Patrick. The FBI has a squad of investigators reexamining the backgrounds and lives of anybody who saw or could have seen that report. It's a 'blind investigation,' of course, since only the FBI Director and his assistant Stan Epworth know the why. By the way, Stan will be your Bureau contact, and an old friend from Brussels days, Dave Byrnes, will be your State contact. Dave is State's rep to ICG also."

"Yes, and I think I did meet Stan—about five years ago."

"Uh huh, you did. Good man. Trust him. Now here's where you come in, Patrick, if you will."

"Yes. Where is it exactly that you'd like me to come in?"

"I want you to handle the control and coordination of the entire investigation for ICG—FBI, CIA, defector, everything. I want you to ferret out this mole, defrock him, identify him, smoke him out!"

"I see. Just like that?"

"You'll have any help you need—or want—and your authority will be absolute. You will report to me and I to the president, and that is the extent of our command line."

Morley's eyes widened. "As the guy in that old joke says, 'Why me, boss?' You must have lots of hotshot investigators."

"Yes, I do, but I don't need another investigator, even a super-investigator; I need a tough controller, an idea man who thinks, and decides, and acts, and operates all these investigative arms. You, Patrick, have a number of unusual qualifications."

"I do?"

"Indeed you do. I'll name some. You're experienced in handling just this type of case. You did it for me twice in Europe. Right?" Morley nodded unenthusiastically.

"You're relatively clean with the Russkies, and you've been off their radar for some years. Any of the good—really good—counterintelligence men from the Agency or the Bureau have KGB files like suitcases. And, yes, you knew Jack Glover." The General looked pensive. "I think you can handle this defector and get him started again."

"Why do you think that?"

"Just a hunch. I think the guy will respond to you and that your personal knowledge of Glover will help. Let's just say it's intuition."

"I see. Any other reasons?"

The General's face was very serious as he leaned closer, speaking in a low but clear voice. "Yes, Patrick. Last, and most important of all reasons, I trust you completely." He hesitated, then went on in the same confidential tone. "This case has me paranoid. I don't know who I can trust. You realize that the names of people who saw that first intelligence report include those of the President, the Secretary of State, the FBI Director, the DCI, the Attorney General, and only a few others! It's crazy, but these people are all suspects! So how can I in good logic, put one hundred percent trust in anyone *they* recommend or send me? With you I have no questions. You're outside the loop. We begin and end on a level of trust I simply can't obtain elsewhere." He grinned. "Now you know why I'm here and why you're here. Will you take the job?"

Morley looked amused. "General, you knew damn well when I agreed to meet you here today that I wasn't likely to refuse your request."

Ashley chuckled. "I only hoped so. I'm delighted I was right. When can you start? Can you fly back to Andrews with me?"

"No, but I'll report for duty tomorrow."

"Good. There will be a jet waiting here on the flight line tomorrow from, say, noon on. Keep using the Brown ID. Contact the C.O. when you have your schedule; he'll give you any details you need. I'll have a car meet you at Andrews." A few minutes later the General waved good-bye as Morley negotiated his car onto and out of the tree-lined driveway. He turned and went back in the house. Morley, in contrast, was frowning, deep in thought, as he sped toward the Homestead A F Base gate and the turnpike beyond.

He drove fast and well. As in any action requiring a high degree of physical and mental coordination, he was very adept. Morley was thirty-six, another transplanted Californian, although he had done most of his growing up in the Midwest. On the surface his curriculum vitae was routine and uninteresting. From life with his widowed mother in Indiana to his graduation from Northwestern to his acceptance of an ROTC commission and a career with the army. He had married and then lost his young wife of three years in a plane crash while they were stationed with NATO forces in Europe. He had resigned from the service not long after the tragedy and come to Florida to live. He was at the moment unemployed.

Behind these bland facts, however, was a very unusual man.

Morley was, for one thing, almost jingoistic in his patriotism; for another, fearless; and lastly, outspoken on the issue of justice for all. The quixotic result of these personality traits had indeed controlled many of his career options and actions. He had spent a lot of his high school free time trying to melt his mother's icy resistance to his seeking appointment to West Point in his father's footsteps. She was, in Patrick's opinion, understandably but illogically bitter: the elder Morley, a much decorated Air Force pilot, was finally declared to have been killed in action in Vietnam, but only after four years of indeterminate status as an M.I.A. Patrick had watched his mother agonize from hope to despair during those four years, which is why he understood her antipathy toward the service; but his own sense of justice branded the antipathy as illogical. For him, the principal result of those M.I.A. years was the development of a high degree of hatred for the Communists whom he, logically in his opinion, had identified as the real culprits. (Nothing he had experienced since those days had changed his mind.)

Patrick's mother had not known of her son's enrollment in ROTC, thinking, logically this time, that his Magna Cum Laude studies and his success as a point guard on the school's undistinguished basketball team were enough to keep him very busy; so it was with shock but resignation that she had given her blessing to his ROTC commission and a planned military career. He had finally worn down her resistance.

Morley's military assignments were anything but routine. He had opted for and been accepted by Special Forces, was trained, and sent to Europe. He was subsequently hand-picked by General Ashley for the NATO Anti-Terrorist Squad in Brussels on the basis of his record and a personal interview. The General developed a deep affection for this talented and intrepid soldier, and came to rely heavily upon him, especially in dicey situations. Morley returned both the affection and trust. There was one case in Germany where the Soviet opposition had attempted to neutralize Morley by a clever and insidious smear operation, which might well have worked, had not the General's unquestioning and unwavering support given Morley the time and tools to expose the operation for what it was. This incident not only cemented their relationship, it also reignited his militant anti-Communist fervor. However, even in such situations there was in Morley that sense of justice, one could even say an overly developed sense of fair play, that not only enabled him to look on the East-West conflict as a kind of game with common sense rules, but prohibited him from breaking those rules even if the other side's action warranted it. The General had always admired this capability, and believed it was the basis of Morley's cool good judgment in crises. Angela Mornay, on the other hand, attributed to this "game complex" Patrick's susceptibility to the call of adventure.

The death of Morley's young wife had hit him hard. He blamed himself. She was killed in the crash of a hijacked aircraft, a ploy between two rival terrorist factions, and Morley felt he should have foreseen it. He resigned from the army not long after the tragedy, but maintained occasional contact with the General. It was a combination of forced inactivity and the entrance into his life of Angela Mornay that snapped Morley out of the past and back into the stream of life, and in the last year he had become again his own self. He had even asked for and obtained the General's help in a borderline ethical matter involving a great deal of money. It was predictable that Ashley would now turn to him for assistance on a thorny problem. It was just as predictable that he would say yes.

SEVEN

MOSCOW, U.S.S.R.

Globitsyn looked up as his aide entered, closed the door behind himself, and walked toward the desk. "Ah, Sergei Mikhailovich, sit down. Pierre has reported, Comrade. His first operation was successful. The CIA man is dead and Telchoff is frantic."

The young man smiled. "Pierre was a good choice."

"I guess so, Sergei Mikhailovich; but I cannot be happy while the snake lives. I want him dead, not just scared."

"I assume Pierre is working on that, sir."

"Oh yes, he has a plan. And I think it's a good one. Now, Comrade—this is confidential, just you and me—his first plan would have started World War Three. He wanted to have a full-scale raid and shoot up the whole U.S. state of Virginia! Well, I've got him calmed down, and he's working on a more modest plan with a great deal less blow-back potential."

"You mean they won't know we did it?"

"Oh no, they'll know all right, but they won't be able to prove it. It will all point back to the Arabs. But I suppose they'll retaliate somewhere in the world; that's to be expected, and it's acceptable. A massacre is not!"

Globitsyn turned those piercing eyes on his young visitor. "But that is not why I wanted to see you. I have a task for you. Go to central records and pull everything they have on an American named Patrick Morley"—he spelled the last name— "last military rank was major in the U.S. Army, last posting Brussels. He worked for that mass murderer from Vietnam, General Ashley, and it appears that he still does. Anyway, I want you to give me a report—no more than two pages—on this man. Tell me where he comes from, what he's done, and why he did it. I want to know everything about him. You may signal any pertinent residentura for help as needed. And, Comrade"—the eyes glinted—"I want this information no later than this time tomorrow. Understand?"

"Yes, sir, it will be done." Again the military aboutface and departure from the room. Again the amused look on the face of a thoughtful Globitsyn. Again, his musings about the damage potential of Telchoff. Sooner or later that treacherous fucker would tell them about the man in Washington, and inevitably they would conclude it's the same one Borodin told them about. But so what? Even if Telchoff poked about, looking for details back in those days . . . it didn't matter because there were no details around. All the same it would be embarrassing to explain to the General Secretary why that snake had *any* knowledge at all.

Pierre's men had almost had the CIA files and notes on the case. They were all over the ground around the CIA man's car. But Pierre had explained that the police were there so quickly, they couldn't take the chance. He said that the Amis *think* there is something fishy, but they could never prove it, and the truck is in five hundred pieces and buried in the middle of a dump by now.

He smiled to himself at the thought of Telchoff, the traitor, who was on his way out but didn't know it yet. Pierre's new plan was workable—and the two Arabs, even if they got caught . . . Not only would it trace back to the Libyans, but that would be *after* they'd killed the snake. With Telchoff gone,

Pierre could get his other business done and be on his way, while the Amis were still trying to figure out what had happened and why.

Globitsyn smiled. The best part was that with Telchoff dead nobody would ever know how much or how little he knew about Kotch—and more importantly how and where he got his information.

He lifted his coffee cup in salute. "To you, my comrade, Pierre—success!"

EIGHT

WASHINGTON, D.C.

Morley was on his way back to the State Department for his third briefing of the day. He had stepped up his departure from Florida—from sad but smiling Angela Mornay—and arrived at the General's office in Washington before 2:00 P.M. Assistant Director, FBI, Stan Epworth was there waiting with the General, and they discussed in detail the direction and results of the Bureau's investigation to date, and agreed on where it was going from here.

Next, he was driven to Langley, Virginia, to meet with the Agency's John Milford for his second backgrounder. They had never met before, but hit it off very well; and after a few moments of routine sparring they were talking like close colleagues. Morley was particularly gratified by Milford's candor. He was willing to show any file or explain any situation in as much detail as Morley wanted.

Milford began with a profile on the source, Boris Feodorovich Borodin. "He was a real comer in the KGB, Pat: a thirty-four-year-old major and protégé of Globitsyn. Smart, poised, already very experienced. Looked like he might be on a rocket to the top of the KGB. His father, the Ambassador, was a legend in the Soviet Foreign Ministry, a man who not only survived but prospered under a series of very different regimes. In the Gromyko mold, you might say."

"Yes, I've heard of the Ambassador. I didn't realize your Borodin was his son."

"Uh huh. And therein lies the tale of a great spy. Young Borodin grew up in plush embassy surroundings, exposed to rich foreigners and advanced foreign schools, and this became the handle for his recruitment. He had seen too much of the 'capitalist good life' to be taken in by the Communists' bullshit in the Soviet Union. Boris was an idealist *and* a realist at the same time: he hated the 'lying, repressive, murderous Party leaders'; and he wanted to live in the West someday with a legacy of cash and good will. We filled his needs on both counts."

Morley nodded silently, his attention focused.

"Borodin was recruited just about two years ago in Japan and had been a prolific and extremely valuable reporter ever since. Unique, really, because he had access to high-level pure intelligence of all sorts, and his counterintelligence production from inside the KGB was superb. He was posted back to Moscow last year, and then four months ago he was transferred to Chairman Globitsyn's personal staff."

"Bonanza!"

"Believe it, Pat. That's exactly what it was. He accompanied Globitsyn to meetings and conferences as his aide and note taker, had access to most of his personal files, but, best of all, they became good friends. Globitsyn would often invite him to his office for drinks and chats in the late evening—Borodin said the Chairman often stayed the night—and in these chats there were no restrictions on subjects discussed."

"The boy must have been a gold mine, Jack. I'm beginning to understand just how much we lost."

"I doubt we'll see another like him in our lifetime. Anyway, you can imagine how tightly this case was held within the Agency." He laughed. "Although we *had* to disseminate his intelligence reports, since that's our business. So over a month ago, during one of these 'vodka and spy' sessions, Globitsyn told Borodin about his prize agent, code-named Kotch. Said he'd recruited Kotch himself, then trained and nurtured him through the early years of his career. Globitsyn boasted that this was a classic case and that it would become the best and most important intelligence operation 'since Klaus Fuchs stole the A-bomb.' Globitsyn was full of vodka and very garrulous that night, but still stopped short of giving our man any real detail about the operation."

Milford shook his head slowly and sadly. "It was a pity because Borodin, having only this titillating glimpse of the Kotch operation, and not even knowing its locale in the world, did not report it right away. Had he done so, we would have—maybe—been better prepared to handle the bombshell when it came in a week or so later."

Again the slow head shake. "Anyway, a few nights later the subject of Kotch came up again—we assume Borodin injected it into the conversation after sufficient vodkas had been consumed—and Globitsyn ended up giving him permission to 'read the files' on the case 'for his education.'" Milford stopped to sip some coffee.

"Well, Borodin learned quickly that this wasn't the pot of gold he had hoped for because Globitsyn had excised all the pertinent agent-identifying data out of the file. Of course, Borodin could tell by the types and levels of Kotch's reports that he was in Washington, in the U.S. government, and that he had *some* access to policy-level top-secret intelligence. He also noted that the spy's access had increased in the last ten or eleven months. There were still no real clues as to the mole's background, position, or identity.

"Despite these negatives, this information was so hot Borodin decided, correctly, that he had to get it to us immediately. He normally reported every tenth day, late evening Moscow time, midday for us—"

"How did he do it?"

"A specially designed system our boys put together just for him, built and perfected while he was still in Japan—we knew he was due for a Moscow posting any time. He brought the two pieces—both well disguised—in with him when he moved back from Japan. No problem. Basically, he had a state-of-the-art miniaturized 'burst' transmitter and he transmitted from his car. The receiver-recorder-transmitter was located in a small apartment, occupied by his eighty-year-old deaf aunt, which was on Borodin's regular route home from work. Our 'collector' merely drove past later in *his* car—it's a normal area for him to be in too—activated the transmitter in the old lady's place, and got the same 'burst' on *his* recorder."

"Uh huh. And it worked well?"

"Like a dream. So, as I said earlier, we weren't prepared for the bombshell. Borodin had stayed late, very late, that night reading the file, so by the time he got his transmission ready, sent it, used his emergency safe system to notify his case officer/collector that the machine in the old lady's place was loaded, the case officer got dressed, went out and got it, came back, wrote the cable, and had it sent, it was very early morning here in Virginia!"

Milford smiled. "I'm giving you a lot of buildup, Pat, and I'm sure you know why. Maybe if the message had come in midday as usual, or maybe if we'd known Borodin had access to the Kotch file before he sent this emergency blockbuster—I say just 'maybe' things might have been different. Anyway, the message came in and everything was handled strictly according to the book: no flaps, no delays, no mistakes. The proper people were called in to the office and took the proper steps to process and disseminate the counterintelligence according to the new statutory requirements. All was completely kosher."

"So what could you have done differently, Jack? Seems to me the U.S. government was 'hoist by its own petard.'"

"Indeed it was—we were. Our staff people followed the law and its spirit to the letter. I'm moaning because if I'd been here and the Director had been here—we were in London for a meeting—we'd have found a way to delay until we could get an exemption to the legal requirement from the President, who *does* have that authority . . . but it wasn't to be, and the report went out, and you know the rest."

Morley nodded. "In the past, I assume such a counterintelligence report would have been held 'in house' under the tightest possible controls. Right?"

"Absolutely. And even with disguise, paraphrase, amputation, whatever, the facts still get through—as we've all learned, to our dismay."

"Yes, I know. It was apparent. Would have been to anyone familiar with the lingo."

"Well, Pat, I won't say any more—it doesn't do any good—but when this is all over you can bet you'll hear some of those headline grabbers up on the hill berating the Agency for the leak!"

Morley nodded assent.

"To go on with my sad tale. Borodin waited till his next regular reporting day to send a short message reporting only a 'red sky'—meaning he was under suspicion and would not be reporting to the aunt's receiver anymore. He asked us to activate the emergency equipment in the Chancery. By agreed procedures this would be done for only three minutes a day, because the KGB knew immediately when it came on; and the three-minute span was different each day according to a schedule which Borodin had. Incidentally, this second report—we did not yet know that the first one had leaked—was deemed by the Director and the President to be *not* subject to that distribution regulation. In fact, the Director said he'd eat the only copies if 'they' ordered him to distribute it!"

"And so to the third and last message."

"Right. We were not really surprised—saddened, yes, devastated, yes, but not really surprised—when the next message became the last. Our people watched while all hell broke loose down there in front of the Chancery when Borodin sent it and took his L pill. We'd figured Borodin had some days before deciding he'd make one final report and then kill himself."

"As you said, Jack, the man was a realist, a very brave realist. Still I'm amazed that he lasted so long and that he was able to get to the Chancery that night to transmit."

"Yes, it was amazing, but we figure the fact that Globitsyn himself had given him the file slowed everything down, because the security guys looked everywhere else first. But by the time he sent the 'red sky' message, Borodin knew it was just a matter of time, so he began planning for the last transmission. We don't know how he did it, but are thankful as hell that he did."

"Without it we were still in the dark."

"At least twilight. Anyway, as you know, Borodin said the internal security types were all over like lice within three days of his sending that first transmission, and his obvious conclusion—ours too—was that Kotch had to have seen the message or the intel report based on it, and told *the KGB*! Borodin sent the 'red sky' message because he was actually under surveillance."

"I noticed he even gave us the benefit of a couple educated guesses in that final message."

"Yeah. I think they are useful points."

"What are your feelings about their validity?"

"Oh, I think they're valid as hell, Pat. 'Course I have great regard for Borodin's smarts, so when he tells me he concludes that Kotch is neither American nor Russian, I tend to think he's got something. I believe that Borodin read enough of Kotch's reports to make an authoritative pronouncement on this subject. I've assumed the pronouncement is based on the wording and structure of Kotch's reports. Borodin had excellent English, by the way. And he was an excellent reporter."

"And the bit about Kotch's access?"

"Same deal. Borodin is an expert. Borodin studied Kotch's reports. Borodin tells me Kotch's access to top policy-level stuff was inconsistent, most of his reports were hearsay, and that the scope and level of his access and reporting were significantly upgraded a year ago. I believe he knew what he was talking about."

Morley nodded. "Now, Jack, I need to ask some security questions."

Milford had the beginning of a wry smile on his face. "Fire away."

"Okay. How many people saw the first cable, the one from which the report was made?"

"An even ten."

"Hmm. How do you manage to keep that number so small?"

"Special indicator, set procedure. Only the Cable Secretary can break and distribute by hand the nine copies. Even the infamous report was made from a paraphrased and disguised summary, and made by two of the ten."

"Uh huh, but ten is ten." Morley smiled, as he knew Milford knew what was coming. "Could Kotch be an Agency officer?"

This time Milford smiled. He seemed not the least bit offended, although he was obviously one of the ten. "No, Pat, positively no. I'm convinced on the basis of logic alone that Kotch is *not* Agency."

"Logic?"

"Unassailable logic. And from both ends—Moscow and Washington. First, here: the ten of us, while surprised at Borodin's disclosure about the existence of Kotch, have known about Borodin—what a disaster he was for the Soviets and what a plum for us—for two years. We've also had access to his file for the same length of time. It is simply unbelievable that if one of the ten were Kotch he would have waited till now to blow the whistle on Borodin. No way."

Morley nodded slowly. "And at Moscow's end?"

"Logic again, Pat. Borodin was a smart, experienced intelligence and counterintelligence officer. He read carefully the file on Kotch's production—we know that—and we know he saw nothing to indicate Kotch was an intelligence officer of any kind, much less an Agency officer."

"How can you be so certain?"

"One, he knew the business so well, and knew how important it would be to us if Kotch were in our intelligence community. He tells us other bits garnered from analyzing the mole's reports, like his access and non-nationality, but would he neglect something he should have spotted even more easily? No way, my friend."

"What if Borodin knew from the file, studying the reports or maybe some other indicators, that Kotch was indeed an intelligence officer, or even an Agency officer? Wouldn't Borodin be afraid to say so in a cable, if he didn't know the mole's status or access to such a cable? Couldn't that fear that the word would be suppressed or turned back against him keep him from putting it in?"

Milford smiled widely. "I know you're playing the devil's advocate, Pat, but it doesn't add up. The answer is no, he wouldn't be afraid. The reason is that he and the officer who recruited him and ran him in Japan (and has handled him this last year by means of trips to Europe) have a code word known only to them, the only written evidence of which is on a card in a sealed envelope in the Director's personal safe. This code word, if and when used by Borodin in any communication, means he suspects Agency treachery in regard to his operation. Our officer is one of the ten who saw everything from Borodin. There was no such indicator."

Morley laughed. "Are you a lawyer, Jack?"

"No"—he smiled back—"just a philosophy major."

"You were well taught, my friend. Your logic seems unassailable; an oddity, I might add, in this business of human frailties where actions do sometimes defy logic."

"Thank you, I think. I had heard you were a logical man, Pat, and hence susceptible to a logical argument."

"You heard right. But a funny thing about logic: sometimes it can lead to the most illogical conclusions."

NINE

WASHINGTON, D.C.

The neat lettering on the door said SPECIAL ASSISTANT FOR SECURITY AFFAIRS, and below in smaller letters, DAVID H. BYRNES. Inside, the first office was small, but quietly plush in keeping with its proximity to the Secretary. There was a seating area to one side and a single desk and chair on the other. Behind the desk sat a very pretty, mid-thirtyish woman, whose flawless, light complexioned face was framed by very curly and very red, close-cropped hair. She looked pensive, her hand on the telephone and her eyes seemingly fixed on some object beyond the far wall of the room. The door to the inner office opened and a man came out. He was slender, medium tall, salt and pepper hair, good looking, well dressed, and frowning. He plopped rather than sat on the small leather couch, letting out a protracted sigh as he did so. "Red, this is one of those days that make early retirement look most desirable."

The woman smiled. He went on. "You know, I haven't had ten uninterrupted minutes all day, and I've got to have that Iran report ready for the boss's five-thirty meeting—and I've got one myself at four-fifteen, ten minutes from now!"

The redhead said nothing, but raised an eyebrow in silent

query. He laughed. "Yeah, I know. What the hell am I doing out here talking to you if I have so much to do?"

Still the woman said nothing, but humor lines had crept into her face. He continued. "Well, the truth is, Red, that I've come to that part where I'm supposed to recommend action and I don't know what to recommend! Any ideas?"

She smiled widely. Her face was even prettier when she smiled. "You're asking me, Boss? What is this, Secretary Week or something?"

"C'mon, Cyn, you know what I mean! Hell, some of my very best plagiarized ideas have come this way."

She laughed. "Yes I know. All right, what is the problem, specifically? I've read the draft, y'know—I typed it; but what part is bothering you? I thought your recommendations for action were reasonable. What more does he want?"

"I guess he wants the restrictions to be tougher. He thinks most of our embassies are like sieves, with secrets sifting through all the time."

"Well? Aren't they?"

"No, dammit, they're not. They're as good as the top management makes them, that's all. Or as bad."

"So make the restrictions tougher. Shape up top management wherever it needs it!"

"Hell, Red, they're so tough now—after the Moscow flap, and the rest—that the staffs complain they can't get any work done."

"Screw 'em, I say. They've got their damn local employees doing all the work and they're not careful what classification of tasks they give 'em. Get everybody off the golf course, the tennis courts, and the cocktail circuit—Americans, I mean. Not only would most of the security problems disappear, they could clear up most of their work backlogs in a month. And I know, Mr. B., I've been there!"

Mr. B. held his chin cupped, thinking. "Mmm . . . maybe you're right." He looked at his watch. "My four-fifteen appointment should be here. More security talk." He winked. "This time a bit closer to home. We'll be talking about the Department."

"One of your people? Someone I don't know?"

"No and yes. Not one of ours and you don't know him, and shouldn't! He's with ICG; that's all I can say."

"I won't ask, boss, but I know there's a big flap going on, and I assume it has to do with that." She smiled saucily.

Mr. B. got up, walked over to her, took both her hands in his, and leaned over to kiss her lovely upturned lips. "Dear Red, your perspicacity will get us both in trouble someday. How do you know that, about the flap?"

"David, love, secretaries always know. They don't even have to see or hear any facts to know. They can feel it in the air."

"What does the air tell you about this one?"

"Only that it's important, and has a lot of important people worried. You, for instance; and the Secretary, for another instance."

"I can't deny that, and I can't tell you why, but I know your advice would be good if I could."

"Tell me this, David, is it a leak?"

"Yes, I can tell you that much—still just between us."

She flicked her curls with a quick gesture of impatience. "I've never betrayed your confidence, have I?"

"No, no . . . it's just that it's different this time."

"Okay, I won't ask anymore."

He shrugged. "Oh well. Yes, love, there is a leak and we are one of the suspect offices—there aren't that many involved—so it is worrisome."

"What's worrisome—you and me and Jane? Hell, she doesn't know what's coming down around here. She lives for lunch hour and quitting time, and smiles only on payday. As for you and me, we know. There are no mysteries. So what's to worry about? The rest of your staff? Don't worry, none of them get in here 'less I'm here. In short, my dear boss, nothing leaks from this office. No way!"

"I believe that, Red, but I've got to convince this man."

"Easy, just be honest. Tell him the truth." She seemed to think a minute, then lit up as an idea surfaced. "Better yet, send him somewhere else to look."

The man looked pensive. "Uh huh, guess you're right as usual."

"This guy that's coming, the one I'm not to know or remember, a good guy? You know him?"

"Yes, he's a good guy and I do know him. We worked together on a case in Belgium a few years ago. In fact, we had a short but successful partnership, so to speak. Yes, good man and a friend. A fair man, I think."

"Then why worry, love, fair is fair."

He laughed. "That's true, but he is also very tough, and relentless . . . yes, good word, relentless. He's like a, uh, bulldog. Also very handsome."

"Uh huh. I see. Civilian?"

He shrugged. "Who knows? It doesn't matter. He'll be whoever or whatever he needs to be."

There was a short knock at the door and the woman buzzed the lock release. The door opened and a tall blond man came in. He was slender in an athletic, sinewy way, and moved like a dancer as he came forward, hand outstretched. "David! Great to see you again." He turned toward the redhead, bowed slightly, and said, "I'm Pat Morley."

She proffered her hand. "Cynthia Ford. Pleased to meet you, Mr. Morley." The two men excused themselves and went into Byrnes's office. Cynthia opened a bottom-side drawer of her desk and pushed the Record button on the tape machine that filled the drawer; then she placed a notebook in her desk stand and began to type from its open pages. The whir of the recorder was totally inaudible; the insulated machine and drawer made sure of that even without the typewriter noise.

Inside, Morley was already down to business. "David, I was delighted to learn from the General that we'd be working together. I've just come from briefings at FBI and CIA, and I'm looking forward to getting your thoughts on this matter. Incidentally, I heard from the General that your job is being up-graded to Assistant Secretary status. He was very pleased and so am I. Congratulations."

"Whoa, Patrick! It hasn't happened yet. But I'd be lying if I said I didn't think it was imminent, and faking if I pretended I wasn't pleased with the prospect. Thanks."

"Great news. Well, Mr. Secretary-to-be, tell me what happened at State."

"The Secretary got the Agency intelligence report and after getting the okay from the DCI, showed it to Richard Millard, his deputy, and me. Actually, we didn't get too excited at first. It seemed sort of a, well, something far away, something that didn't concern us. But then the Secretary got more upset the more he talked about it, and we kind of caught the fever. It's been that way for the last month. It seems to be the core of any discussions we have with the Secretary or with any other of the, uh, recipients of the report."

"And you know who they are, these other recipients?"

"Of course. It's a government regulation—all spelled out in there. Craziest damn rule ever devised. British can't believe we have it; Russians think it's some kind of scam."

"Your investigation has been confined to the Department?"

"Investigation is not the word, Pat. It's concern." He laughed. "The investigation is all being handled by the FBI. We're left with concern as to what they're unearthing about departmental employees. We're in the dark, you know. There has been no further information since the initial report, al-though we assume the Agency's source has made follow-ups."

Morley looked thoughtful. "And you don't see any of the FBI reports, either in your capacity here at State or in that of liaison with ICG?"

"Nope. Stan Epworth has called a number of times for inci-dental information on people, jobs, routines, etc., but Stan's a pro, a one-way street."

Morley smiled. "Just like you'd be, David, if the roles were reversed. Anybody else contact you for information?"

"Oh yeah, but not really for information. I'd say it's more like misery loves company. As I said, everybody knows who was on that distribution list. But of course, all this means is they know there's a Soviet illegal around—or so the Agency's source says. Hell, there's no reason to think the suspects have to be in any particular place or job, only that the report indicated policy level."

"It said, 'access to policy-level intelligence.' Quite a different thing. That may go a lot deeper than the distribution list. Right?"

"Of course. Secretaries know lots more than they're supposed to. So do assistants!"

"At State too?"

"I hope not, Patrick, but human nature is human nature. I still can't figure why FBI's investigation is so narrow." He laughed. "Guess it's because I'm on the list."

"Another angle and a candid question: does Miss Ford know about the existence of that report?"

"Nope. Not from me anyway. Funny you should ask, though. Just before you came in she had mentioned to me, apropos of my bitching about my busy day, that she knew there was a quote flap going on end quote. Said all secretaries have this ESP capability. Said she had no idea what the flap was, only that it existed."

"Interesting . . . and believable. I had to ask that question, but I knew your office would run by the book; just wondered if you've run across any other offices, here or elsewhere, which have access to policy-level information and *don't* run their security by the book?"

"That's a yellow dog question, Patrick Morley, and you know it. In State, I don't know of any. I've got one hundred percent backing on all security matters from the Secretary, and if I did know of any offices which were lax, I'd damn well read 'em the riot act."

Byrnes smiled and went on. "Okay. Now that's out of the way, I can go on. Yes, I've run across sloppy security and I think the worst place is in the White House, and the worst people—across the board—are the political appointees. I know it's an old cry of the bureaucrats, but it's an old cry because it's a legitimate one. Like in any other walk of life there are good ones and bad ones, but I think you have more of this type of security problem when you have more top-level people who are, one, essentially amateurs in a professional business, dealing on a temporary basis with very esoteric, complicated, and dangerous matters. Two, because it's a professional field they are dealing with experienced professionals from other countries; and three, their hearts aren't in it—after four years or less of dabbling they go back to their old lives."

Morley nodded thoughtfully. "Very persuasive. I'll keep them in mind as things progress. I am certainly not unmindful of the lessons of the 'Irangate' affair, which certainly fits your description. While we're on the subject of principles, philosophy of government, whatever, what is your feeling about ICG? How do you think it's working out? What do the Department and the other members of the 'USG Intelligence Community' think of it?" He smiled. "I ask out of personal curiosity—General Ashley couldn't care less."

Byrnes laughed. "I know. I'm sure that's why he's so valuable. Well, I get a lot of feedback here, as you can imagine, and I'd say it's about, oh, seventy-thirty *for* ICG, which is a remarkable tribute to the General. Those numbers were reversed six months ago. You know, ICG came into existence because the various agencies simply refused to play 'team' games. Simply put, the General has said, 'Be on the team or out of the game' and he's got the power to make it stick. They respect him, and they are beginning to admit the need for him. Who knows, maybe they'll even come to like him."

Morley nodded slowly. Byrnes went on. "Maybe this case will convince them once and for all. It's a damn cinch none of them want his responsibility on this one."

"I'm glad to hear all that, David."

"Now let me ask a question on another subject, but it's professional, not personal. There is a defector named Telchoff, former chief of the KGB Residentura in New Delhi. I assume he is being handled by ICG?"

Morley nodded. "I would assume, so, yes. It is certainly ICG's responsibility." He waited, eyebrows raised.

"Well, as you probably are not aware, we've had a bunch of security problems at the New Delhi embassy in the last year, and I'd much appreciate being able to ask him some questions about them." He laughed. "Hell, Pat, he probably engineered some of them!"

"Shouldn't be any problem. Give me or send me your questions, and I'll see they get to the right person and get answered—that is, if the guy will answer."

"Thanks. I'll send them on to you tomorrow, but no hurry. Whenever your man finishes with the important questions."

"Fine, David. I'll stay in touch."

Cynthia Ford watched Morley leave. He looked back and smiled as he went out the hall door. Handsome devil, she thought. She was still watching the door when her boss came up behind her chair and reached his arms around her. She turned for the kiss.

TEN

LOUDOUN COUNTY, VIRGINIA

The farm house was two hundred feet from the two-lane road and surrounded on three sides by a thick windbreak of tall pines. It looked much like other farmhouses in the area, but closer inspection pointed up some important differences. There were more people around—all men—and while they were dressed in farm clothes, they didn't "wear them well," nor did they seem to be engaged in any kind of farm work. Then there were the windows: thick tinted glass, heavy closed drapes, and bars. These unusual modifications were not visible from the road. The neighbors, far removed as they were, knew the farmhouse was some kind of a secret, guarded meeting place, and assumed it was government or military business. They neither asked questions nor ventured answers.

It was early afternoon when Morley drove up the narrow gravel lane and parked in the cleared area to the side of the house. A man in blue jeans and a light denim jacket that did not quite hide his holstered sidearm watched him park and then motioned for him to leave the car. Morley got out and approached, ID card in hand. The man looked at it carefully, turned, and nodded toward the bay window that overlooked the parking area, then gestured for Morley to follow him. Once past the heavily bolted, steel "terrorist" door, they were in a large kitchen, then a long hallway, and finally a den or library.

The lights were on even in the brightness of the day, as the heavy drapes admitted none from outside. There were two men in the room, and at first glance Morley was not sure which was the defector and which the case officer. Then one man stepped forward, shook hands, and said, "I'm Farley." Turning to half face the second man, he added, "And this is Pete."

Pete got up slowly, frowning, and offered his hand. He said nothing. Morley, also silent, turned toward his escort and Farley and gestured for them to leave. They did. He sat down in the twin lounge chair facing Pete, who had returned to his chair after shaking hands, and smiled. "I've heard a great deal about you and I'm glad to meet you. May I call you Pete?"

Pete nodded, still serious, then seemed to relax, and slowly a smile began to transform his face. The dour, sharp-planed Slavic features softened, the dark eyes took on a sparkle, and the deep creases on either side of his mouth disappeared. The man was good-looking in almost a Latin manner: dark, thick wavy hair, olive complexion, black mustache, and very white teeth. He looked younger than his fifty-plus years, as his eyes sought Morley's. "Ah, you are Godfrey, eh?"

Morley returned his smile. "Yes."

"Good. You are friend of Jack Glover, uh, Farley is telling me."

"Yes, for many years. Jack and I lived in the same city."

"Hah! Chee-cah-go, eh?"

"Yes, a long time ago."

Pete spoke with a well-modulated but heavily accented voice. "Now, Godfrey, tell me. You think friend Jack, uh, he is killed auto crash—you think is accident?" The smile had gone.

"I don't know yet, Pete, but I intend to find out."

"But what do you think? I think it was no accident."

"Well, Pete, I begin by thinking it was *not* an accident. It will have to be proved to me—by facts and evidence—that it is just an accident, or I will continue to believe it is murder. Do you understand?"

"Oh yes, Godfrey, I understand." The Russian looked serious and thoughtful as he went on. "So, friend Godfrey, if no facts, no accident, eh? KGB assassination, huh? What do you think?"

Morley, looking at the man's anxious face, realized this was an important, maybe even a watershed, question, and he answered without hesitation. "Exactly, Pete. We must assume that Jack's murder was a KGB wet operation." Morley's instincts told him immediately that this had been the right answer.

The Russian smiled. "Hah! I like you, Godfrey! You don't bullshit me, try make me feel good. Everybody here they say Jack was just accident, say not to worry. No KGB, no murder. But I know this was KGB murder. A message for 'old Pete,' Godfrey. KGB says give secrets and we kill you! I know KGB, Godfrey. I see too many years too many 'accidents.'" His mercurial disposition went from sad back to happy. "Yes, friend Godfrey, I like that you tell me no bullshit. You call spade spade. . . . I use okay, spade?"

"Yes, you did. I will not bullshit you, Pete. You and I both must call a spade a spade—no bullshit between us. I suspect Jack was killed to slow down your debriefing and to scare you. In fact, I think they would like to kill you if they could."

"Hah! You are right, Godfrey, when you say this is to scare old Pete." He laughed. "They did a good job, that is certain. I am, as you say, scare shitless!"

"I'd be scared too. In fact, I *am* scared; after all, I'm not only taking Jack's place, I'm a friend of Jack's and just as dangerous to them. But you know what I say, Pete? I say fuck you, KGB! I say I'm not playing your game. This is *my* country and I can beat you. You can't scare me, you cowardly bastards. I'm going to get revenge for Jack. That's what I say, Pete."

"Hah! Yes, I like it, Godfrey. I like that part 'fuck you, Yuri Aleksandrovich Globitsyn, you murdering cowardly bastard.'

You can protect me, Godfrey? These people, these KGB thugees, they are smart and very, uh, tough cookies." He smiled. "Yes, very tough cookies. You can protect okay?"

"I can only promise to do my very best, Pete. As you say, these people are smart, but I think we can be smarter. First thing, I would plan to move you today—tonight—to a better place—more secure, where you will be safer. Also, both you and I will start using disguises to change our appearance, several times if necessary."

"Yes, I see. And I like that part about revenge for Jack. How do we do that?"

"Simple. First we find that driver who killed Jack, and we trace him back—or better yet, get him to talk. Then we go after the KGB agent who hired him, and so on. We roll up the whole cowardly plot, you see?" Pete nodded his head vigorously.

"But most of all, Pete, we get immediate revenge by disrupting KGB plans. They killed Jack to scare you, to shut you up. We fuck them by not being scared, by continuing as if Jack were still alive. You and me, Pete, we get the best revenge for Jack by not playing the KGB's game."

Pete began that slow smile again, and brought it to its peak. "Yes, I agree. You are a smart man . . . like Jack, and I think you have right idea. Sorry I did not understand before. Good! We finish what we started. When you want start, Godfrey? Right now maybe?"

"I don't like this place too much, Pete. I think it will be better to get started on moving you first, then you and I can begin working together. I need to go and check personally your new home and make sure all is good, then I'll come back tonight—late—and we'll move. Okay?"

"Sounds okay to me. I am like the airplane on television—'ready when you are.'" He smiled again. They shook hands.

The small gold lettering on the door said EGIL KREEGER, CAPTAIN, METROPOLITAN PD. Inside, the office was spartan, but roomy and comfortable. The large desk and a good-sized table next to it were almost covered with file folders; and the man sitting behind the desk looked weary enough to have just read them all. He stood up slowly and came around the desk to shake hands.

He was a big man, big enough to be a Redskin linebacker, with the craggy, weather-beaten face of an outdoor sports lover. His gray hair was mussed and unruly as if it hadn't been combed in a couple of days. His eyes were very blue and very shrewd-looking. He came off overall as a large shaggy bear, maybe a prototype cop of the previous generation. Morley liked what he saw, at once convinced that the General was right when he had said, "Egil Kreeger is a special man and a special cop. You can trust him."

Kreeger's face softened as he pointed to the leather chair at the corner of his desk. "General Ashley recommends you very highly, Mr. Morley, and in case you're not aware of it, that's not a frequent occurrence."

"Thank you, Captain. I'll do my best to live up to it. Did the General brief you on our problem?"

"No, he said you would." Kreeger smiled. "Matter of fact, he said you'd give him hell if he told me too much, so you'd better handle it."

Morley proceeded to give Kreeger a very detailed briefing, ending with his talk that morning with Telchoff. He left nothing out. The General had told him that Kreeger had saved his life in Vietnam and was the bravest soldier he'd ever had in his command; they had agreed then and there that Morley would play no security "games" with Kreeger. He would be given all the facts.

The captain listened carefully, asking a few pertinent questions, and when Morley finished, he leaned back, obviously pondering. "So we need a secure safe house, in the District, for your boy Pete, and we need it a week ago yesterday?"

"Right. I'd like to move him as quickly as I can. That place down there scares the hell out of me!"

"Okay. The General did tell me you might be needing such a facility. He didn't say why, just that you might. So I've been doing some checking. I've got one down in Foggy Bottom. The building's unique: It has four apartments, each with its own entrance, and nobody in it sees or wants to see what the other three are doing. I'd suggest we use one of our police matrons and put your man in as a happily married husband, one who's recovering from a heart attack, should anyone ask, and who needs a driver—normal for the standards in the area—and who has a nephew attending nearby George Washington U., who spends a lot of time with his favorite uncle. These three will be my top people—that matronly looking wife can shoot your eyes out at fifty feet—and I can assure you they are not known to the Russkies like those guys down in Virginia probably are."

Morley shook his head slowly, smiling widely. "You're way ahead of me, Captain. Sounds even better than I'd hoped for. When can it be ready?"

"It's ready. Just take a phone call, say two hours' notice."

"Okay, let's make it ten tonight. I'd like to do the whole thing after dark."

"Fine. I've got a plan for that too, subject to your approval."

"You know, Captain, I bet I'm going to like your plan. Tell me about it."

"First, what kind of car will you have?"

"An eighty-eight blue four-door Taurus, Virginia number ADT three, six, one. There will be three of us in it: driver up front, me and Pete in back."

"Good. Okay, I want you to come up One twenty-three all the way to Chain Bridge, controlling speed so that you arrive at the Virginia end of the bridge no earlier than nine thirty-five tonight. A minute or two later won't matter, but don't get there any sooner.

"At exactly nine thirty-five—we'll synchronize on Observatory time in a few minutes—my people will block all District-bound traffic at that end of the bridge, letting them go through one at a time after we examine visually the car and occupants. As soon as *you* go through—I'll be there to make sure—we will stop traffic completely for three minutes. Then we will pretend that we've found whatever it was we were looking for and return traffic to normal.

"Meanwhile, with that three minutes' head start, your car will proceed along Canal to the first turn on Arizona and up all the way to Loughboro. Go left on Loughboro to Sibley Hospital, turning in the first parking lot, on your right. There will be a white four-door eighty-eight Chevy with D.C. plates, six, two, one, dash, four, eight, seven, parked with hood up and a man checking wires in the engine. This will be Lt. Toby Williams. Toby is black, average height, just over forty. Your code is 'The Bird sent me'; his reply is 'Fantastic.'

"Pull up as close as you can. The matron will be in the backseat; put Pete in there with her and you get up front with Toby. He will then drive you to the safe house by an inefficient but well-covered route. We'll know if anyone has been able to follow you—we have plans for that too.

"When you and Pete get into Toby's car at Sibley, the two other men in his car will replace you in the back of yours. They'll direct your driver on a red herring route to the Kalorama area where they will pretend to put Pete into a safe house. One will be dressed like Pete.

"One last thing. I think it would be better if you didn't go all the way to and into the safe house tonight. So Toby will let you out along the route—soon as he gets word from us that all is clear, and then you can cab back to your place or wherever. Any problems?"

Morley shook his head, smiling. "No, no problems at all, Captain. No questions. . . . Hold that, one question. Will there be any neighborhood or area coverage by your people? I know there won't be tonight, I mean later."

"Yes, we'll have two designated but unwitting patrol teams making frequent passes in the area, but we don't want to risk calling attention by overdoing it."

"I understand. I'm sure the three you'll have inside will be more than adequate. Sounds great, Captain. I'll see you at the bridge shortly after nine thirty-five tonight."

Morley was staying in a high-rise apartment in Chevy Chase, not far from the D.C. line. The place had a reasonably effective security setup, and twenty-four-hour message service. The red light on his phone cradle greeted him when he came in. The message was to call Farley as soon as possible. It was an audibly shaken Farley who answered the phone. He had good and bad news. The bad was that two men had tried to kill Pete; the good that they had failed. The thoroughly cowed Farley admitted it had been sheer luck that had saved Pete—not their protective measures—but fortunately the intended victim was not aware of what had happened. Farley suggested they move Pete quickly, and was not offended when Morley said curtly he'd taken care of it.

The attempted murder was well conceived and well executed. It was indeed only luck that had let them avert disaster. There had been a power interruption in the area in midafternoon, and two electricians, in Virginia Electric Power Co. (VEPCO) uniforms and truck, had responded to the request of several local customers to find and repair the problem. The outage had been real, the electricians looked genuine, and they could be seen going from farm to farm checking, as they approached the safe house. Farley had called the company and verified that two electricians—they gave him the names, employee numbers, and the license and ID numbers of their truck—had been dispatched to investigate. When the men drove up and all the numbers matched, Farley had let them in, after an admittedly cursory pat down of bodies and inspection of tool kits. He assigned an armed escort to accompany each of the electricians, who had said that in the interests of time they would work singly in opposite directions from the circuit box.

Evidently, the electrician who had begun tracing toward the rear of the farmhouse west wing, where Pete's quarters were, enticed his guard into a lapse of concentration and slugged him with a heavy tool—the guard was still in the local hospital under observation. Then the man must have beelined it for Pete's bedroom, where he usually took a nap about this time. Fortunately, he had deviated from this procedure this day. One of the men had loaned him a Bolshoi Ballet videotape and he was on the other side of the house playing it on the VCR.

Farley and his men were able to establish that the phony electrician must have known Pete's routine and the layout of the house because of the time element—it was too fast to be hit or miss. In like manner they could establish that the killer decided to abort rather than seek further when Pete wasn't where he should have been. So he left the unconscious guard in the closet, doubled back to the kitchen, called his partner in, and told Farley he'd found the problem, but couldn't fix it with the tools they had. He said they'd return next morning.

Farley wasn't buying, especially when the man explained the guard's absence as a call of nature. He searched the man at gunpoint. The assassin was equipped with a silenced pistol, which had presumably been disassembled and hidden on his person and in his tool box. He and his partner were already in an interrogation room, and Farley was sure their initial sullen arrogance would melt quickly under persuasion.

Farley's men had backtracked and found the real electricians bound and gagged, but not permanently harmed, in a neighboring barn. They were working on all the other questions and angles, and Farley promised to report any significant discoveries. He was pleased when Morley said he'd be there before 8:00 P.M.

The next morning, in a new apartment/office, Morley continued his study, research, and reasoning. Telchoff was safe and cozy in his new quarters too. As before, he was virtually a prisoner, but now understood and accepted the need for it, and was compensated in large part by the comparative luxury of the apartment, including a box of Russian music tapes and a top-grade audio setup to play them.

The assassination attempt had to have been the product of considerable planning and support action, not to mention a good bit of inside information. This kind of thing took time. So Morley was immediately sure of two things: one, Glover had indeed been murdered; and two, the other side had the farmhouse covered and hence could well have spotted and followed him yesterday, after his visit. He had been very careful on his way back, but couldn't guarantee that he was clean. So he would never return to the Chevy Chase apartment, not even to pick up his bags. (That would be taken care of securely and shortly.) He also had alerted Kreeger to possible low-key inquiries in the P.D. concerning his visit there. He believed he was clean now and that this new apartment was as well, so he spent a great deal of time planning to maintain this status quo.

About 10:00 A.M. the phone rang. "Godfrey?"

"Yes."

"It's Farley. Scramble, would ya?"

Morley hit the red button on the phone. Farley's voice came back on after three seconds, firm, clear, and secure. "Our birds are singing—they think they're up on a murder one rap for the real electricians—it's very interesting. They're Arabs from Syria, although they were recruited by the Syrian embassy in Algiers, some guy named Samir. The deal was money and they claim they don't know who they're working for or why. Name checks are working both on their Syrian passport names and what they claim are their real names. We suspect we'll find that they're Palestinians and the rest is bullshit, but we'll wait and see.

"Anyway, they arrived about three weeks ago, came to Washington and reported by phone—as instructed—to somebody named Farid. We checked out the number they gave us and it was a pay phone in a shopping center on Connecticut Avenue. They rendezvoused with Farid at a restaurant in Georgetown, and then all subsequent meetings were in his car.

It was a tan, four-door, late-model Ford with D.C. plates, and that's all they remembered. . . . Y'know, Godfrey, I believe 'em! They are not too smart.

"They said Farid gave them the whole drill, drove them down to look at the farmhouse, and then set them up in a motel in Warrenton. The day before the attempt he brought them uniforms, the silenced pistol, and the money, seventy-five hundred dollars each, and they did an 'on the spot' dry run for familiarity and timing. He took them into D.C. where they rented a car, and the next day they received a phone call at the motel when it was time to intercept the real electricians. They had hoped to get clear of the farmhouse and away before the victim was found. Farid was to pay them twelve thousand five hundred dollars apiece on successful completion of their assignment. The motel phone call was from a woman, a voice they hadn't heard before.

"We assume they were chosen—in addition to the fact that they are killers—because they both have good English, especially 'George,' the one with the pistol. He is fluent enough so that none of us suspected anything when we talked to him in his VEPCO uniform. They insist they only met Farid, nobody else, though their description of him would fit half the Arabs in D.C. Oh yes, Farid had a floor plan of the farmhouse, and they were told to arrive between four-thirty and five P.M. because the target would be in a particular bedroom at that time! Who told them? Why, Farid, of course. That's about it, till we get the name trace results. Questions?"

"Yes. This one guy, the leader who spoke fluent English, where'd he learn it?"

"He says in school, but it's too good. He'll probably turn out to be Lebanese and to have spent time in the U.S. And the other guy's English wasn't bad either. I 'spect they'll both be Lebanese or Palestinians from Lebanon."

"And they saw nobody but Farid? Sounds like a very professional arrangement. How'd they rent that car and where?"

"Place near Dulles. They had—George had—a Virginia driver's license. From Farid, of course."

"What about Farid's language? How did they converse when they talked among themselves?"

"Arabic. George said he heard Farid speak English several times but he couldn't place the accent. Said he was good but far from fluent."

"And the description was worthless?"

"Yeah, they couldn't come up with anything unusual, and we led them through the whole book exercise, and we've got an artist with them now."

"I assume you're working on the question of inside help—at the farmhouse and the electric company?"

"You assume correctly. Anything else?"

"No, seems you've got it under control. Just let me know soonest when you come up with anything."

"Will do."

Morley called Kreeger and invited him to lunch in Chinatown, then went back to his files and the latest investigation reports. It was discouraging. The number of people who were entitled to see, and saw, that first Borodin intelligence report was small and very distinguished. The number who were not entitled to see, and saw, was even smaller. That is, there were three people who had (inadvertently) seen it and admitted same to the FBI. How many there were who had seen, were not entitled to see, and who had *not* admitted it was a matter of conjecture. There was of course the fourth category: those not on the original distribution but to whom the report had been shown later with the proper authority having been obtained. Morley himself was in this last group.

It was very difficult to "clear" people or to zero in on others as suspects on the basis of what he had. If only Borodin had been able to pull a few more clues out of the files. Damn! Morley began to get anxious for his first substantive interrogation of Pete Telchoff. Maybe the guy could lead him into some light. He smiled wryly. Maybe the opposite.

Kreeger was waiting at the Chinese restaurant when he arrived. They had lunch, talking about various things, and then walked back to Kreeger's office. Inside, Morley briefed him in detail on the attempted assassination, which of course had not been reported to police channels as yet. Kreeger was fascinated by the Arab angle, since militant aliens—read terrorists—were part of his sphere of responsibility with M.P.D. He said he'd look into the Farid business very quietly and see if they had anything. Morley promised to get him one of Farley's drawings of the suspect. They discussed the security problems of Morley's debriefing visits to Telchoff and hit on a good plan involving the use of one of the other apartments in the same building. The owners were on a cruise and would be gone about three more weeks, and there was a way to go from apartment entrance to apartment entrance inside the building if one knew how and had the proper keys. Getting to the building securely from his own was left as "Morley's problem."

Back in his apartment poring over more FBI reports, he was again interrupted by the phone. It was Kreeger.

"Patrick"—they had agreed at lunch to dispense with the formality of titles—"there was a maid killed out in Chevy Chase a little while ago. I saw it on the news tape and the address sounded familiar. It was your apartment—I mean the one you gave me yesterday. I assumed you'd moved when you gave me the new number this noon. Anyway, as best they can piece it out so far, the gas stove exploded when she opened it to clean the oven."

"Jesus!"

"According to the cleaning service, a wipe out of the oven is normal procedure. There was no evidence of a bomb, but neither were the Maryland boys looking for any. They're happy to leave it as a tragic accident, and I suggest we do the same, as we don't want to high profile the thing; however, you and I should treat it the other way and jack our security condition up another notch. I'll try to get some details out of the Montgomery County P.D. but I'm not going to push very hard. Okay?"

"Right on target. The General assures me there is no way anybody could ident this new apartment—or get into it—but that's always a relative statement because every time I go out I take a chance of being followed home. . . . Uh, come to think of it, though, if you have anybody topside in the Montgomery County Police, it might be worth the chance to have them do a quiet check at the Chevy Chase building. You know, was anybody strange around yesterday or last night—especially an Arab, anybody just nosing, hanging around the manager's office, whatever. But use your own judgment, Egil. That's your bailiwick."

"Let me think about it, Patrick. It could be feasible. I'll be in touch."

Back to the reports. In the next couple hours he pulled out several pages of questions he felt needed further resolution. Most regarded security practices in specific offices, sign-out procedures, access to safe combinations, and similar items. The offices singled out were in Justice, State, FBI, and the White House. He called Stan Epworth and read the list into Stan's recorder. The Bureau official didn't seem the least bit annoyed—or even surprised—that one of his own offices was on the query list. He promised Morley definitive resolution, where possible, within forty-eight hours.

"You know, Patrick, I have a sinking feeling we're opening one hell of a can of worms."

"Yeah, I know. I feel the same way myself. Let's just hope once we pry the lid off we can get it back down again."

ELEVEN

WASHINGTON, D.C.

The dapper, gray-haired man in a gray pin-striped suit walked quickly from a taxi to the southernmost entrance of the corner apartment building, entering with a key. Going down a half-flight of stairs he faced another door bearing the lettering MAINTENANCE ONLY—DO NOT ENTER. Inside, another half-flight led to a long hallway that made a ninety-degree turn, bringing him under the easternmost apartment around the corner. He repeated in reverse the half-stairs and locked doors routine, then climbed a full stairway to the formidable-looking door of the east second-floor apartment. He rang the bell and shortly the door was opened by a large, handsome fortyish woman with short, curly blond hair and a good figure. She greeted him with a stiff smile. "Mr. Godfrey, I presume."

Morley nodded. "I bring greetings from the Bird." At once the woman's smile relaxed and her face became softer, prettier, more feminine. "And you, ma'am, Miss Orchid?"

"Yes, and I'm pleased to meet you, Mr. Godfrey. The, uh, Bird speaks well of you. Please call me Pansy." Her eyes danced.

Morley smiled. "Pansy Orchid!"

"My mother was a flower person."

"No explanation required, Pansy. It's a lovely name. And how is our friend, Pete, tonight?"

"Frankly, he was a little testy last night and earlier today, then he settled down. He has enjoyed the tapes a great deal, and we had a special Russian dinner this evening so I think you'll find him in a mellow mood. He likes you, Mr. Godfrey, and I think he was impressed by the move from Virginia."

"He can thank the Bird for that, but I'll take the credit for the time being."

"Fine. Let me take you to him. He's looking forward to seeing you."

"First, if you please, I'd like to check the layout of the apartment."

"Of course."

The building was large and solid. She told him that some years before it had been the mansion of a very rich senator, later divided into four spacious apartments. Two—one up, one down—were entered from the cross street, and the other two from the busy avenue, all by separate entrances. There was a central area: foyer, living, dining, den, and a large kitchen and pantry off the dining room. Three bedroom suites led off the living room. A door and stairway went down from the kitchen to a delivery area in the back of the building: both the kitchen door and the outside door below were steel and steel-bolted "terrorist" models—as was the front one. The windows were decoratively but effectively barred, and featured glass that would resist magnum fire and sledgehammer blows. There was also an impressive smoke and fire control system.

In the central one of the three bedroom areas sat Pete Telchoff listening contentedly to the rolls, blasts, and booms of his gifted countryman Khachaturian. So engrossed was he that he was startled when Morley touched his shoulder. He looked around, his face breaking into a smile, and jumped up to shake hands. "Aha, my dear friend Godfrey! I am glad you come. I see you have meet Pansy, eh?"

"Indeed I have, Pete. I'm very glad to see you too. You are comfortable here?"

The Russian laughed slyly. "How can I be no happy, my friend? Number-one quarters, Khachaturian, and a beautiful lady?" He smiled contentedly. "And there is my favorite, uh, nephew, Alfredo, who is also an excellent chess player!" He winked at Morley. "Not too excellent, Godfrey, but challenge. Yes, good challenge. Ah, sit down." He pointed to the facing twin to his large lounge chair. Morley sat, Pansy stood by, waiting.

"Maybe you have small vodka with me and Pansy?"

"I'd be delighted."

After Pansy had delivered the generous glasses and a plate of caviar, lemon, onions, and toast points, and they had toasted Uncle Sam and Mother Russia, she left, closing the door to the sitting room behind her. Pete and Morley talked a bit about the previous night and Pete was lavish in his praise of the planning and execution of the move, confiding that he had never been comfortable in the farmhouse.

Morley moved their talk into business channels. "Pete, I've read all of Jack's notes on your talks with him and I am familiar with all the background information you gave him. You've had a very interesting career in the KGB."

Telchoff nodded. "Yes, Godfrey, many interesting years all right." He laughed. "One time I think I could be KGB Chairman, in future you know. But things, as you say, change." He laughed again. "Now it is an enemy, Yuri Aleksandrovich Globitsyn, who is Chairman."

"Tell me about Globitsyn. What you know about him as a person, a man. When and where you met him and have been with him over the years."

"Aha, yes, Godfrey, he is interesting man. Very smart, very ruthless! I think he wanted be Chairman KGB since boyhood. Nothing must interfere, you know! He is tough, a smart cookie, you say?, who never forgets if you hurt him or get in way.

"First meet Yuri Aleksandrovich in Djakarta nineteen fifty-nine, sixty. He is already KGB bright hair boy, how you say? I say okay, Godfrey?"

"Yes, almost." Morley smiled. "Fair-haired boy."

"Yes. Fair-haired boy. He was acting number one Djakarta Residentura, very young. Yuri is very smart, as I say, very merciless. Do not sell short, this man. He is powerful and strong man, Godfrey, and he hates everything about the West. A fanatic."

"We never underestimate our KGB opponents."

"Good! Never do that."

"So when did Globitsyn leave Djakarta and where did he go?"

"He leaves about summer nineteen-sixty. Yes, we were there, same, about six, seven months. He leaves August, maybe September sixty. Back to Moscow training."

"He received training?"

"No, no, Godfrey, he teach. A regular assignment for KGB sometimes. But Yuri is not long at training. Goes to Roma I think sixty-one late, early sixty-two. Big flap Roma with Communist Party Italia, bad flap! Yuri, he cure the problems, make Party happy, make Italianos happy, make Politburo happy. A big boost Yuri's KGB career! Big! He come back Moscow, umm, about sixty-four early, assignment number-two American section. This is in line for number-one job Washington Residentura."

"Yes, I see. Now, Pete, you came to Washington in January nineteen sixty-nine, right?"

"Yes, correct."

"And Globitsyn?"

"Maybe eight, ten months after. Maybe September sixty-nine. Yes, I think September."

"Uh huh. When you came Malik was boss?"

"Yes, Malik he in D.C. Good man, Godfrey. He leave, go back Moscow maybe April, then Dashkov acting number one."

"Dashkov was number two under Malik?"

"Ah yes. Dashkov is asshole. Not smart, like Malik, not like Globitsyn. Dashkov expected to be number one Washington but no chance. Dashkova she is daughter Marshall Bakharin, but Marshall hated asshole son-in-law. Dashkov get sick when Globitsyn made to replace Malik; did not come to the office much. Dashkova call offices every day, say Dashkov sick, no come in. I say Dashkov sick of working under Globitsyn."

"What happened to Dashkov?"

"Back to Moscow summer sixty-nine. Leaves KGB. Goes somewhere, I don't know."

"What was your status in the Residentura under Malik and Dashkov?"

"I am senior of junior officers. I handle security of Residentura and general duties. Maybe number three I am. Then Malik leaves and asshole Dashkov take over. He makes me number two. I think he knows nothing about spies and intelligence, even security. I bullshit him many times."

"And when he became sick, who ran the Residentura?"

"Most times, me. Have it very good, you say? Admin staff, very good. I run spy work before Globitsyn arrives September. When he does, I turn all over to him in good order."

"He was a good Residentura chief?"

"Very good."

"And then you and Globitsyn became good friends?"

"It is true, Godfrey. We are the bachelors. We know each other from Djakarta and sometimes Moscow. Yes, good friends." He laughed. "Yuri and me we live the capitalist good life. We swim, we ski, we golf, we drink the vodka, we bed girls, and in between we do work." He laughed again. "Not *too* much work, friend Godfrey. Not too much so we are too tired for going out nights!"

"And so it was one of these friendly vodka nights that Globitsyn told you about this illegal agent in the U.S. government?"

The slow smile began and expanded on Telchoff's face. "Aha, friend Godfrey, we are now get down to business, eh? Yes, I wait for your question about mole."

Morley matched his smile. "Pete, my friend, this is the most important information you have given Jack and me. No problem to talk about it, is there?"

"No, no problem, Godfrey. Only I am afraid you expect too much. It was only one night almost twenty years now. Globitsyn—and me—have many vodkas. Hard remember, Godfrey, but I try my best!"

"That's all I will ever ask, Pete, try your best. Can you recall more about this one occasion? When exactly was it, in time I mean? How long after Globitsyn arrived in Washington? Where were you that night? What had you been doing? How did the subject come up? What did you usually talk about? You know what I'm getting at, Pete, I'm sure."

He smiled again. "Of course, Godfrey, many times the same questions. . . . I think this one night is maybe year, mmm, at least a year after Globitsyn came here. We are going out on town maybe once in week, sometimes twice. This was October nineteen seventy . . . yes, before Revolution Day, I remember. We drink at restaurant, uh, at Carlton Hotel, yes, walk back to Chancery. Globitsyn office has refridge and vodka. We sit there and drink many vodka toasts. On other times not much time to talk business when drink, chase girl, or such; but this night Globitsyn has much to drink and we talk business, then we talk war, then he say he will shows me something. He opens his personal safe, get out medal, show me. Is Central Committee medal—high honor—exceptional service, you know type?"

Morley nodded silently.

"Yuri is proud of it, but says cannot wear because is top secret. Medal is for top-secret operation. He say sorry cannot tell more. But after more vodka, he tells. Yuri speaks of special operation with illegal agent. He has trained this man years before—I think Russia—and now agent is in place in USA government! Yuri laughs that agent very smart and will go top of USA government. Central Committee pleased! Globitsyn pleased! Everybody pleased! Even illegal agent, who full of Globitsyn bullshit, pleased!"

"Now, Pete, take your time and think about the conversation that night. Try to get it straight chronologically, then try to remember the exact words Globitsyn used talking about the agent."

"Yuri is very careful man, Godfrey. Even full of vodka he is very careful. Umm . . . he say he 'made special operation with illegal agent.' I think that is exact quote."

"So what did you make of this, Pete?"

"I think Yuri recruited this man for this job. I think he was to be illegal agent in U.S.A. government from start."

"Would this case, this operation, be unusual for the KGB?"

"Yes, unusual. . . . I say not many, but I hear of others, one, maybe two, three. Yes, Godfrey, there is much my KGB can do if an agent has good potential."

"Good. Now, Pete, you said you thought the training of this agent took place in Russia. Why do you think that?"

"Because that would be usual procedure for this kind of operation. Also, probably training was during time Yuri was in Moscow headquarters, but scheduled for coming to Washington next posting. That would be usual procedure."

"So we could pin down the time of the agent's training to sometime between nineteen sixty-four and sixty-nine?"

"Yes. Maybe closer to sixty-four because I think there was long time between training and contacting this agent again in Washington."

"Do you remember any time Globitsyn was away from the American section for long during this period?"

"No. We did not work that close, Godfrey."

"I see. Now why, Pete, why did you think it had been a long time between the time Globitsyn trained the illegal in Russia and then saw him again in the U.S.—in nineteen sixty-nine?"

"A good question, Godfrey, I think myself—hard. Yes, I think it is because Yuri is pleased with this man, this agent. He is pleased, and I think he is surprised. I get impression he did not expect this man to be so very good, even better than he expected. He could not do this in a short time."

"That makes sense, Pete, but *how* did the agent improve? What way? Did Globitsyn say?"

"I don't think so. Just an impression. I think . . . wait . . . yes!" Telchoff's face lit up with satisfaction. "Yes, is about this man's speech. I think Yuri expected a commun-i-cay-shun problem but did not have one."

"Communication problem—is that your phrase, your words, Pete, or Globitsyn's?"

"My words, Godfrey. An impression. I do not remember his words."

"What languages does Globitsyn speak?"

Pete laughed. "The KGB Chairman has, you say?, the tin ear. Not good at languages. He studied English for years. He is in London and Washington but his English is not too good. He speaks Polish a little, I think. He was in Poland long time ago."

"Was his English good enough to handle an agent? In nineteen seventy, I mean?"

"Maybe—if agent have good English."

"Pete, we have this illegal agent, probably a transplant illegal, who is pretending to be an American so he can have a career in the U.S. government. This man has to have fluent American English, so Globitsyn cannot expect problems with the agent's English. So his communication problem could only be with the other man's Russian or his own English. I'm assuming these are their only common languages. So when you say that the agent's language made Globitsyn happy—even surprised him—it must have been that the agent's *Russian* had improved."

Telchoff nodded, smiling. "Yes, Godfrey, it must be so. Also I have impression this agent is not Russian and not American. I do not remember words but it is a definite impression."

"Aha. We must discover why you got this impression. This is very important, Pete. Think about it."

"Yes, I will."

Telchoff sat, brow furrowed, for almost five minutes, silently rocking the chair. Then his head began to nod slightly and his lips moved silently, as if he were trying to convince himself of something. He began to speak slowly. "I think, Godfrey, sometimes I say 'impression' I get, when it is a *word*. You know, I *think* Yuri not speak too much even after too much vodka. Then I think but Yuri *did* speak. He *did* tell me secret he was not supposed to tell! Hah, I think, Yuri not so strong. It is something he himself said to me. Yes. I remember. He say when talking about Central Committee medal, Yuri, he run whole operation from beginning. First he recruits an agent outside Russia, then talked KGB into bringing agent to Russia for training. He say man was easy recruit because he is Slav and is Communist from small boy.

"So, all time I am looking for impression but forgetting words. Now I am sure, Godfrey. Your man is not Russian, not American. He is East European Slav from satellite country. Now I am sure!"

Morley smiled and poured them both a lot more vodka. "Now we are getting somewhere, Pete. Let me say what you have remembered and what we can conclude from this about our agent. One, he is a man, a Slav, an Eastern European who has been a Communist from youth, a good linguist, well educated. He was recruited in Eastern Europe, presumably his homeland, at an early age by Globitsyn himself, sent to Russia for training, and is now—posing or real—an American with a U.S. government position and much potential value to the KGB. Okay so far?"

Telchoff nodded happily. "Good, Godfrey, yes."

"All right. Two, we can conclude this agent's Communist-satellite background is not 'open' because he would not have been admitted to the U.S. Therefore, he must either be a transplant, impersonating—taking over the identity of—some native-born American who died, or he is an immigrant with a phony background. Right?"

"It is, again, the classbook procedure, Godfrey."

"One more thing we can conclude, Pete: if he is a transplant agent, recruited at an early age by the KGB, given specialized training by a senior KGB officer, handled personally by the Residentura chief, object of a medal from the Central Committee, he was from the start a special case. He must have had some kind of special connection in the U.S. or special abilities to make the KGB spend so much time and effort on him. Agree?"

"I think that is correct. Yes, procedures are classbook, but not usual. He had unusual potential, you say?"

"So in this case I must assume this agent learned English as a child in America. It is the only way he could cope and keep his real background under cover."

Telchoff nodded. "Yes, is true, Godfrey. But maybe his European background open but not true. This is chance also?"

"Exactly, Pete. In which case he may or may *not* be a transplant! The only lie could be one about his early life in Europe. So we know this about him: he is probably over forty years of age and under fifty; he was born a Slav and was a young Communist. As of sixty-nine, seventy, he was residing in the Washington area and had a U.S. government job with 'KGB potential.' He speaks good Russian. That is it for facts, I think. All the other identifying factors are guesses."

"What about recruitment by Globitsyn in Eastern Europe and training in Russia?"

"Well, Pete, we don't have exact dates for either of those events, and even if we did, it *could* only mean that the illegal was in Europe or Russia—on an open visit or secretly."

"Yes. Is true. This can be."

"Let us leave the illegal for a while, Pete, and talk about you and Globitsyn. When did you leave Washington?"

"Nineteen seventy-three, summer. I was posted to Japan, good job, number two, Tokyo, with chance get number one after a couple of years. Good, uh, very good, recommendation from Globitsyn." He laughed. "I am not still the 'boy,' Godfrey, but I am fair-haired, yes!"

"Uh huh. And Tokyo, did it go well for you there?"

"The work, yes; the play, no. You see, Godfrey, Yuri Aleksandrovich stayed Washington, but he settled down. He is serious man, and decided before going back to Moscow in nineteen seventy-five, he will be serious *married* man. As I say, he was fun fellow but wanted to be Chairman KGB some day. Yuri think always 'if not good for career, don't do it.' This is fact, Godfrey. So he meet Voroskaya—'Talia Voroskaya—in Washington. He sees Voroskaya, she is pretty woman, and decides she is good for Yuri's career, because her father is Marshall Vorosky, hero of Soviet Union, once Red Army chief and all that."

Telchoff sighed and shook his head. "Only trouble, friend Godfrey, 'Talia Voroskaya came to Washington transfer from Tokyo where she share for six months king-size bed with number-two KGB Residentura! Yes, Godfrey, she is old Pete's live-in girlfriend, you say?"

Morley could not repress a smile. "Why didn't old Pete marry 'Talia? Wouldn't she also be good for old Pete's career?"

Telchoff laughed. "Ah, Voroskaya is nice girl, but I am not marrying kind. I have no desire for settling down. I say she nice girl, but also 'spoiled brat' in American. Big trouble, Godfrey."

"Sounds like you were looking for excuses?"

"Yes, I think is so. Anyway, Voroskaya say I seduce her, betray her virtue, say she tell Marshall Vorosky old Pete is shit. So she transferred to Washington, and married Globitsyn. Soon friend Yuri he hate me just like 'Talia—never mind Yuri and Pete sleep with same girls before. They get married, then in nineteen seventy-five back to Moscow. Globitsyn he going higher and higher in KGB, and higher he goes the more he hates old Pete. My career is, you say?, down tube. I am finished, but must stick it out. For a while. I hope Voroskaya go bad, Globitsyn divorce her and like old pal Pete again. No dice, Godfrey.

"So I am at the end of career. I am transferred from civilized Japan to Africa, two stinking posts full of snakes and fucking bugs, then to India, to work under chief who is much junior, and even though acting chief for time, I know is over, my career. When I meet Jack and we talk about problem, he tried to recruit me, but I say no, and Jack is still friend. Good man. Yes."

"So Yuri Globitsyn was intent on wrecking your career, Pete? And then he decides no more playing around, he will call you back to Moscow and kill you?"

"Yes, I think so. Just like that."

"But why now? What had changed? Why all of a sudden must he kill you rather than just let you go on as you had for many years?"

"I think about this long time, Godfrey, and Ivanova—my friend in KGB headquarters, you know?"

"Yes, I know of her and we'll talk about her later."

"Ivanova say Globitsyn is angry because Project Delta almost blew up and he thinks Pete did it. I tell Ivanova no way! Yuri Aleksandrovich knows this is pet project of his shithead assistant, Megov. He is hoping to split off Punjabi/Sikh territory from India and Pakistan and make new country. This shithead is crazy, and Globitsyn was crazy to listen to him. I was speaking against this shithead idea from beginning, but no one will listen. Now these two shitheads almost lose India's friendship when Indian CIB find out about project, and so they blame old Pete. No way, I tell Ivanova. I am against shithead idea on official report. 'No way,' Ivanova tell me. She say, 'What report?' It is Yuri Aleksandrovich. Old Pete's report no longer in the file! So I think maybe Globitsyn, he did not want to have old Pete appear in person to tell his story. What you think, Godfrey?"

"Yes, that all makes sense to me. But suppose, just suppose, that Globitsyn wanted to, uh, shut you up permanently, for an even more important reason. Suppose this illegal whom Globitsyn had trained, transplanted, and then run in person for five or six years was in very bad trouble, say, in fear of being identified by the Americans; and suppose also that since nineteen seventy-five when Globitsyn left Washington, this illegal had progressed in his career to the point where he is an *extremely* valuable source at the policy level of the U.S. government."

Telchoff was excited, almost bouncing in his chair. "Yes, yes, I think it could be so. If this illegal is in danger, then Central Committee knows it, and Yuri Aleksandrovich remembers he told old Pete about this agent one time some many years before! Hah, yes, he is scared old Pete can say, 'I know who is the illegal because friend Yuri Aleksandrovich told me!'"

"Exactly."

"Is true, friend Godfrey? Is this illegal in trouble?"

"Yes, Pete. It is true just as I said—all of it."

"Aha. And how will you find him, Godfrey? He will not be found from what I tell Jack and you. Not enough facts. Right? Can you tell me? Is too top secret?"

Morley laughed. "Yes, it is top secret, Pete, but we have great trust in you and I can tell you. We learned about this illegal through our own agent in the KGB, Moscow. He gave us many facts, but couldn't identify the illegal except by the cryptonym Kotch. You have heard this name before?"

Telchoff frowned, thinking, then slowly shook his head. "No, I think not. It is not familiar. I not hear this from Globitsyn, or anywhere before now. Maybe, friend Godfrey, there are two illegals, maybe one this man Globitsyn has in Washington, and another, this Kotch man."

"That is possible, but don't you think it is more likely that Globitsyn wants to kill you because these illegals are *one* man— the same man he told you about?"

Telchoff nodded silently and Morley went on. "I haven't yet told you, Pete, that there was a very serious attempt on your life, down at the farmhouse yesterday afternoon. Two armed men disguised as electricians, but Farley and his men foiled the plot and captured them."

Telchoff seemed interested but not impressed. "Who is paying them?"

"We don't know yet, but we will find out. My guess is that there's a trail back to the KGB."

"Mmm, yes, I suppose so. This is why you move me, God-frey?"

"Yes. Not this particular attempt—you know I'd decided we should move even before this—but this kind of threat. I think you are safe here, Pete. And I think this makes it even more important that you and I work together to foil Globitsyn and his murderers."

Telchoff pepped up a bit at this. "Yes, yes, Godfrey, I agree. I am happy with this, help you fuck these people. Yes, we work together this important job. We drink toast, okay?"

"I would be honored, Pete."

It was very late when Morley retraced his steps back to his apartment, and even later when he finally got to sleep. He set the alarm. He wanted to listen to the tape of his talk with Telchoff first thing in the morning.

The Egyptian frowned as he picked up the telephone. He knew a call this late at night could *not* be good news.

"Hello."

"It is Aribi."

"I know. What is it?"

"Only to report, sir. You were out earlier."

"I know I was out, what is it you wished to report?"

"We have not yet been able to close that deal."

"You called to tell me that? I'd figured that out already."

"Yes, sir, but you told me to report daily."

"So I did." His voice softened. "No leads yet?"

"One, sir . . . maybe. There is a man, a waiter, who possibly saw our, uh, friend yesterday. He is not sure from the photo-graph, but he thinks it could be. We'll be checking out the neighborhood this morning."

"Good. Stay with it, Aribi, and do report every day. I am always anxious to hear from you. Good night."

"Yes, sir, good night."

TWELVE

WASHINGTON, D.C.

Morley had barely laid out his papers and files on the desk when Kreeger called. He said that his people had routinely reported the arrival of an Egyptian businessman a few weeks ago. The man had set up an office in an apartment near Dupont Circle and seemed to be legitimately involved in some import/export deals, for which he had all the necessary permits. Although they immediately put him on their watch list as a routine procedure, they had made a special notation on the file because the Kuwaiti couple who had previously occupied the apartment had been suspected drug traffickers. FBI and CIA traces on the man's name, Fuad Maksud, were negative.

Yesterday, however, Kreeger's men had been tailing a Libyan alien who was under suspicion for all the usual reasons, not the least of which was acting as paymaster for some suspected terrorists. This Libyan had led the police to the Egyptian's office, where the two were together for more than half an hour. Kreeger said it could mean nothing, since the Libyan also had a legitimate business operation. He added that the Libyan and the suspected terrorists were under continuing "loose watch" and were being allowed to run free in hopes they would lead the police to bigger game.

Per Morley's previous request Kreeger had rounded up all the photographs he had of pertinent Arabs in the D.C. area, so that they could be shown to the two would-be assassins in cold storage down in Virginia. He said he would add a few more, make sure that the Egyptian and Libyan were included, and send them by messenger to the General's office.

Kreeger had nothing new on the Chevy Chase apartment stove explosion, but was hoping to hear something later in the day.

Morley then called Farley and arranged for his people to pick up a set of the pictures from the General. On a hunch he called Epworth and Milford and told them he was sending copies to them for checking their respective files.

Back to work, and it was two solid hours before the phone rang again. This time it was David Byrnes at State, asking how Morley was doing with his list of suspects. Had he been able to whittle them down a bit or not? Morley said he'd been a bit pressed on other things, but that he'd seen enough to "whittle" some, but not many, names off the list. Byrnes then told him that there was an interesting event coming up that Morley might want to use, and asked if they could get together and talk about it. They agreed on ten o'clock the next morning at Byrnes's office.

By midafternoon Morley had been over all the latest FBI reports, and had again called Stan Epworth to ask further checks on certain items. He decided that there was really no way to clear totally most of the people who qualified as suspects, nor was there any way to condemn them. He would have to be very patient and very lucky. Maybe Byrnes would have a good idea. Thinking and making notes, he continued through the afternoon, no closer to a solution, but with his conscience assuaged by the hard work. About four o'clock he stopped to take a slow relaxing shower, and then lay down on a towel on the couch to catch the TV news.

The door chimes sounded miles away and he realized he'd fallen asleep. As he snapped into full alertness, adrenaline flowed. Nobody should know where he lived! He approached the door from the left—it opened right. "Who is it?"

"Open and see, klutz," replied an amused feminine voice.

Morley opened and saw, and the beautiful dark-haired woman stepped forward into his arms. He reached around her to push the door shut and click in the two dead bolts, by which time her mouth had relented and let him take in air. He held her at arm's length and looked. She was doing the same. She smiled. "Surprise!"

Morley forced a frown. "Surprise, yourself! What took you so long, girl?"

"I have a busy schedule."

"I know. How'd you get away? Did they close Worth Avenue and block off the beaches?"

"You're not glad to see me?"

"Do I not look glad, lady?"

"Hmm. I dunno. Maybe if I lifted your skirt I could tell." She reached for the bottom edge of the towel that was loosely knotted around his waist, and lifted. He raised his eyebrows, waiting silent and unmoving. She undid the knot. "Ah, yes, I see . . . indeed."

She took his hand, leading him toward the bedroom as she shed shoes.

THIRTEEN

WASHINGTON, D.C.

Telchoff seemed tired and distracted that evening so Morley shortened the session. At least that was how he tried to rationalize it, ignoring the fact that Angela was waiting for him in the apartment. However, there was one possible gem, about which he had a good feeling. He had brought copies of Kreeger's Arabs' pictures to show Pete on the long shot that he had seen any of them around the farmhouse or anywhere else. Telchoff examined each of them carefully, shaking his head, and then returned to the picture of the Egyptian. He stared at it a while, turning the photo different ways, holding a fingertip over various parts of the face and head, and muttering to himself in Russian. Finally he handed it back to Morley, still shaking his head and frowning in puzzlement.

"There is something here, Godfrey. This man I think I have seen before. I cannot remember, but face—I know it from some old time. Maybe he just looks same as old friend. I do not know. Can I save and look again in morning?"

Morley left him with the Egyptian's picture, still staring at it with that disturbed, puzzled look. He used a new route back to his apartment, shedding his disguise in the elevator.

Angela was in the shower when he came in. He signaled through the glass door for her to hurry up, but she crooked her finger in invitation and began to relather. He repaired to the kitchen where he mixed two traditional "three to one" Wyborowa martinis with Martini & Rossi vermouth and a dry twist of Florida lemon. He poured the mixture into two frosted "straight up" cocktail glasses just as Angela appeared in her standard "après shower" garb of two towels—one wrapped Sikh style around her head, the other around her body. She took a long sip from the proffered glass, grimaced, took another, and then moved bouncingly back toward the bathroom, drink in hand. Morley was smiling as he watched her provocative form disappear around the corner.

He called Kreeger while Angela was dressing, and on impulse asked him to join them at the Bristol Grill for a late dinner. Kreeger said yes, obviously pleased with the invitation. He was a widower and his only child was with some high tech firm in California.

Angela and Kreeger hit it off well from the start and the outing became a fun night, so they decided to extend it with a visit to the Ritz-Carlton (née Fairfax) Lounge to enjoy the performance of the latest musical prodigy from New York's sophisticated nightclub circle.

They watched, listened, and sipped through the very enjoyable show, then said a reluctant good-bye outside. Angela kissed Kreeger's cheek and invited him to Florida. He accepted, and then got a cab back to where he'd parked earlier.

Morley and Angela began what she called their "Mickey Mouse journey" back to his apartment. She understood and accepted the need for all the cab changes and so forth, but the fact that Patrick felt they were necessary increased her worry about what he was into this time. She found herself wishing Egil Kreeger would stay around Patrick more.

Both Kreeger and Morley would have been chagrined had they noticed the man in the far corner of the Ritz-Carlton lounge, who, shielded from their view, had been observing them during the show. They would have regretted the lapse of security in being there together, and they would have deplored the sheer nasty coincidence that had led them to that particular night spot on that particular night. The man was very good at tailing.

The phone was ringing when they came into the apartment. It was Farley. He began by apologizing for calling so late, saying that he'd been trying for the last couple hours. There had been a good bit happening—all good. One of the captured would-be assassins had folded completely when faced with his own M.P.D. mug shot with his real name and pedigree, and the other one joined him shortly. They admitted knowing Farid from way back, in Lebanon, under the name Aseem Otar. They didn't know if that was real or just another alias. He was living, as Morley had learned from Kreeger, under a third alias in D.C. with all the proper papers. The killers swore on their mothers' respective graves that they did not know anybody in the command line above Farid-Aseem, but were sure there was someone.

Farley's second item was similarly interesting. Farid had also recruited and handled the two penetration agents involved in the assassination attempt. The first was a woman at the electric company who supplied the information, stolen uniforms, and ID's, and handled the phony outage complaint. She claimed that she'd been conned by this friend of a friend (she identified Farid's picture right off) into helping him pull off a "big practical joke." She admitted that her conscience *and* her curiosity had been stifled by Farid's generosity: five crisp one-hundred-dollar bills. Her motivation was greed, her judgment atrocious, and her employment terminated.

The other leak was a more serious matter. He was a security-cleared assistant cook who had worked at the farmhouse as a replacement during the regular cook's time off. He'd been employed in this capacity off and on over the last few years. His motivation was also greed—fifteen of those crisp bills in his case; his judgment was also atrocious, and his employment also terminated. However, in his case the punishment promised to be a bit more severe.

Both readily identified Farid's picture as that of their corrupter, and both maintained there was no further information they could supply. Farley's people had accepted this from the woman, but the assistant cook was slated for a little pharmaceutical memory jogging tomorrow. Farley promised to call if there were any results or other new developments.

When Morley awoke next morning in the tousled bed he was looking at Angela's scowling face braced against her fist, staring at him. He decided to use the nonchalant tactic. "Good morning, darling, I thought you would sleep late."

No go! Her frown just deepened. "Sleep late? I haven't slept all night!"

"Oh, I'm sorry. Was it the food? No, I know, it was that damned brandy! I shouldn't drink it late at night either. It'll kill the tum—"

"Patrick, how can you be so full of manure so early in the morning? You know damn well why I can't sleep! How could I?"

"Hmm. Not indigestion then?"

"More like indignation."

"I see, you're angry I let Egil come between us and our romantic evening."

"No, Patrick, not Egil. He's a love and I enjoyed him immensely. Are you dense this morning or are you just baiting me?"

"Dense only, darling. Elucidate please."

"All right. I'll play the game." She shook her head slowly in resignation as one might do with a bright but recalcitrant child. "You've been here six days and—"

"Five."

"Whatever! And you've called twice, and—"

"Three times."

"First time you were nasty, positively overbearing. Wouldn't answer any of my questions. I don't count that as a real call! As I said, you called twice and did nothing but blow smoke at me. I get up here and have to threaten the General's secretary with a habeas corpus suit to get your address—even then I'd still be looking if his nibs hadn't walked in! I find you, you look terrible. You haven't been eating or sleeping right, and I s'pect you've got your shapely little arse in a big jam that you're not telling me about. So dammit, what the hell is going on? Tell me why I shouldn't just pick you up and take you back to Florida?"

She was so angry her lips trembled, but Morley just kept smiling at her. Finally, he said, "I love you."

That did it. Her beautiful eyes narrowed, the full lips firmed, the voice steeled. "You arrogant bastard! Do you think you can cut me out of your life, let me in for a damn supper and a roll in the hay, and send me back to Florida purring like a damn lovestruck cat? Who the hell do you think you are? Dammit, I want some answers, Patrick; and I want them now!"

Morley continued to smile, then repeated, "I love you."

She started to sputter in fury, but it was too much, and she began to laugh and cry at the same time, finally collapsing in his arms. Her eyes opened and her face clouded again. "Patrick, darling, you can't just brush me aside with kisses—no, I didn't say stop—but, dammit, *I am* worried. You only get mysterious when it gets dangerous. I want to help. What *is* going on?"

"Seriously, darling, I—"

"Hey, that's a good start—seriously, good! Go on."

"Well, I'm working on a top-secret case for the General."

Her eyes rolled upward, pleading with heaven for the gift of patience.

"Yes, I know you know, but I don't think you should know anymore."

"I see."

"I don't think it would be safe for either of us."

"You're not kidding?"

"No way. I *can* tell you this. We are playing with the KGB

first team here and they play hard ball. If they think you know too much you become a target."

"And you're a target."

"Yes."

"Do they know who you are?"

"Yes, I'm afraid they do . . . and I'm more afraid they could know by now who you are."

"I see. So I could be a target too?"

"Not if I can help it, my love. I'm going to see to it that you're a missing target."

"Oh?"

"I want you to leave here today, this afternoon, and in such a way that they can't follow you."

"Uh huh. And how will I do that?"

"You'll fly on an air force plane out of Andrews that will file an open flight plan to Homestead, but a covert one for O'Hare."

"And I'm going to Chicago?"

"You are indeed, love. You're going to stay with Dana for a few days till we get things cleared up here."

"Maybe Dana's away."

"No, she's there. I talked to her last night. She's expecting you—and excited about it."

"Isn't that nice. You've been a busy boy, haven't you?"

"Yes."

"And when am I leaving?"

"Two this afternoon."

"You're serious, aren't you?"

"Never been more so, my love."

"Mmm. And you can't tell me why?"

"I've told you why, darling. I love you and don't want the bad guys even to think about using you to get at me. That's all I think it's safe to tell you." He laughed. "As the villain said, twisting his mustache, 'Trust me, baby.'"

"All right, Patrick, I'll trust you. But I want your promise that you won't take any foolish chances. I want you around for a lot of years yet!"

"Deal, darling. I intend to be around for all those good years with you, but I have to do this job first and I need to be on it one hundred percent. To do that I need to be sure you're safe. That's the whole . . . and the sole . . . idea."

"And I'll only be away a few days?"

"Week at the most—maximum ten days!"

"I'll need clothes for Chicago."

"Use your plastic. Have fun shopping."

"Will Egil be with you?"

"Sometimes."

"Make it all times. I'll feel better."

"Okay. I'll ask him."

"I don't believe you but I feel better already."

"I'll do my best."

"When did you say my plane leaves?"

"Two P.M."

She smiled and reached out her shapely arms. "In that case, as you were, my love! Carry on!"

At 9:45 A.M. Morley set out walking as the day was mild and the Department only ten minutes away. David Byrnes was waiting for him when the pretty redhead ushered him in.

"You look well for a man deep in research, Pat."

"Half my life's been in research—at least it seems so to me."

"Thought you were an action man."

Morley smiled. "Well, David, I'd like to be. Of course the kind of action I'd like involves water skis and fishing tackle. But such is life! Nowadays, my boy, any other kind of action—to be effective—seems to require an inordinate amount of preparation."

"Those are indeed true words, friend, and strangely enough they fit—well, sort of—what I'm about to suggest." He picked up a ballpoint and began to doodle on his ever-present yellow pad as he talked.

"There is a NATO Energy Committee meeting this weekend in San Francisco. There will be representatives from seven European countries, plus Japan, South Korea, and Thailand—and of course the U.S.—attending. The subject matter is known— onward planning for the oil crunch we are all expecting in the mid or late nineties—but the agenda, discussions, and especially any agreed action lines are very high-priority intelligence items for the KGB. From all the CIA has told us over the last year, it is hard to believe that the KGB will 'pass' on this opportunity.

"What I'm suggesting—and I know I'm overstepping the bounds of *my* professional interest in the matter—is that the easiest and most foolproof way for the KGB to get this information would be to tell their illegal to get it if—and this is a big if—he is attending. Agree?"

Morley laughed. "I agree on some parts, not on others, David. First of all, you are not overstepping at all. This is a foreign policy matter, and as such is within your ball park. It may also be a departmental security matter—depending on the rest of your, uh, proposal. Also, as departmental liaison with ICG, I consider it your duty to pass on good ideas whenever they come up." He smiled. "And lastly, if I were KGB I would most certainly want this information, and I would certainly consider activating my mole as the easiest and most foolproof way of getting it—if, as you said, the mole is attending. Okay?"

"Yes, Patrick, thank you. I was hoping you'd see it exactly that way. And be assured I'll pass on anything that looks interesting, regardless of origin. Now, my idea is this: there is a four-man delegation representing the U.S. at this meeting—actually five, since General Armbruster, the C.O. of the Sixth Army, will be hosting it. Of the other four, three either had or could have had access to that CIA intelligence report that started all this." Byrnes paused to look at Morley.

"You have my undivided attention, my friend. Carry on. Don't be bashful about naming names."

"All right. Name names the man says, so names it will be. First there is the number-two man in the department, my boss,

Richard Millard. He has seen it, legally, as I told you. He's the leader of the U.S. delegation. Secondly, there is Steven Mattison from the White House. Steven is the number-two or -three assistant—depending on the subject matter—to the chief of staff; however, one of his areas of expertise—he's a very bright guy—is energy, so he'll be representing Sixteen Hundred Pennsylvania at San Francisco. Third is Marshall Berenz, who will be representing the Defense Department for much the same reasons as Mattison for the White House.

"Okay. I have no idea whether or not Mattison and/or Berenz saw that CIA report, but I'm sure you do; and of course I have no idea whether or not you have focused in on either or both of them. My idea was that here you have three—shall I call them possible suspects—going into a situation where they may be given a tasking, so why not cover them tightly and see what happens?"

Morley nodded slowly and seriously. "I like it, and what's to lose? One question. though. The mole has to be the top KGB operation at the moment. So even if they do decide that this conference merits the risk—again, at this time—would the KGB let him take the risk of communicating with them in a strange—to him—town? Is there anything to prevent our mole, if he *is* one of the three you named, from holding his report, doing *nothing* in San Francisco, and then transmitting it to Moscow in whatever routine—and obviously secure—method he normally uses, *after* he comes back to Washington?"

"I thought about that, Patrick, and decided that luck was on our side here—for a change. There is a Warsaw Pact meeting with, I suspect, a very similar agenda, in Prague on Monday. Normally this kind of information is not perishable, but I have a feeling that the Soviets would love to have the results of the NATO meeting to discuss at Prague. In addition, the Prague meeting has been set for some time and has had some publicity, so I think they'd be loath to change the date this late."

"Uh huh. I see."

"And, Patrick, as a routine matter I worked out the security ground rules for the meeting with Millard, and I can assure you no one will be able to carry papers or even notes from the conference room. So I think the onus will be on the Soviets to get a report—orally—while it's fresh—there in San Francisco!"

Morley grinned. "David, if you get unhappy here at State, I can recommend you to the General."

"Delighted to help and am ready to do more . . . anytime. Just ask."

"Will do, and thanks again."

The day was still pleasant, a warm, soft breeze, puffy white and blue sky, so Morley decided to walk back to his apartment. He came out the front entrance of the Department, turned left, and started up 21st Street.

Partly because his senses were attuned to such irregularities, and partly because he was particularly alert to such a possibility on this case, he immediately noted that a well-dressed young man, dark hair and complexion, who had been loitering near the elevator when he emerged on the ground floor, had come out the door and turned left behind him. Coincidence? Perhaps, even probably. But he'd lived this long because of a healthy and fervent distrust of coincidences.

He crossed busy Virginia Avenue and continued north on 21st Street, crossing E Street with the light, still heading north on the west sidewalk. The usual heavy traffic whooshed by, heading south on one-way 21st. Morley brushed his forehead with his left hand, head turned slightly to the right, using a tiny mirror on the band of his watch to look behind him for an instant. The dark young man was there, a bit closer now; his head was bent down toward the lapel of his jacket, his lips moving.

Morley smiled inwardly. They weren't *that* good at all! Then a warning voice reminded him that pride did indeed go before a fall, and his whole body went on red alert. He decided that whatever was going to happen would depend on his route. They couldn't know it in advance, so the trailer was communicating route information, transmitter inside his jacket pocket, to his teammate, probably motorized. Thinking quickly as he walked, Morley decided that the trailer was the "setter-upper" and the car the attacker, because the sidewalks were too crowded for the man to attack and then escape in the car. He figured further that he would be set up and attacked at an intersection. Lastly, he estimated that the car would be the weapon, not firearms from the car. This from the simple logic that these people would probably not want his death to appear other than an accident.

Morley brushed his forehead again. The man was about ten feet back and on the street side of the walk. They were approaching the F Street intersection. Traffic was one way, left to right, and moving with the green light. He brushed his hair part this time. The trailer was still about eight feet back and on his right side. The light changed and Morley, the trailer, and three other pedestrians crossed and headed north for the G Street intersection. Morley chanced another look. The man's head was bent to his lapel again.

He's going for it at G Street, Morley thought. The car will be coming from right to left, east to west, which will give him a chance to set timing with the attacker. The only question was which side will be favored by Murphy's law. Who will have the light?

The yellow flicked on as they approached the intersection. The usual number of vehicles ran it even as it turned red, then with a roar and whoosh the G Street traffic began to move. He sensed rather than saw the trailer about three feet behind him as he waited at the curb, and then he saw the attacker. Two innocents were just clearing the intersection and then there was a gap in the curb lane traffic as a large Cadillac with heavily tinted windows slowed down, then with the space ahead began to accelerate across the intersection, tires squealing.

The trailer tensed and began his move. Morley dropped to all fours, hooking the heels of his shoes on the curb edge for added stability. The man's momentum carried him over Morley's back, hands and arms scrabbling for holds on the yielding air, his body a screaming, spread-eagled target. There was no squeal of brakes, no slowing of speed, just a hideous cracking sound as the car met the hurtling body in midair, carried it fifty feet, and shed the broken mess in the gutter. The Cadillac raced to a green light at 22nd Street, turned left, and disappeared into the south-bound traffic.

There were no sirens yet. (Excuse me, Egil, thought Morley, but where are they when we need them?) The other pedestrians had run toward the body and the curb lane traffic was stopped and piling up behind as the bloody mess blocked the lane. Morley knew that nobody but he really knew what had happened, not even the killers. They were probably well on their escape route, confident they had hit the target and expecting to see their teammate later for a victory drink. That, he thought, was a good idea.

He turned and walked back south on 21st to Virginia Avenue and caught a cab. Going north on 23rd he rode through Washington Circle and got out in front of the nearest hotel. By the time the police had sorted things out back on G Street, Morley was sipping his second Wyborowa on the rocks. There were, after all, *some* things the Eastern Bloc did well. The lounge was starting to fill up, and he watched the newcomers carefully.

Half an hour later he had zigzagged back to his apartment via cab, bus, and foot, confident that he had not been followed.

After he returned from seeing Angela off at Andrews field, Morley continued his busy day, mostly with phone calls. Farley reported that the traitorous cook seemed to have been telling a true story, except that he thought the man was not coming completely clean about how he'd met Farid, claiming the Arab had simply called him on the phone and asked for a meeting.

Morley called Kreeger and briefed him on Farley's reports and the Cadillac murder attempt. They decided to push Interpol and NATO traces on Farid and the Egyptian, Maksud. Then, just as he was setting out for his evening's chat with Telchoff, he was called in rapid succession by both Epworth and Milford with negative reports on the Arab name and picture traces, including the newly discovered Aseem Otar. None of them had been optimistic because "those people" seldom use the same cover names or aliases very long, and never their real names. Milford cited as an example the fact that Agency files contained some sixty-three references to cover names using Farid. There was one potential ray of promise: the Agency's Libyan desk officer thought he'd seen Farid/Otar's picture before.

FOURTEEN

MOSCOW, USSR

"He missed! Pierre has missed! Twice—even three times. Two gunmen captured, one killed, and Telchoff is alive, laughing at us! Sergei Mikhailovich, this is a bad day—for you, me, Mother Russia—all of us."

The younger man remained silent, nodding each time Globitsyn made or repeated a point, but too wise to interject a comment. Finally, the torrent subsided and Globitsyn, chin cupped in hands, stared mutely at the far door of his office. Then a wry smile began, and he turned toward his handsome young assistant. "Ah well, Comrade, we must take the bad luck with the good, eh? In both actions we were seconds away from success; it could have gone either way. The Telchoff operation was well planned and well executed. How could Pierre's men have known that snake would not be where he was *every other day* at that time? At least that's what Pierre's inside man told him— too late, of course. And the Ami fucker, this Morley, he has a charmed life. He leaves a flat he's been in but a day or so, and then never comes back! How can you plan against luck like that? Fortunately, Pierre stumbled on his new apartment, so the next day picked him up and the execution looked easy. At the last second the fucker bends over to tie his shoe and Pierre's man goes poof! Even Pierre is a bit rattled." Globitsyn laughed. "He is so rattled, Comrade, he is *asking for orders!*"

Globitsyn sat moving his head slowly from side to side. Finally the young man spoke. "Yuri Aleksandrovich, it is neither your fault nor Pierre's. Your plans were good, very good. As you said, only your luck was bad. Next time, it will be those two enemies whose luck is bad. It is the law of averages."

The KGB Chairman did not appear to notice the familiarity with which this very junior officer had addressed him; rather, he seemed to accept eagerly this glib explanation of the events. "Yes, of course, Comrade, this is true. We must not lose faith in Pierre or in his operational planning. The best plans can go bad on luck. I think I had better give Pierre a signal telling him this. I'm afraid his morale is low. His ego has suffered a terrible blow. . . . And there is always the problem of overreaction. You know, the man gets desperate for success, and begins to cut corners on security to get it faster. You see, now that the Ami, Morley, is alerted he will be twice as watchful. I do not want Pierre to rush about flailing his arms at this moment."

"I am sure that is correct, Comrade Chairman. It is my understanding from what you said that Pierre could not act at the moment anyway, as he does not know the whereabouts of both men?"

Globitsyn nodded and the younger man went on. "And also, sir, we must note that this Morley has had no success in identifying Kotch, nor has the snake, Telchoff, been of any help to him in this regard. You said that Kotch himself has so reported to you. Is this not good? The Ami has no clues or he would be following them up. And Kotch says he has not done so."

"If we can believe Kotch!"

"And why not, sir? What would Kotch have to gain by lying to you?"

"You're right, Comrade. What indeed? Still I think I will call a halt to Pierre's action—as you noted, he's got to find them first, anyway."

"Can Kotch do that, sir? Can Kotch find them?"

Globitsyn's face clouded quickly and his eyes became hard again. "That is an impertinent question, Comrade. Do not ever mention again anything about Kotch's capabilities in America. That is not a subject on which you should be knowledgeable. Understand?"

"Yes, sir. I apologize. I didn't mean to pry."

"Don't do it again. Now, Sergei Mikhailovich, I want you to go back to the records. I want to know if this Morley has any vulnerabilities, any problems we could exploit. Then I will go back to Pierre with a signal advising what kinds of action we wish him to take."

"Aha. Very good, sir. Anything else?"

"Well, while you're in records see if there is any information on Josef Shola, a Hungarian national, born mid to late forties, or Thomas Gulyas, similar background and timing. Bring this information to me personally. Do your own typing. No secretary should be aware of this request. Understand?"

"Yes, sir." The man made notes on his ever-present small pad.

"And immediately."

"Yes, sir."

The younger man stood, made a perfect military aboutface, and left the room. Globitsyn smiled at his back. His expression slowly became serious and pensive. He mused, muttering to himself angrily, recalling Kotch's advice. The smart bastard said, don't kill the Ami, use him! Use him to get the Amis off my back for good! Let me think about it, he had said, I've got an idea. But Pierre has an idea too. Pierre wants to kill the Ami. In fact, Pierre says it is a debt of honor. Maybe Pierre was out in the hot desert too fucking long. Maybe he's thinking like one of those crazy rag heads now.

FIFTEEN

WASHINGTON, D.C.

The phone rang insistently as Morley struggled back to sensibility from a deep sleep. He reached for the source of annoyance, sneaking a glance at the clock as he did so. Nine-fifteen! No wonder the phone was insistent. No matter that he'd had a busy day and then gone on till dawn working over Telchoff's memory on the subject of KGB transplant illegals in general and particular. "Hello."

"It's Egil, Patrick. Sorry I woke you, but Pansy called a bit ago. She was excited. Caught it from friend Pete, it seems. He's had a brainstorm—says he remembers who the man in the picture was. Said you'd know which one he was talking about. Seems he actually saw the guy, years ago, and he's frantic to talk to you about it."

"That's good news, Egil. I thought he might come up with something. Last two times I left him he was staring at that picture, Maksud, muttering to himself. Let's see. My first reaction is to get over there—I'm as anxious to hear as he is to tell, and I've got a hunch this is going to be important; but my better judgment tells me that the time press on this item does not justify breaking the cover routine I've established, and which is working well. I should wait till tonight as usual."

"Whatever you think, Pat. What would you like me to tell Pansy?"

"I don't want to upset Pete—he's excited for a good reason. Let's have her tell him I'm out of town for the day but plan to be back for our usual. . . . Oh, hell, Egil." Morley chuckled. "Maybe this is one of those rare moments in the annals of intelligence work when the truth is the best way to handle something! Have Pansy tell him I'm very anxious to see him, but that the security of his location and the cover story for my being there should not be compromised. She could put this to him as a proposal—he's an experienced professional—and if he insists that time is of the essence I'll stretch cover and meet him right away. Okay?"

"Fine with me. We'll put it to him just that way."

"Good. Anything else?"

"Just a glimmer, Pat. My Montgomery County contact had a man sniff around your old apartment house in Chevy Chase yesterday. The girl who holds down the manager's office after hours said she let a guy in to deliver flowers to an apartment on your floor that evening. Says there was no one home, but the man said it was some kind of surprise and he was supposed to just leave them by the door. The guy had on a uniform jacket that quote, looked real, end quote, so she didn't question him further, and of course he had a big expensive basket of flowers. The part that may interest you most—as it did me—is that the girl chatted a bit with the guy. Seems he said he was her countryman. The girl is a Lebanese American."

"I suspect you've got our security hole, Egil. Is there anything we can do about it?"

"Nothing beyond the usual—fingerprints around both apartment doors and inside yours, and some interviews to see if anybody else saw the man or his vehicle. You never know, maybe we'll be lucky. The girl's description wasn't worth worrying about. It would fit half the Arabs in town. I'm not ready yet to have the Maryland boys show her the pictures. Maybe later."

"No sense spending any more of your time on that one, Egil,

but I'll be grateful for any leads the County lads dig up. I think we know what Farid's been up to and that whatever the drill was it'll lead back to him. I am amazed at the speed of their reaction. Scared too! These people are pros with a hell of a lot of capabilities, especially for working in enemy territory."

"Enemy territory?"

"Hell, yes, Egil. I can smell KGB. We're not dealing with Arabs here—not bottom line anyway. This thing is being run out of Sixteenth Street."

"You're probably right, Patrick. Makes Pete's story—whatever it is—more tantalizing."

"Sure does. While we're on the subject, Farley called me last night. I asked him to call you and give his info. Did he?"

"Yeah, first thing this morning. Very interesting. We've expedited the national and foreign trace on Aseem Otar."

"Will there be any pressure on you to arrest him, Egil?"

Kreeger replied, "None of the 'pressure people' are aware of the case as yet. We'll keep it that way for a while. Besides, we can't arrest what we can't see."

"Right." Morley laughed. "I'll be in touch."

Before resuming his studies Morley called the apartment reception desk and told them to permit no visitors' entry into the building without his *prior* approval, and absolutely no workers unless he, Morley, personally escorts them. They assured him their compliance.

Back to his research. Morley had decided that Mattison, Berenz, and Millard were interesting subjects and certainly possible candidates for "mole," before the San Francisco thing came up. It really was one hell of a good opportunity, though it was also one hell of a coincidence. Amazing that out of the forty to fifty people in the U.S. government who had realistic, if not legal, access to the Borodin report intelligence, there would be three who had Eastern Europe in their backgrounds. And that two of the three had actually spent part of their lives in the same satellite nation. And then, all three going to San Francisco. Morley smiled to himself. Damn those coincidences! And of course last but not least, the assurance of both the Russians in the case—Borodin and Telchoff—that the mole was not a Russian and not an American. He began to pore over the three files again.

Mattison was born in the U.S. in 1945 but that was a fluke. His pregnant mother had come from Czechoslovakia to New York right after the war to see relatives and Steven was born a month earlier than expected. His was a wealthy landowning family from the Bratislava area, and one with a not uncommon intermingling of Magyar blood over the years. They were anti-Communist for obvious practical reasons, and Steven had been involved as a student leader in the ill-fated Prague Summer uprising of 1968 to the point of getting himself on a KGB "wanted list." He had escaped to Vienna and then to New York. The problem blew over eventually and as a U.S. citizen, Steven had visited Czechoslovakia and Hungary several times since.

He had been sponsored on his arrival in the U.S. and then adopted by John E. B. (Jeb) Mattison, a very successful and influential New York international lawyer. Jeb Mattison had married Steven's maternal aunt before Steven was born and it had been a happy marriage until her death in 1967 in an auto accident in Hungary. Steven's mother, her younger sister, was killed in the same crash, and his father had died earlier. Jeb Mattison was childless, and it had seemed natural that he would adopt his orphaned nephew, who went on to complete his interrupted education in the U.S.

Jeb Mattison had been the confidant and adviser of a succession of U.S. presidents in the field of Eastern European finance, law, and politics. A person of considerable reknown around Washington, D.C., he had been for years, and still was, active in Czechoslovakian affairs; always, of course, on the side of the anti-Communists, and specializing in fund-raising for refugees and escapees. Despite his uncle's obvious ability to help, Steven's progress in Washington appeared to have been on merit. He had gone to Wall Street after graduate school, then accompanied his boss when the latter became Assistant Secretary of

Commerce. He got Washington fever, and when his boss moved back to New York four years later, he recommended Steven—by then an accepted expert on trade matters, especially in the field of energy—to the White House chief of staff. In his three years there Steven had proved worthy of the recommendation.

Yes, Morley thought, Steven Mattison has the access to qualify as the mole; and the timing and background were compatible with Telchoff's story except in one respect: the government position in 1970. But there were many possible explanations for that discrepancy. Only one thing bothered Morley—no, two things: Mattison had a long, well-documented, and credible history as an anti-Soviet; and he had limited potential in the U.S. government because he was a political appointee, not a career bureaucrat. Again, Morley felt, these were surmountable problems.

Neither could he dismiss the possibility of Jeb Mattison. There was no question about his access to high-level information, but it was spotty as hell. There were, in effect, the same two negative factors—to a much greater degree—that existed in the case of his nephew. Nevertheless, Morley thought, if *he* were a KGB officer, he'd like to have Jeb Mattison for an agent! He kept Mattison's name on his list of peripheral "could be somethings," but not as a mole candidate.

Marshall Reid Berenz was a career government bureaucrat, one of that elite group of talented *and* dedicated public servants who float or remain just below the top level of the politically changeable hierarchy of the old—and new—line agencies of the government. These invaluable cadre members provide the continuity, stability, and—again—the dedication without which the American form of quadrennial government could not exist. Often these superbureaucrats had a specialty that transcended the boundaries of any single agency or department, and they were in constant demand by several. Such was the case with Marshall Berenz. His expertise was in budget matters and he had been serving with distinction, as well as frustration, on loan to the Defense Department for the last year.

Berenz had arrived in the U.S. after World War II as a displaced person—a Polish refugee. He was not yet twenty years old, a bewildered, nonpolitical, frail "child," who had already been through more heartbreak than most Americans saw in a lifetime. His family had been wiped out early in the first Nazi attacks, and he had lived by his wits in the Warsaw ghettos for several years as a member of a teenage "wolf pack." Shortly before the end of the war, he and several others of his group had been picked up by the Russians, "conscripted" into the Red Army, and used as cannon fodder. In the mad confusion of April 1945, Berenz had escaped to Vienna and then on to Italy and into the DP channels that led eventually to the wonderland of the United States. According to the file Berenz had become and still was a rabid American jingoist.

At first glance, Morley had concluded that Berenz did not have the kind of access or the potential for it that would qualify him for mole status—at least this particular mole—but his background was so interesting that Morley dug deeply. He discovered that during the last three years this budget expert had worked on a temporary basis with top-secret materials of CIA, Treasury, State, Defense, and the White House. He had all the necessary clearances and, buttressed by all the recent "no secrets" legislation, had had unbelievable access while doing his "planning and advisory" stints in these sensitive posts. It seemed that in the aftermath of the "Contra-Irangate" scandal of '87 everything—even the most secret expenditure—had to be recorded somewhere, and Marshall Berenz was very often the recorder.

Yes, Morley decided again, if he were KGB, he'd love to have Berenz as his agent.

Richard Dennis Millard, number two in the Department of State, by nature of his job alone was a candidate. He saw everything that the Secretary saw, all the cables, intelligence reports—everything.

Millard was the only one of the three who had been born and lived all his life in the U.S.; but he *did* have a Czechoslovakian connection. His parents had emigrated from there and had Americanized their Czech family name, Mladar.

Richard's father, a steelworker, was killed in an industrial accident when Richard was just a small child. His mother was a smart, tough woman who kept her family together by working two or three jobs at a time. Richard was the youngest child and the others seemed to have chosen him to be the best educated and most successful, and they contributed much of their money and time toward this end. He in turn never forgot them, never marrying, and returning the love and money in many ways over the years.

Richard was all they could have asked, kind of an ex-emplification of the American Dream. Phi Beta Kappa at Pennsylvania, Rhodes scholar, top of his class at Georgetown Foreign Service, etc. His State Department career progress was not spectacular but steady, with no blots, and his appointment as Assistant Secretary had received the approval of his peers. He was, in sum, universally respected as a hard-working, talented, and competent officer. However, this high appointment was almost in its second year and his status was still "acting" rather than "confirmed." The reason was sentimentality, nothing else: his predecessor was still in a "vegetable" status in Walter Reed Hospital after a series of strokes, and although it would be apparent to a first-year pre-med student, as Millard himself had been heard to say, that the man would never function as a human again, his long-time friend, the President, refused to send up Millard's appointment for congressional confirmation. A note in the Bureau file indicated that several colleagues had stated that Millard was "very bitter" about this slight to the point of having considered resignation.

As he finished reading, Morley once again, but this time acceptingly, marveled at the coincidence of these three men. Then he questioned himself. Was he being led by Pete Telchoff or were they legitimate candidates who just happened to have similar backgrounds? He opted for the latter explanation, reasoning that there are millions of Americans who have a relatively recent foreign family background.

And San Francisco was just a lucky opportunity, that was all. Not a trap, not a KGB mirage, just a meeting that happened to come at a convenient time and was being attended by people of possible interest. So he would take it and be happy.

He had discussed the "San Francisco opportunity" at some length with Stan Epworth, who was all for giving it a try, and had alerted the San Francisco FBI office. Tomorrow would be the principal session of the conference.

SIXTEEN

WASHINGTON, D.C.

Telchoff was excited. "Like I say, Godfrey, the damn Stalin mustache confused me, yes. Sure I see this man before, maybe many years ago, but no mustache. I think also he was not dark-skinned when I see him. So I think, Godfrey, maybe is cosmet-i-cal, you say? I think maybe he could be Russian! You see, before I think sure he is Indian or Arab I know before; but without mustache and dark skin, maybe he is Russian.

"So I think, maybe I know him as KGB if Russian. I run like movie picture through head, huh? See maybe hundred faces— from not long, from long, from very long time ago. Then it comes, Godfrey, it comes—I remember! This is face from many years ago. No mustache, younger man, hair shorter, and military. I make picture him in military uniform, KGB. Same ears, same eyes, same shape head and jaw. So, I know I see this man before. Long time, maybe twelve, fourteen years. Yes, he is KGB officer, major, I think. Is in uniform.

"He was in office of KGB Chairman, Yuri Vladimirovich Andropov, I see him, maybe nineteen seventy-five. I was in Moscow short time seventy-five, before Africa posting, yes, seventy-five. See this man, no mustache, KGB major uniform, he is there, waiting to see Chairman. I do not know his name. Just see this man. Yes, and he has dark complexion, like Arab or Indian, I remember. But he is KGB major."

Telchoff had been pacing the floor excitedly, the words tumbling out. He stopped and smiled at Morley.

"And Pansy, she take brush, take away mustache and I remember this man, he is Circassian, dark like Arab, and too, Godfrey, he is Moslem. Many Circassian Moslems. Most, I think. This is why I think before he is Arab."

"How did you know this man was a Circassian Moslem, Pete? Who told you?"

"I think about this, Godfrey. Maybe, yes, for sure, is secretary in Chairman's office she say so."

"You asked her?"

"Oh, yes, she is friend. Tashi Mishkova is friend of Ivanova, and I know. I ask about this major, she say Circassian Moslem, but no give name. Maybe he is illegal and did not give secretary name."

"Tell me, Pete, was it normal, usual, in those days for an illegal to be at KGB headquarters in uniform and visit the Chairman?"

"Nooh, Godfrey, is good point from you. This man is not from KGB headquarters, I think, but not illegal too. Maybe he is just being posted as illegal. Not yet illegal, I think. Also, is late this day I see him. I think he is surprised to see anyone in Chairman's office, you know?"

"You mean he was just being posted as an illegal?"

"Yes, I think."

"Because he did not give the secretary his name?"

"Yes, but there are other reasons. I know many officers KGB headquarters at this time, Godfrey, but not him! His visit to Chairman at late hours was unusual. No name too is not usual. Is impression I have this night, friend Godfrey, this is officer going for illegal posting—important posting or he would not be talking to Chairman. I have impression this man had been posted somewhere as legal, but now being changed."

Morley laughed. "I'm learning to trust your impressions, Pete. But tell me, why did the secretary know he was a Circassian Moslem and not even know his name, or *a* name?"

Telchoff laughed. "Is easy question, Godfrey. She is, you say?, nosy! She talk with man. He tell her, but still not tell name. Is usual. Boss he say no tell name, he not say no tell where from or religion."

"Okay, Pete. Here we have one Circassian, who is dark-skinned, major level many years ago. He was being posted, probably as an illegal agent . . . uh, somewhere. I would guess in the Arab world—because of his background, his looks, his religion. So next we see him masquerading as an Egyptian businessman in Washington, D.C., and he arrives coincidentally after Pete Telchoff does, and after the mole is partially surfaced. Back to Mishkova, Pete. Can you remember where and when she told you about this man? Was it in the office? A social occasion? Another time? Was Ivanova there? Anybody else? Any particular occasion? How often did you see Mishkova outside the office those days? Did she tell you other things?"

Telchoff cocked his head to the side, looking at Morley, then slowly his frowning face relaxed into a smile, ending up with a loud laugh. "Aha, friend Godfrey, you are very good. Yes, *very* good. You know right questions, yes. I am thinking you must be CIA first team—I say right?—yes, first team number one." He frowned again. "I remember. Mishkova she tell me many things those days. Often we stop her apartment after work, drink some vodka. No sex, Godfrey, no sex. Tashi separated from Sasha Mishkov, but I try, uh, repair, as you say, repair this marriage. They both good friends, and I think they can make new start, huh? But, yes, Tashi make lots, uh, vodka talk, tell many office things, not big secrets, but gossip, you know, huh?

"Must have been around time, maybe few days past I see Circassian major, Tashi tell me about this 'great man,' she say. He is for true KGB major, but he is Moslem she say, so he placed in some foreign city. Yes, he is illegal. He is to pretend to be some Arab or such, you know. Tashi she tell me this, I think, to show she not fooling around, as you say, with this major. She say because he Moslem, but I think she is being true Mishkov. But thing is, friend Godfrey, this Moslem, yes, he must be good to be major and illegal who talks to head boss. You see?"

"I understand, Pete. So if he was a major in nineteen seventy-five, and a promising illegal, then I would think he is maybe a KGB colonel by now, no?"

"It is possible, Godfrey. Say for sure a lieutenant colonel. Yes, probably colonel."

"So my next question follows closely, Pete. Why would KGB, Globitsyn, send a KGB colonel, a very successful illegal, probably a natural for cover work in the Arab world—why would they risk him for a job in the U.S. at this time?"

Telchoff put on his thinking scowl, chin cupped in hand, looking through the subtly barred window at the light rain that had begun to fall. Finally, he raised his head and looked at Morley. Again he was smiling. "Godfrey, you are the very good question man. I think I am glad we are friends. I would not like to have you as enemy. . . . Yes, you are right, Globitsyn has very big, I think you say 'stake' in this case, if this illegal man is here, in Washington. I think he has big stake because he personally is involved, and because this illegal man is very important to KGB. He must say, 'I have to put KGB first team in,' huh? Also, Godfrey, if Circassian has flap, as you say, and the operation fails, KGB can deny, because to rest of world this man is Arab, and uses Arabs—you show me many Arab pictures—so who is get blame for flap? Arabs, of course! Very smart, this Yuri Aleksandrovich Globitsyn!"

Again the cocked head, again the sly look. "Too, Godfrey, Globitsyn wants Pete Telchoff dead, and he wants friend Godfrey dead too. Is not so?"

Morley nodded. "Yes, Pete, he's tried for both of us already. And each time there were Arabs involved."

"Aha, it is so. Indeed, friend Godfrey, I think maybe this is so. Maybe these Arabs' pictures you show me, maybe they come for me at farmhouse?"

"Yes, Pete, it was those Arabs that came for you, and I am now sure they were sent by your Circassian comrade."

"And you, he sends them for you too?"

"Yes. I only saw one, but he looked like an Arab."

The cocked-head sly look came again. "He is name Gorbal something, I think. He is killed hit-run accident, huh? Day or so ago on Washington street, is not so?"

"Correct. I was meant to be the victim but he was good enough to change places with me at the last minute."

Telchoff roared with laughter. "Ha, Godfrey, you change places, huh? Very good. I like that. The Circassian he is active, I think."

"I think you're right, but I also think we can stay alive if we're careful. And it shouldn't be too long. I hope we can get you out of this confinement in a couple of weeks."

"That is good, Godfrey. I stay long as you think I must."

"Fine, Pete. Now I think I'll let you listen to some Tchaikovsky before going to sleep. I'll see you tomorrow."

"Good! Good night, friend Godfrey. And be careful. Remember you are playing against KGB first team."

Morley nodded seriously before he turned and closed the door behind him.

SEVENTEEN

SAN FRANCISCO, CALIFORNIA

The young woman turned quickly, swiveling her chair, at the sound of the inner office door opening. "Yes, sir?"

William McC. Armbruster, Major General, U.S. Army, Commanding, Sixth Army, paused, smiling, in his rush toward the far door. "Nothing else, Kathy. Just lock up for me, will you? I'm late for my appointment." He laughed, and the woman joined him—they both knew his "appointment" was the Friday afternoon poker session at the Officers' Club, half a block away.

"Yes, sir. I'll finish these letters first."

"Good—and have a good weekend. You have my itinerary in case any of those Washington types need me before the wrap-up tomorrow?"

"Yes, sir, I do."

"Fine. See you later."

"Good-bye, sir."

The woman turned back to her typing, a half smile on her face, watching the door out of the corner of her eyes. It was only ten seconds before it opened again and the General spoke. "Kathy? Give my wife a call, will you? I may be a little late tonight. Tell her I'll ring her if it'll be after seven. Okay?"

"Yes, sir."

"Thanks. See ya." And this time he was really gone.

She made the phone call and then got up quickly, stripped the paper from her typewriter, crumpled it, and threw it in the "unclassified" trash container. She thumbed the bolt on the front door and turned out the light. From outside the office would now appear to be unoccupied. Then she let herself into the inner office, and after closing the heavy drapes, proceeded to pile—neatly—the mess of papers on the General's desk into his classified tray. She carried the full tray to the open safe and placed it in a drawer. She returned to inspect the desk and conference table to make sure there were no stray papers around, then shut the drawer and spun the dial, locking the safe.

She looked nervously about, as if assuring herself that no one was there, then moved quickly to the outer office and picked up a small camera that was sitting on her desk. She took from her purse a new roll of film and went into the clothes closet, shutting the door tightly. She was out in a minute or two and walked back into the General's office.

Again, a quick look around, then she went to the corner of the General's desk, reaching under and pressing a small button concealed by a decorative wood overlap. Nothing visible happened. She went to a picture of the President on the far wall and pulled its edges toward her. It turned noiselessly through an arc of about 120 degrees revealing a wall safe. Quickly, she spun the dial—right, then left, then right again, then left back until it clicked, pushed in on the dial center, click again, and opened the door. She sorted papers, found the ones she wanted, and brought them to the General's desk. Placing them one by one in the middle of the desktop and using the gooseneck lamp at about eighteen inches, she took two exposures of each of the six pages. Then she reversed the whole procedure, replacing everything—including the original roll in her camera—to where it had been five minutes before. She put on her coat and, locking both doors behind her, proceeded down the hall to the security station, the second roll of film securely taped to the inside of her lower thigh.

The young corporal smiled—she was a very attractive woman. "Good evening, Miss Kalinn, may I have your purse, please?"

She smiled back and handed it to him. He opened it and looked inside, removing the camera and setting it aside while he completed the inspection. He laughed. "I'll sure be glad when we get off this Class II alert and back to normal. You too, I bet?"

She smiled and nodded.

"Film in the camera, Miss Kalinn?"

"Yes—and exposed. I took some pictures of the ceremony this afternoon."

"Hey, that was great, wasn't it? Bet you got some beauties."

She laughed again. "I hope so—if I didn't goof up the focus or something."

He laughed with her. "Sorry though, I'll have to let the signal guys develop it for you. Orders, y'know."

"Sure, no trouble. How soon do you think they can get to it?"

"Oh, say, Monday evening, Tuesday at the latest."

"Hmm. Better than the drugstore."

"And cheaper!" He laughed again, handing her back her purse, and putting the camera in a marked envelope.

"Well, have a good weekend, Miss Kalinn."

"Thanks. You too."

She drove to the Union Square garage, parked, walked out the north exit, turned left, then crossed the street to the St. Francis, climbing the short flight of steps to the lounge off the lobby. A dark, good-looking, and expensively tailored man stood and welcomed her to a corner table for two. "Kathy! I was afraid you were caught in traffic, or had to work overtime, or something." He looked concerned, not smiling.

"No, just Friday, I guess. Everything seems to take longer on Friday afternoon."

"Well, sit down. What may I order you?"

"Oh, an old-fashioned—in one of those pewter mugs."

He beckoned a waitress and gave her the order. She was back in minutes, although the lounge was fairly crowded. Kathy took a long sip of her drink, then sat back.

"Did you get the tickets?"

"Oh, yes—the seats are beautiful. You'll love 'em." She opened her purse and took out a small white envelope, handing it to the man. He turned it upside down, shook it, and two blue printed tickets fell out. The woman moved closer and he held the tickets so they could examine them together. Her near hand, below the level of the table and shielded by her turned body, found the side pocket of his jacket and deposited the film roll she'd palmed from her purse.

"Hey, these are great! Thanks again."

"My pleasure. Sometimes the army does come through with flying colors. I almost wish I were going with you."

"You've seen it? No?"

"Oh, yes, but I'd enjoy it again." She took another long sip of her drink. "Mmm, that *is* good!"

"Another?"

"Well, just one. Then I have to go. Got a lot to do before my date."

The man signaled the waitress again, gave the order, and asked for the check. When she returned with the drink he gave her a bill and waved away her attempts to make change.

Shortly thereafter the young woman finished her drink and they left quietly together. The waitress, ignoring a raised hand from another table, cleared their table immediately, carrying the glasses to the service bar, where, masked from most of the lounge, she removed the film roll from the pewter mug and placed it in her apron pocket. Then she pretended to see the outraged patron, going quickly and apologetically to his table. Two neatly dressed men at a table in the far corner watched this whole charade with silent but not obvious concentration. They watched while the waitress finished serving another table, then after whispering to the hostess, started for the employees' exit, leading to the rest rooms. They were on the other side of the double doors, waiting, when she came through.

Outside on the street in front of the hotel the handsome man kissed Miss Kalinn's cheek, then climbed on a northbound cable car. A young man and woman who had been waiting on the Square side followed him onto the car.

EIGHTEEN

WASHINGTON, D.C.

At 9:00 the next morning—6:00 A.M. San Francisco time—Stan Epworth called Morley to report the results of the previous evening's surveillances in Washington and San Francisco. Nothing in Washington—all suspects had dull nights; but in San Francisco they'd struck pay dirt. The KGB *had* wanted the information from that NATO conference badly enough to activate the "marina net" to get it! Epworth was surprised because he felt the KGB boys *had* to be aware that this net was receiving "spasmodic Bureau attention." As he put it, "The big question is whether the Russkies are curious, careless, or cunning." Anyway the Bureau agents had watched the whole transaction, intercepted the film, "turned" the courier—a waitress—making her their double agent, and then had her send a substitute film on its way to the KGB case officer. They had a line now on the entire net, including the identity of the KGB case officer, T. A. Gerasimov, an official of the USSR consulate. Epworth asked Morley to keep the "doubling aspect" to himself for the time being as the Bureau intended to let the net run for a while and see where it took them. They had agreed on just how much of the report Morley would pass on where necessary.

Milford called a short time later with more good news. The Libyan desk man had found the picture of Farid. The Arab's name was indeed Aseem Otar, or at least that's what the Tripoli newspaper cut called him. He was pictured as a "Palestinian freedom fighter" who was being decorated by Col. Qaddafi on the anniversary of the Libyan revolution five years before. Morley marveled at the memory of the desk officer, not to mention his excellent files.

Next he called Kreeger to give him the update on Farid/Aseem. He had called last night to tell him that their Egyptian friend was taking on a much greater importance in view of Telchoff's information. In answer to Morley's question Kreeger said there was no pressure—yet—to arrest the Egyptian. Morley decided to brief David Byrnes personally, figuring he owed him a report on San Francisco.

David looked relaxed, lolling in his large leather chair. Then he leaned forward, his face serious. "What happened, Patrick? Sounded interesting over the phone."

"It was indeed *very* interesting. I don't know exactly what to make of it, but it sure was interesting."

Byrnes said nothing, just raised his eyebrows in an invitation to proceed. Morley complied. "Well, as I mentioned to you over the phone our three targets were spotless as lambs. The closest they came to questionable action was attending a 'skin and groan' show up on Broadway last night—two of them, that was. The other, Millard, was in bed by ten after a dinner with the Japanese delegate. Anyway, they didn't even make a mysterious phone call, none of them."

"Uh huh, I see." Byrnes smiled. "I assume you are getting to the 'very interesting' part soon, Patrick."

"The very interesting part is that while our pigeons made no moves someone else did."

"Ah so. A guy we didn't suspect?"

"A whole damn team we didn't suspect. But luckily, the Bureau did. They had a line on a couple of the team members. Thinking that the bait was too tempting for the KGB to resist, they put tight coverage on them. Sure enough, the team moves in and grabs the goodies."

Byrnes nodded thoughtfully. "A team, eh? Then it wasn't anybody from *any* of the delegations?"

"Nope. It was a local net, and I'm sure—and the Bureau's sure—that the KGB would not have activated the team, since it's undoubtedly a good one, if they could get the intelligence the easy way via a delegate. Of course the mole could have been there but under orders not to do anything at this time. They *would* risk the team to protect the mole . . . or maybe they didn't think there was much, or any, risk."

"Yeah. Could be. Lots of 'could be's,' though, aren't there? Did the team get anything?"

"A fistful of 'top secret' papers that look good but aren't. As you told me earlier, none of the real 'meat' ever left the conference room."

"Did the Bureau wrap the net up?"

"No. They're letting them run a while. They've been on to this bunch for quite some time. They know where to pick them up."

"So our three boys are off the griddle?"

"No way. I think they're even more interesting than before. Patrick smiled, but his eyes were serious.

"They could be innocent though. Suppose the illegal simply wasn't on the delegation and the KGB had to activate that team to get the info for the Prague meeting. Maybe the illegal's access in Washington does not include this type of info, so it was now or never."

"There are lots of possible explanations for what happened."

"So which possibility does the redoubtable Pat Morley go for?"

"Well, it's early, but my hunch tells me the mole was there, or at the least has access back here to the meeting results, and that Prague is not that important. I think they activated the net to protect the mole, but did not expect it to be compromised."

"Who are the team, Pat? What kind of people? How valuable?"

"The principal member—for this operation—is the secretary to the Commanding General, Sixth Army; the others are a young lawyer in San Francisco and an importer of Oriental goods from Oakland. Their control is a KGB officer from the consulate."

"And what happened?"

"Friday afternoon, after the principal session of the conference, General Armbruster, the secretary of the meeting, took the papers to his office to be picked up the next day by departmental courier for Washington. You know the security arrangements; you and Millard set 'em up."

"Yes." Byrnes smiled. "We sure as hell didn't expect the General's office to be compromised, though!"

"Of course not. They even had an upgraded security system in the Presidio for the weekend."

"Right. That was part of the deal. Oh, well, best-laid plans."

"True. If everything went according to plan there'd be no jobs for guys like us."

"I suppose; but still it's embarrassing."

"Anyway, the girl photographed the papers after the General left for the day—she got into the safe he said was 'foolproof'—and she got them by the guard by a simple switch of film rolls. She meets the Oakland importer at the St. Francis, slips him the film roll under cover of a cozy cocktail stop, then goes home. Half an hour later the lawyer calls and they go out to dinner in Tiburon, and who's at the restaurant but KGB officer Gerasimov and his wife! They all say 'surprised hello's' and change their two deuces to a table for four. So that's that— anything could have passed over the course of the evening."

"But you said the girl passed the film to Oakland."

"Right. I should have said the Bureau guys *thought* she passed *something* about the size and coloring of a film roll!"

"But they trailed Oakland, didn't they?"

"Sure did. He goes to Fisherman's Wharf on the Powell Cable Car, meets a woman who turns out to be, disappointingly, his wife. They have dinner and go home to Oakland in her car. What happened? Did the film roll get to Gerasimov? We don't know. We assume it did, but how it did was very slick! Oakland could have passed it to anybody at the restaurant—he went to the john twice—and there's always the waiters, bus boys, and so forth. He went home and went to bed. No telephone calls. Could have already passed, or Oakland could still have it, waiting; or maybe the girl didn't even pass it—especially if she knew she was seeing Gerasimov that night, which seems possible."

"What about the girl and the boyfriend lawyer after dinner?"

"Back to her apartment in the Marina and lights out."

"Will the Bureau pull these people in eventually?"

"Sure, eventually. They've gotta have solid evidence, though. The Bureau was complaining that Justice—the D.A.— made all three of them 'no touchee' without a warrant. You know the vocal capacity of the lunatic fringe in San Francisco."

"Oh yeah, I know. We've got lots of those untouchables around here too. So we end up no closer to our boy than before?"

"What else is new? That's the way I've ended every day since I've been here—no closer!"

"Tomorrow is another day." Byrnes opened a side drawer in his desk and handed Morley three thin manila folders. "Here are the U.N. Mission files you asked for on those three musketeers. Good hunting."

"Thanks. I'll be in touch."

Morley had a busy afternoon, mostly on the phone. First, he called the General to fill him in on San Francisco and its aftermath, and to confirm that he had a "go ahead" on the coverage he had proposed on certain senior U.S. government officials. Next he called Epworth, to make sure the Bureau's role in this scheme was moving along, then Milford at CIA.

"Jack, how's our pet project?"

"No snags, Patrick. The Director approved everything this morning, and you and I can do the briefing this afternoon, your convenience, time and place. I think we have the right woman for the job and that she can make something happen; and better yet, so does the boss."

"Good. How about, say, four-thirty at your place? I'd rather risk that—I mean my going there—than having you all come to a safe house. Okay?"

"No problem. Come into the underground area. I'll be there at the first guard post at four-thirty watching for you. I'll call the gate too. Use Godfrey."

"Great, Jack. I appreciate the trouble you've gone to on this."

"My pleasure. I liked Glover and I hate moles."

NINETEEN

MOSCOW, U.S.S.R.

"So where is the snake, Telchoff, sir?"

"We"—he laughed shortly—"that is, Pierre and I, believe we have located him in Washington, but even Pierre concedes that it would be madness to try to take him." The Chairman looked at the young man opposite him.

"And the Ami, this killer Morley?"

"We have been able to locate him too; but again we feel it would be better to let him continue."

"I see . . . I mean I don't see, Comrade Chairman! Not many days ago you are demanding their deaths, damning Pierre for failure, and now you very calmly say let these snakes and killers live. I don't understand."

Globitsyn chucked the young man under the chin, affectionately. It was late. All office forces had gone home, leaving the huge dark building to the night watch and a few—like the boss—who always hated to leave. He answered in mock severity, "My dear boy, the impertinence I accept from you astounds me—I who have on many occasions rewarded insubordination with demotion, or much worse."

He sighed, again touching the younger man's too handsome

face, this time even more affectionately with his fingertips. "Mishka, Mishka, do you not see? It has now been how long since the traitor Borodin first reported on Kotch?"

"Over a month, sir."

"And nobody has come to arrest him. See? Yes, Mishka, he is safe. It is true. I had our records revised so that no one except me can ever identify Kotch from them. I confess! I was a fool to think the traitor Borodin could have outsmarted me."

He held out his glass and the younger man filled it from the icy vodka bottle. "And so why are we to risk anything to remove the snake Telchoff and the killer Morley at this time? Wait till it is easier, less risky, my boy! You see?"

"Yes, Yuri Aleksandrovich, now I see. The Ami is no threat, Kotch is safe. Why trade the devil we know for one we don't know by killing the first?"

"Exactly, Mishka! And why take enormous risks—and maybe lose Pierre, who is very valuable—just to kill the snake Telchoff tomorrow rather than a month from tomorrow?"

"Of course. Telchoff is no threat at the moment either. He has told them all he knows and they do not even suspect Kotch!"

"And besides, Mishka . . ." The Chairman stopped to drink deeply. "Ahhh, good. Besides, we have a most important task yet for Pierre."

"I do not know about that, sir."

Globitsyn laughed. "Of course you don't know about it. I haven't told you . . . yet." He took another deep drink, held his glass out to be filled again, then patted the seat of the huge leather couch beside him. The young man obeyed and the Chairman put his arm around his shoulders, drawing him close, while he talked in a lower, confidential tone.

"We have a much more important, uh, removal to make, that is, for Pierre to make; and we do not want to chance his being unmasked before he can do it!"

"Another person, sir? Another threat to Kotch?"

Again the Chairman touched Mishka's cheek playfully. "You

are very perceptive, my boy. Exactly! A very real and dangerous threat—even though the man himself does not yet realize it. You see, Mishka, this is a man who can identify Kotch as our illegal, who knew him in his home country, and knew he came to Russia to be trained as a transplant!"

"Why hasn't this man done anything?"

"As I said, my boy, he does not yet know that he knows. Kotch has never been photographed much or well, and it was many years ago. And Kotch has been careful all these years to avoid the man—which was easy as he has lived far from Washington."

"But now . . . now he is a threat?"

"Yes, he will be coming to Washington and in a capacity which makes it inevitable they will meet. So we must remove him. Pierre and I, that is. And we must remove him in such a way that it will not point at Kotch or at us. A way that is foolproof."

"Aha. Could it be an Arab terrorist attack, Yuri Aleksandrovich?"

The Chairman laughed gleefully and long. "I have chosen well in you, Mishka! Yes, very well." His finger on the younger man's cheek forced his head to turn, facing the Chairman, then the pressure forced him forward to meet the older man's lips.

TWENTY

WASHINGTON, D.C.

Steven Mattison gave his tie a gentle twist with thumb and forefinger, pulling it just slightly off line—just slightly. His uncle had taught him that the really well-dressed gentleman's sartorial correctness was never 100 percent. There should always be some slight irregularity, be it tie, handkerchief, cuff visibility, whatever. He remembered how Jeb had chuckled when he'd explained, "Just to show you're human, my boy."

Steven sighed. Jeb had taught him many things, from helpful to vital, and scarcely a day went by that one of them didn't crop up. He looked at his watch. Six-eighteen. He'd better go. He smiled, remembering Jeb's alliterative rule on social timing: "Cocktails—casual; dinner—dot!" Yet it wouldn't do to be too casual in arrival for Ethel Andrews's cocktail party. Of course she'd invite him again—one of Washington's most eligible bachelors, special assistant in the White House, fancy Georgetown address (never mind it's Jeb's capital home). Hell, she'd invite him again if he arrived at eight and pissed on the doorman's foot. Besides, she liked him . . . a lot. And he sincerely liked and enjoyed her, and wouldn't think of embarrassing her in any way.

Steven drove automatically over Reservoir Road, right on Foxhall, and then to the gates of Ethel's mansion. The valet service took his car, a small Olds in the stream of Mercedes, Rolls, Cadillacs, and Jaguars. Actually, it was becoming a "reverse snob" prestige thing in Washington to drive a non–gas-guzzler, and if it were used-looking, all the better.

Ethel was near the door chatting with some elegantly dressed late arrivals. She saw Steven approaching and, without missing a syllable, signaled with her upraised finger for him to wait. She was free seconds later, as she passed her other guests over to someone else. Steven moved to her more than polite embrace, dutifully bussing both powdered and perfumed cheeks in the pseudo-European manner of the day. "It's been too long, lovely boy!"

"I know, dear, I know. We're both much too busy. I promise to reform in the near future. How about you?"

She stepped back, holding him at arm's length, her eyes suddenly serious, even sad. "Yes, my dear, we must, as you say, reform. I, especially—I've not as many years left as you."

Steven laughed, his fingers reaching to caress her smooth, unlined cheek. "Not too likely, Ethel dear. Even Jeb refers to you still as 'the Andrews girl.'"

"He also let you kiss that Blarney stone he keeps in his wall safe." They both laughed, then the woman became serious again. "Steven, I'm having a small luncheon for Arthur Sedgwick and his guests from London—they're here this evening, by the way; you'll meet them—on Sunday at one in Middleburg. Can you come? Please. A favor?"

Steven smiled. "I'd be delighted, Ethel, but as a favor to me, not to you."

"Ah, that Blarney stone. No matter, I'm pleased you'll come." She waved to another arrival and, squeezing Steven's arm, moved off toward the doorway.

As with most Washington cocktails, this party was a mixture of government, business, diplomatic corps, and the arts; and as with most Ethel Andrews's cocktails, the quality of the mixture was very high. Then there was the casual embarrassment of quantity and variety of extremely expensive food, and a plethora of moving trays offering everything from Cokes to Courvoisier.

Steven made all his "duty hellos," moving from group to group in the smooth, quick fashion of a cocktail veteran. He saw Marge Sedgwick talking to the senior senator from Wisconsin in an alcove off the library, and the senator's wife nodding animatedly to another woman whose back—a very slender, attractive back, being shown in some detail by the rather striking dress she was wearing—was toward him. Marge turned and stopped in midsentence. "Steven! Where have you been? You're positively the most difficult person to find in all of Washington!"

"I wouldn't say that, Marge." He laughed. "Good evening Senator." And as the other ladies turned, he bowed slightly. "Mrs. Arndt." He couldn't tell whether the senator was annoyed or pleased with the interruption. The man's cold blue eyes never showed any kind of emotion.

Marge Sedgwick broke the spell. "Steven, this is Leslie Antrim from London. Leslie, meet Steven Mattison, who denies, quite unconvincingly, that he runs the White House. We know he does."

"Don't let my boss hear that, Marge. I need the job!"

They all laughed, even Senator Arndt. Marge went on, speaking to the lovely young woman. "Steven's uncle, Jeb Mattison, was at Oxford with your Uncle Roger and the minister. I'm sure you've heard them speak of him."

The woman's eyes sparkled with inner amusement. "Indeed I have, and often. It seems Uncle Roger and his friend Jeb are the principals in many tales of heroism among the last generation of London debs! I'm pleased to meet you, Mr. Mattison."

"Steven, please." He took the proffered hand. It was cool, dry, and small, but surprisingly firm. The amused look still dominated her face, and she made no attempt to hide it. Then Steven realized what it was—Marge Sedgwick, the notorious matchmaker of Washington society. And with a bit of assistance, or was it connivance, from her friend Ethel Andrews. "The Sedgwicks' friends from London," indeed! Could the lovely Miss Antrim be one of them? She certainly didn't need any matchmaking help with those looks; and just as certainly she had perceived what Marge was about. Miss Antrim's eyebrows, beautifully arched, and just a shade darker than her hair, raised perceptibly, and Steven realized he was still holding her hand. He released it, smiling. "My pleasure, Miss Antrim."

She returned his smile. "Leslie."

Marge moved in right on cue. "Steven, be a dear and show Leslie around a bit. Introduce her to some of the younger people, talk about boating or skiing, or whatever. That's a good lad."

Ethel, also on cue, arrived at that moment and hustled the older folks away toward a group at the far end of the room. Steven, as if it had been planned, was alone with the cool, beautiful, and now intensely amused Leslie Antrim.

Her laughter was light, but real and infectious. "I must say, they are not too subtle, Mr. Mattison. Please don't think you must escort me. I'm sure you have many friends you wish to see."

"Please. 'Steven'—and it would be a pleasure to show you around a bit, even to talk about boating or skiing, though I'm a bit wobbly on skis."

That laugh again. "All right then, Steven. We'll obey our orders—with the exception of conversational subjects." She took his arm with a light touch and they strolled toward the main room. "I don't need to ask many questions." She smiled conspiratorially. "Marge has briefed me on whom I would meet tonight."

"Including me?"

"Definitely. In fact, I would say especially you."

"I sensed that from your amusement."

"I knew you knew! That made it even more amusing."

"Yes, as you said, subtlety is not one of their strong points."
They both laughed.

"But really, Steven, I'm sure you know, Arthur and Marge
are 'old school,' and your uncle was one of the favored and
familial group. Besides, they all subscribe to their grandparents'
philosophy that all young people are fools in general and in
particular when it comes to making matrimonial choices."

"Sounds very old world."

"I suppose it is. They both feel that if the oldsters didn't
make the choices, there'd be no marriages, and the whole
blasted race would die out."

"Perhaps. You've been to these parties before? Often?"

"Yes, though they're the same in any capital."

"You have the advantage of me. I wasn't briefed on *you*. Are
you a party attender by profession?"

"If you mean am I what your Foreign Service people call a
cookie pusher, I must plead guilty. I reckon I am. I've been
with Her Majesty's service for almost five years now."

"I should have known."

Her head came up slowly, but her eyes were no longer smiling. "Oh! Why?"

"Your poise, diplomacy, friendly manner, you know."

She pretended a curtsy, smiling again. "Put that in writing—
preferably on White House stationery. It'll do wonders for my
career."

"Have you been posted abroad?"

"Yes, I was in Cairo for two years and New Delhi for the
same. I am posted here temporarily for a semester's course at
Georgetown."

"Language? No, of course not, you have better facilities in
London—unless you're taking a crash course on the American
idiom."

"Prep'ratory to what, Steven?"

He laughed. "Damned if I know. Do you like languages?"

"Love them. Main reason for joining the service. You know,
see the world and talk to it too. Do you like them?"

"Yes, but I doubt I would ever be a linguist of your class."

"You don't know my class!"

"Oh, but I think I do." They both smiled at the underlying humor.

"Do you speak other languages?"

"Yes, Czech, of course, and—"

"Of course?"

"Aha, your briefing was incomplete! I was born in the U.S. because, as they say in the joke, it was where my mother happened to be at the time; but my parents were Czech and I had dual citizenship until I came here to stay twenty years ago."

"You have no discernible accent, other than a bit of Boston."

"I came by that honestly at Harvard, but my aunt, Jeb Mattison's wife and her sister, my mother, were very close and we visited each other often and long. I spent a good deal of my youth in the U.S."

"You started to say something before, to list another language."

"Oh yes, like all good Czech lads in school after the curtain came down, I speak good Russian; and, of course, German and Magyar, necessities of growing up in the Bratislava area."

"What was that you said about 'my class'? I'm not sure anymore that it was a compliment."

Steven laughed heartily. "Oh, but it was. I'm not really very proficient in any of them anymore. Rusty as the devil."

A smiling young couple approached, a very handsome pair. The woman spoke. "Steven! Good to see you. It's been forever. You must settle down and stop working so hard!"

Steven smiled back. "Alice, Don, please meet Leslie Antrim, from London. Leslie, meet the Crutchers from Omaha. Don is the junior, in seniority only, senator from Nebraska, and Alice is his guiding light."

They all nodded happily and began to talk animatedly. The trim and very good-looking young senator wasted no time zeroing in on the lovely Englishwoman, and watching, Steven began to feel a very strange emotion. Could it be jealousy? Of course not, he thought, he hardly knew the lady.

TWENTY-ONE

MOSCOW, U.S.S.R.

The Chairman was pleased but puzzled. He was pleased that Kotch had reported no suspicion had been cast on him, but was puzzled by Kotch's request for a meeting with Pierre. Kotch said he had an idea which—if it worked—might get the Amis off his back for good. Said it was a bit far out and he wanted to run it by Pierre first to see if he agreed it was feasible. Then of course, they would propose the operation to the Chairman—for his approval or rejection. He chuckled, thinking it was nice of them to give him a first refusal! He shrugged. He hadn't intended that they would *ever* get together when he sent Pierre in! It sure as hell would be a breach of security. But both the hot shots say no problem, so what to do? He decided: okay, children, have your way, but be careful.

He was beginning to think he'd created a Frankenstein in Kotch. The man shouldn't even know who Pierre was, must less meet him. And to discuss how to handle *my* operation! Those two will probably propose the first battle of World War III. Oh, they're smart, all right. Maybe too smart. Well, they promised not to *do* anything until he okayed it, specifically. Kotch said he knew I had a "case officer running things." He didn't want to know anything about him, just to meet him and discuss his idea. So discuss, he thought, and tell me about it.

Globitsyn shook his head slowly, and then his face relaxed into a smile. He reasoned that he had taught them to be aggressive spies, so why was he crying when they applied what he taught them? The Chairman can't sit here behind this Moscow desk and run personal operations all over the world. He has to let go. Has to let the boys he taught run them by themselves. He picked up the phone and hit an intercom button. "Irina? See if Colonel Asimov is still in the building. Ask him to join me if he is. . . . No, don't call him back if he's left. Yes, just a note to remind *me* in the morning. Fine."

He poured an iced vodka from his refrigerator, while he waited for her to call back. She didn't. He was getting annoyed when there was a light knock on the door. It was Asimov, of course; the girl never did anything right.

Colonel Asimov entered quietly as always and made for the chair near Globitsyn's right side. The Chairman pointed toward the fridge and Asimov went over and poured himself a drink. He came back, touched glasses with Globitsyn, and sat down.

The Chairman sipped, then spoke. "V.V., I need your advice. I may be premature, but I think not; and anyway, I want to be prepared. Now, V.V., this problem, in fact the existence of any problem at all, is between you and me alone! No others. Understand?"

"Of course, Chairman." Valeriy Vladimirovich Asimov was a small, slender, very dark-complected man. He had a thin, serious face, dominated by large dark eyes and heavy eyebrows, and framed by bushy black hair that made his head appear outsized for his body. KGB scuttlebut maintained that V.V. had never smiled, not even as a child.

"Good. You are one of the few people who know that we have sent Nadim Sadimoff to America and why. You know Sadimoff better than anyone else. In fact, it was on your strong recommendation that I sent him. So now, my friend, Nadim and our most sensitive agent in America are meeting in Washington—maybe at this very moment—to discuss an 'idea'—yes, that's what they call it—which, if successful will get the Amis off the agent's back forever! Or so they say."

Asimov's huge dark eyes watched the Chairman's face unblinkingly, not even moving as he lifted his glass for a sip. Globitsyn went on. "I've had enough hints from the agent to anticipate what it is they want to do, and while it's a good idea, it has considerable risk. What I want from you, V.V., is your opinion, principally on how Nadim will react if worse comes to worst. You know, if something goes wrong and he ends up in an American court on a murder charge or something like that. See?"

The large head nodded slowly. "You mean would Nadim crack too easily? Eh?" He scratched his chin. "Let me tell you, Chairman, why I recommended Nadim to you. And why I recommended Nadim ten years ago for the Hummous job." He stopped to take another sip. "It was in Hanoi, late in the war. The Amis didn't know it, but they were very close to winning. I was running NLF terror and intelligence nets into all the cities, especially Saigon. Objectives: sew confusion and report results. You know the routine better than I, Chairman."

Globitsyn nodded, glass at his lips, and Asimov continued. "Nadim was my number two. He was a superb agent handler, but a frustrated agent, always wanting to be where the action was. So this one time, we had an action unit going into Danang—aircraft attrition—and the leader got himself killed in an auto accident in Hanoi two days before push off. Of course Nadim volunteered, and reluctantly I let him go. He had a pretty good disguise—you know the Circassians sometimes have the Mongol look to their eyes—and a good experienced unit. This was an important raid and was tied into a big offensive coming up. Anyway things went bad—maybe a traitor, maybe a leak, maybe just the bad luck—but the Amis and their lackeys are waiting at the strike point in force and wrap the whole team up, taking them into a small base near Danang for questioning. They pick Nadim and one other NLF man for first try and let ARVN sadists loose on them, you know, torture because time is fleeting."

Again Globitsyn nodded. He quaffed the last of his glass, got up, and got the bottle from the fridge, bringing it over to fill both their glasses. Then sitting down again, he signaled for Asimov to continue.

"Well, Chairman, to shorten the story, an NLF patrol attacked this base about the time they were attaching the electrodes to Nadim's balls, and all hell broke loose. Nadim got one of the torturers' auto pistols, shot up the place, got his whole team out intact, and escaped."

Asimov stopped to sip his drink. Then with a look that was very close to a smile, he went on. "End of mission, eh? Nadim is a hero, saved his whole team, eh? Not so, Chairman! Nadim took that team, got back their explosives, and completed the aircraft attrition job at Danang! He is the tiger, the bulldog, the ferocious Russian bear. I do not know this other agent and I do not know what it is they propose, but I say if Nadim is running the show it will be successful; and if it needs it—if it is for the good of Russia—Nadim will give his life!"

Globitsyn looked thoughtful. "So you still recommend Sadimoff?"

"Unreservedly, Chairman."

"He has good political sense?"

Asimov shrugged. "I'm not sure of your meaning, Chairman. No, Nadim is not a political animal. Oh, he is very aware of the politics of any situation—such as his present one—but does he have good political sense? I don't know. He has never needed it. He has always followed the orders of those who do have such qualities. If he and this, uh, agent make an action proposal they—or at least Nadim—will expect Moscow to determine whether or not it is politically correct. Did I answer your question, Chairman?"

"Yes, V.V., I think you have answered all my questions— about Nadim. Now let us have another vodka and I'll explain to you what this is all about. I feel the need of your good advice."

TWENTY-TWO

WASHINGTON, D.C.

Morley and Kreeger had agreed that Telchoff needed a night out, and then collaborated on a way of doing it securely. So it was a well-disguised and very excited Russian who spent the evening at the Charlestown Racetrack, and had a late supper in the private dining room of an excellent Chinese restaurant near Rockville on the way back. Pansy and her cohorts were supported, unobtrusively, by another team, and the evening went off beautifully. Telchoff seemed to have a great time: betting too much, eating too much, drinking too much. Then he topped the outing with a serious seduction pitch that Pansy didn't really turn down, but was able to defer.

Meanwhile, Morley sat in his apartment and read, thought, wrote, researched, and generally stayed up late wringing out his mind. He had decided before the San Francisco episode that on the basis of the FBI investigative reports, Telchoff's information, logic, and reasonable conjecture, there were actually eight solid suspects who could be Kotch. Of these, despite their open Eastern European backgrounds, and their flawless behavior in San Francisco, Mattison, Berenz, and Millard continued to be the most promising. All the others seemed to have at least one glaring discrepancy with the list of qualities he had ascribed to Kotch; but he had not yet cleared any of them.

Morley had taken secret and logical steps to cover the general activities of the main three as well as two of the remaining five whom he considered leading contenders. There had been no concrete results as yet. He bemoaned the fact that Kotch could be anybody—that is, anybody who had seen that report. Did he have to be high level? Conceivably not, if he had constant access to his boss's desk and/or files. Did he have to have an Eastern Europe satellite background? Not unless you believed Telchoff. Was Telchoff a phony? Sent as a red herring to protect Kotch? No, Morley had decided early on that Pete was legitimate and could be believed. Therefore, Kotch *did* have to have an Eastern Europe background; but as they had both figured out, this didn't mean that this background had to be open, or if it were open, it didn't have to be correct. Kotch could be a beautifully clean transplant or an open guy with phony credentials.

Morley's list of important leaks—limited to those that had been discovered, of course—and the side-by-side names of people with "time and place" access was totally inconclusive. He'd gone back about two years in view of Borodin's report that Kotch's access had improved dramatically about a year ago, and now saw no need to go back further *or* deeper. There just weren't any suspicious conclusions to work on.

Morley agonized. He kept coming back to those three Eastern European types and San Francisco! Was everything as it seemed? That is, that the mole wasn't there so they had to activate the Marina net to get the information? Or was the mole there, and everything else a charade to get me off his back? If the mole was there, he could think of lots of reasons why the KGB would have told him to be cool. If he wasn't, and they had no other way to get the information—that is, no other asset in the delegation—and they thought the Marina net was clean—it would have been routine to use the net. Bullshit, Morley thought, they've got me going around in circles!

Was that not the important question? *Who* had him going around in circles? The "why" he knew; the "how" he could figure out; but the "who" stumped him. He thought, am I being paranoid? Am I being manipulated *into* a particular line of thought or *away* from another? Or is it just that things are really what they seem to be, and logic is leading me inevitably to a conclusion that is inescapable? Another thought struck him. If I'm being manipulated, why try to kill me? This was closely followed by the fact that they hadn't tried again recently—at least to his knowledge.

Then he tried thinking like the KGB: okay, I'm Yuri Globitsyn, and my pride and joy mole has been damn near unfrocked by my fair-haired boy, Borodin. Okay. I know Borodin sent two reports—we intercepted part of one and Kotch read the other; but I don't know if there was a third, or even a fourth!

Furthermore, Morley reflected, Globitsyn knows he fixed the Kotch file so it was titillating but not revealing. An ego like the Chairman's would preclude him from believing Borodin could have outsmarted him. So, Morley reasoned, Globitsyn figures it's been well over a month. Nobody has come around to arrest Kotch. *He* says there is no change, no suspicion, no problems. So, Borodin shot blanks; Telchoff can't remember anything worthwhile; and Morley hasn't got a clue. Why do anything? We're in the cat-bird seat. Let the Amis do what they will.

Morley shook his head. There had developed, just in the last day or so, a little buzzer in the back of his brain that kept going off at odd times. He figured it was trying to tell him he was missing an important point, something that was small but not small. It had to be something that happened to him—or that he had learned—since he came to D.C. He mulled over each day's events. He stopped at San Francisco—again. Suppose there were two moles. Would the KGB give him one to save the other? No, doesn't make sense, he thought. If I were KGB, wouldn't I love to have a man in any of those three positions! Would I throw him to the wolves to save somebody else? Hell no, I'd protect him and still get the necessary intelligence by using my Marina net. Morley shook his head slowly, realizing he was once again back at square one.

A new tack: If Kotch was safe—if Borodin's report(s) had not identified him, and Telchoff couldn't help—why didn't Globitsyn pull the Egyptian/Circassian out while he was able? The guy must be a hell of a valuable agent. The answer had to be that Globitsyn *did not yet* consider Kotch home free. Kotch was still in danger. It had to be.

Okay. Kotch is still in danger, but from whom? It couldn't be Borodin. So it had to be from Telchoff, or from an unknown. Yes, he thought, that's it. There must be a Mr. or Ms. X that I can't do anything about at the moment, but Telchoff can. Pete has a superb memory once he gets it started, so I have to start it—push the right button, and. . . . The buzzing went off again in his brain. Yes, I have an idea what that button might be!

Meanwhile he still hadn't solved the enigma: was he being manipulated into concentrating on Mattison, Berenz, and Millard because they did *not* include the mole; or was his own logic leading him to them because one of them *had to be* the mole? Who's manipulating him? Telchoff? Byrnes? San Francisco was his idea. Epworth? He pushed hard for one of these three being the mole. Milford? He briefed him on the Borodin case; did he color it? Who knows? Another Mr. X? The General?

And then of course there was the "reverse double twist" where one of the three—say, Mattison, for example—is really the mole, and the KGB is pushing him, Morley, in this direction because one, they knew he'd be drawn there eventually and inevitably; and two, they knew he could never prove it! Well, he thought, maybe that CIA girl, Amanda, can shed some light on this aspect. She sounded competent, and certainly a looker. Morley fell asleep on the couch in the middle of these mental games. He dreamed badly.

The phone woke him up. The clock showed 8:32 A.M. It was Egil Kreeger. "Patrick, things are beginning to simmer a bit. As we thought, if we leave enough inflammables around, sooner or later somebody will start a fire. Per your request we put a light cover on the Egyptian starting two nights ago and then 'upped' it last night based on what Telchoff told you. Lucky we did. He goes out last night about eleven—from a dark apartment— and heads leisurely for Georgetown. Goes into the Four Seasons, sits in the lounge, and has a couple of quiet drinks. Nobody approaches him or seems to notice him. Then he goes to the john and doesn't return! After a reasonable time our man goes to see and, of course, no Egyptian. He stays put because there's nothing else better to do, and lo and behold about forty-five minutes later here comes the Egyptian back in, emerging from the john area. Picks up his drink, melted ice and all, just as casual as you please. Fifteen minutes, he heads home and goes to bed. Slick, eh?"

"Very interesting, Egil. Your man figure he went out via the men's room or something?"

"Yeah, it was or something. You can get outside from the john area if you know what you're doing and can crack a couple of simple locks. I figure the Egyptian is capable on both counts."

"If this guy is the pro we think he is anything can happen. I guess all we can do is keep watching and hope we get lucky."

Kreeger chuckled. "What else is new? Standard police procedure. I'll stay in touch."

Fifteen minutes later the phone rang again. It was the General. "Patrick, my friends on the tight little island have reported that someone, a suspected Soviet illegal, low to medium support type, was nosing around the real Amanda's neighborhood yesterday."

"Get anything?"

"They don't know yet."

"That's not a very good answer, sir. They assured us that their end was wrapped up. 'No problem, Yanks,' as I remember."

"We mustn't jump to judgment; however, like you I suspect they're stalling to get their story together. I'll let you know as soon as I hear from them."

"I think I'd better alert Amanda about this. Maybe we should even pull her out."

"Agreed you should tell her, and the decision to pull her out or not is yours, Patrick; but you may wish to delay that decision for a day or so. It could all be smoke, and to be practical, this is the kind of a development we've been hoping for. Possibly the KGB is considering another move to protect their mole, who may or may not be Mattison. But the fact remains: there must be a connection. The question is whether their action is their own idea, or a reaction to our provocation."

"Yes, I agree. We have to let Amanda do her job. She's one hell of a lady, and I don't want her hurt, but as you say, this is why she's there."

"Right. By the way, since you're going to set up a meeting with Amanda anyway, I'd like to join you and meet her, if we could do it securely."

"I'm sure we can. Give me your schedule for tomorrow and I'll try to set it up."

"Anything else?"

"Yes, Egil just called. Our so-called Egyptian, whom Telchoff thinks is Russian and KGB, ducked his surveillance for about an hour last night."

"That guy gets more interesting, doesn't he? I don't think there's much doubt anymore about who he is and why he's here. Your hunch was right."

"Looks like it to me. Wish I could get one on the big mole operation."

"Big? Is there a little one too?"

"Mental cog slip. Just a thought I had last night. A possibility that there are two and we're being herded toward the little one."

"You don't think Mattison could be our man?"

"Oh yeah, he *could* be our man. I mean he *could* be a Soviet agent, but I don't think he's Kotch."

"Then why inject Amanda into the situation?"

"I don't *know* that he isn't Kotch, and of course any Soviet mole is worth catching; but mostly, I guess I want to make waves and see the KGB reaction. I'd say that their nosing around Leslie Antrim's place in England is very interesting, even though it could be motivated by a variety of objectives. At least something's happening, and if we get them reacting often and fast enough, they'll goof up somewhere."

"All right, I guess. Keep me posted."

"Count on it, General."

TWENTY-THREE

WASHINGTON, D.C.

"Marshall Berenz is an asshole. This is the worst waste of time since old Pottsy had us on that one-oh-five case out near Glen Echo. Hell, I'm not sure I wouldn't rather be fighting those mosquitoes by the canal than sitting here watching the clock and listening to you scratch your ass—while Marshall baby and his wife play tiddledy winks or grab ass or whatever in there! Shit, I'll bet it's tiddledy winks."

"How soon we forget! Two months ago you were cursing Pottsy for putting us on the China squad to fill in. Said you couldn't tell Orientals apart. Before that you bitched about the TDY in Frederick. In fact, I think you said you'd rather have those Canal Road mosquitoes then too. But as I recall, Bobby Joe baby, when those mosquitoes *were* biting your patrician neck you were moaning about goin' back to Austin and practicin' law again! Shit, man, I bet when you *were* down there in court you used to wish you were in the North woods goosin' a moose or some. . . . Hey! Wait, Bobby. Our man is movin'. How the hell'd he get out and into that car so fast? Bar one to bar two—'Archie' is moving west on Rabbit from garage area. We'll take him to Badger and one block past, then turn off. You're lookin' west, right?"

"Roger, bar one. Looking west on Rabbit half block from Badger. I see Archie. Okay, we're on your tail now."

"Bar three, you read?"

"Rog. Five squared. We're at Quick and Badger, ready to go either way."

"Good. Bar one coming up on Badger. Oh shit, Archie's straddling left lane. . . . Cute! There he goes straight through on Rabbit! You get him, bar two! I've got to go left or I give him the message. I'll parallel on Quick to three-eight. Bar three, precede me—slowly—so you'll be ready to go either way on three-eight. Bar two, coords?"

"Bar two, roger. He's coming up on three-eight dead end . . . Hang on . . . okay, south on three-eight."

"Got that, bar three?"

"See him coming, bar one. Got him! You behind?"

"Coming up for turn on three-eight. Bar two, I have you in sight. Stay with it. I'll bring up the rear."

"Bar three comin' up on Rez. Archie's stopped waiting for light. He's in right lane with blinker on. . . . Okay. Turning right toward Sick Bay."

"Bar two on Rez. Have Archie and bar three in sight."

"Good. Bar three, stay on him if he goes straight or right at Foxy. If he goes left at forty-four or at Foxy leave him for us, but double back when clear. Bar two, he's your baby whenever he goes left. Got it?"

"Bar two, roger."

"Bar three in. We passed forty-four, next chance Foxy."

"Bar one, going left on forty-four. Got a hunch he's going left on Foxy. I'll be waiting at Canary."

"You got it, bar one. Archie waited 'til last moment, then went left on Foxy. He is really hauling ass, bar one, hurry up!"

"Bar two in. Got 'im in sight."

"Bar one in. I'm on Canary ahead of him. I'll let him pass, then speed up. B two, you can lag and be ready in case he takes the bridge."

"Rog. He's yours, bar one. I see you both."

"He's passed the bridge, gang, heading for Whitey . . . moving fast down Whitey. Be ready, bar two. He's got some choices comin' up!"

"Rog. Ready."

"Bar three, coords?"

"Just got on Whitey, coming up on your tails."

"Looks like left branch into Park. Oh shit, he cut over to the right, going down toward the Lady. I've got to go straight. He's all yours, bar two! Move up to spell him, bar three."

"Rog from bar two."

"Bar three in. Looks like the game is over. He's moving into JFK parking. Can you believe it? We'll follow him in and put foot three on the street."

"Bar two in. Right behind you. Sending foot two to rendy with foot three."

"Bar one in. Good! Bar two, don't go in, use first exit, circle, and cover cab stand on river exit just in case. Bar three, block Archie's car and wait for foots two and three to report. I'll be there in thirty seconds."

"Bar three in. Foot three reports Archie met woman in entrance lobby, entered main door, now inside. Foot three going in on badge for look-see."

"I'm right behind you, bar three. Bar two report."

"Bar two in place cab stand area. No Archie."

"Foot three reporting. Archie and woman appear set to watch show. Four minutes to curtain. Security's giving me seat behind and to side. No further reports till they move."

"Where's foot two?"

"Lobby door. I'll be able to see him too."

"Fine. Carry on. Sending foot one to join foot two. Bar three stay in posy. I'll join bar two near exit."

Epworth gave Morley the gist of the evening's adventure over the phone next morning. "All for naught?"

"I guess so. It gave my boys something to do, relieved the boredom, but that's about all."

"You talked to them this morning?"

"Last night. I've got a standing order to be called if there's any unusual action on this case."

"Right. And what did they think?"

"The squad leader, Burley—you've met him—said that in retrospect it could well have been innocent. The route he took to the Kennedy Center was a bit unusual, but it did avoid the congestion of Georgetown at dinnertime. The woman turned out to be a cousin of Berenz's wife, and the wife *had* been to the doctor that day with a strep throat, so it does look innocent."

"What did Burley's gut tell him? He's an old hand at the game."

"That's the rub, Patrick. Burley says the guy was trying to lose them. Whether he was playing games, screwing his wife's cousin—not a bad-looking gal, Burley's boys said—who knows? He says the guy knew they were there and tried to lose them."

"So what can we do?"

"You mean that we're not doing?"

"Yeah."

"Well, we just move the case up a notch. We get the ears inside as well as out, wire his offices and car, add a team to take the wife, and take a closer look at the cousin. Those kinds of things, you know."

Patrick nodded. "Sounds good. Hell, he now knows—or does he?—that he can't shake the tail; he's got to step his operation, if there is one, up a notch too."

"Exactly. That's why we have to concentrate on identifying anything that could be contract or commo."

"Good. And what about the third little bear? Snug at home?"

"Like hell! That guy almost never stays home, and when he is he's never alone. Now there's a guy who could indeed run an espionage operation right under your nose and get away with it. He sees so many people during the course of the day and night, there's no way you could check them all out. And half of them, maybe more, are foreigners, from Soviets on down. He goes to at least two cocktails and a dinner most nights and he could have ten quick case officer meetings at each one, and dammit, we'd never know."

"Bug him?"

"Movie stuff. Not practical."

"Why not? Shoes, suit, whatever?"

"I say not practical. He doesn't *have* any *clandestine* meetings. I said he *could* have agent meetings in any of the public places, but even computers and state of the art can't overcome nature. We've tried the shoes thing, the cuff links, tie pins, studs, whatever. It hasn't been successful under these kinds of conditions."

"Hmm. Okay if you say so, Stan. The woman inside?"

"Yes, she's in, but nothing's happened. She's been over the place, every inch, and nothing suspicious. I think she's done everything and nosed everywhere she can. But we'll keep her in place and see what goes down—if anything."

"And the other two guys, no action?"

"Nothing worth reporting. Strictly routine."

"Ah well, they also serve, Stan."

"Sure. I know. It only takes one slip, and it always happens when you least expect it."

TWENTY-FOUR

WASHINGTON, D.C.

Steven Mattison was excited. Perhaps "elated" would be a more accurate description. Whatever the shades of his emotional condition, the cause was indisputable—Leslie Antrim. The weekend had been super, to the point where he, who ordinarily eschewed the "horse country" life, hated to see it end. There had been a few times in Steven's active bachelorhood in Washington when he had the word "love" around his tongue—and once even "marriage"—but he'd decided quickly that he didn't like the taste very much. Now he found himself doing it again and, this time, liking it.

It had happened very quickly, but then he understood that it often did, even the tritely described "real thing." And, he thought, best of all she'll be here another four months. No, best of all was that she seemed to reciprocate his feelings, at least up to a point. He smiled to himself. Wouldn't do to push too hard too soon. She had a promising career. The Brits wouldn't blow the kind of dough it takes to keep a young Foreign Service officer in G.U. for a semester—of economics, no less—without expecting a return on it. And she seemed to be happy with her career prospects.

He'd have to play this one very carefully. Already he figured he had much more than the usual to lose. He didn't want Leslie to say no when he asked her; and he surely didn't want her to be annoyed. She was living on campus by choice, and had set stringent social limitations for herself, both with the intent of emphasizing her studies. Now, while he got the definite impression these rules could be bent, he found himself afraid to coax. He was bemused by the fact that he was scared to death she'd say no.

Tonight, of course, was different. He couldn't just bring her back to the campus and drop her. Nor could he tell her why he hadn't the time tonight. *That* she *really* would not understand— a secret meeting with a Russian spy! But the Sedgwicks had bailed him out by insisting that Leslie stay the night in Middleburg and ride in with them in the morning. Steven was able to plead the press of an 8:00 A.M. breakfast session at the White House quite convincingly.

He came across Reservoir Road to Wisconsin, then right to Q and left to 30th, into the alley, and his electronic control opened the right half of his large garage. He moved quickly through the dark yard, skirting the drained and covered pool, to the patio that joined a screened porch. The porch door was locked, as was the impressively solid door to the rear entryway. He entered and went immediately to the library, turned on the soft lights on either side of two lounge chairs, sat in one of them, and waited. . . .

The man was late. Unusual. Promptness up till now had been one of his hallmarks. Steven laughed wryly. The man, promptness and all, was still a mystery. There was a slight sound at the rear door and seconds later the man was in the library doorway. He nodded, said "Good evening" in Russian, moved to the other chair, and sat.

TWENTY-FIVE

WASHINGTON, D.C.

Morley was upset. The General had just called to say that he'd
finally heard from his British contact. The latter had been very
apologetic, but the damage had been done. The General said,
"Tommy allowed as how there seemed to have been some kind
of a 'balls up'! The Antrim servants were all well briefed and
the whole place was operating on a business-as-usual basis.
Then one of the servants came down with mumps. Anyway,
the replacement servant was brought in quickly and there were
two days before Milord decided to tell Tommy's people about
it. (Seems Milady was in a snit because they were on the eve of
a large dinner party when the cad of a servant began to swell.)
And so, Patrick, under the terms of the British version of Murphy's law, it was inevitable that the Soviet agent would come at
just that time and seek out just that servant."

The General said that Tommy told him that all the agent
could have learned was that the new servant was confused as to
the present location of Miss Leslie, having never actually met
the lady, or been told about her. However, Tommy's people
were embarrassed and offered to pull the agent in and "stick"
him if we so desired. The General had nixed that obviously

counterproductive move, which could only jeopardize further Amanda's cover. Ashley said he'd make sure Tommy was more careful from now on.

Amanda didn't attend her class that evening so the professor couldn't give her the emergency signal (which he, of course, did not realize was an emergency signal). Morley then moved procedures to the phone calls next morning, first from the ostensible classmate and then from the ostensible professor. They both reported that a man had answered the phone, and while he was pleasant, he did not identify himself nor offer to take a message. Both callers insisted he take a message saying it was important that they contact Leslie as soon as possible.

Morley was worried, but not alarmed. The next step in emergency contact was electronic. Amanda had a tiny receiver that was supposed to be worn at all (reasonable) times. It had a short buzz to it and an even shorter electric jolt, so it was best if she were alone when it was triggered. There was also the risk that the signal could be intercepted, although the interceptor would probably not realize what he had. Anyway he thought the problem merited the risk, so he sent the signal. It worked and Amanda made the appointment for that afternoon with the "cleared" beauty salon.

Morley was there watching securely on closed circuit TV from the upstairs office when Amanda arrived with Steven Mattison in tow. Steven was openly curious about the place, looking here and there, but finally kissed Amanda's cheek and left, promising to be back in an hour. As soon as he left she came up to the office and immediately took the offensive. "Have you ever felt the shock from one of those little bleepers, you sadist! What's the deal? Can't you guys afford a phone call anymore? Damn, that thing gave me a heart attack, and the bleep could've been heard a block away. Hell, Patrick, I jumped a foot!" Then she relaxed and smiled. "Good thing Steven wasn't around. He'd've thought my excitement was from something he'd done and would be looking for a way to repeat the process. Seriously, what's the matter with Ma Bell's gadget?"

"Ma Bell couldn't get you, love, and if you remember the procedures you memorized, the next step is the buzzer."

"Hmm. When did you call?"

"This morning, twice."

"I was there!"

"Does it ring in your room?"

"Uh, no, it doesn't. Nobody answer?"

"Oh yeah. A man answered and took a message for you to call—urgent but not emergency."

"Umm, obviously the message was not delivered."

"What men were there this morning?"

"The, uh, cook-butler and Steven for a while."

"All right, let's not waste any more time on it, but if you can do it securely, it might be interesting to find out why no message. You could legitimately ask tonight after your class. It was Professor Blake and Beth Huston who called."

"Will do."

"Now, where did you have it?"

"Have what?"

"The bleeper, of course."

"Oh, right under my boob."

"Which one?"

"Left. Easier to place for a right-hander."

"Uh huh, and what did the audio man tell you about not putting it near the heart?"

"Oh, to hell with it, Patrick. I still think you could have called again."

"Procedure three, my dear, is not to keep trying the phone, but to—"

"I know, I know. Push the button and shock the little broad. Stop her heart, whatever."

Morley just shook his head in wonderment. Amanda laughed. "Oh well, I was about to call you for a meet myself. Had a strange one last night and need a spot of consultation."

"Your stage, 'Manda."

"Okay. I've been staying over at Steven's for three nights now. Don't leer, you male chauvinist pig. My virtue, such as it is, is intact—different bedrooms, chaste good night kisses, and the like. The man's a perfect gentleman."

"He brings boys in?"

"No, at least I haven't seen any. I think the guy reveres me, y'know; doesn't want to sully my spotless soul, whatever. Wants me to go to New York with him and meet Uncle Jeb— who hung the moon and made the mountains.

"Anyway, what happened last night might interest you. We went to dinner at this fancy place downtown. Came home early as Steven had an appointment. Said he had to keep it, very mysterious. Said he wouldn't be late, and I should go to bed.

"I did as bid, but about an hour later I woke up. Suppose it was all that fancy food, French sauces chasing each other up and down my alimentary canal. Anyway, I got up to eat a couple Tums and drink some water, but there was no glass in my bathroom. Lazy damn maid! (Do I sound to the manor born, Patrick?) So I went silently down the hall to Steven's bathroom to borrow a glass of water; but as I passed the stairway I could see light from the first floor. Since I am a highly trained and multitalented spy, nothing to do but sneak down a couple steps so I could see what was going on down there. 'Course I never dreamed Steven would be trying anything right in his own house under the eyes of a highly trained and multi—"

"We know. Get on with it."

"Well, seems I hit an opportune moment as Steven and this other man had apparently been talking in the library, and were now saying good-bye at the open door. Steven was talking but I couldn't see him. The other man I could see only from the back, and really, Patrick, the light wasn't that great."

"You could hear Steven but not see him?"

"Yes, I'm sure it was he."

"And the, uh, stranger. Description?"

"Medium and medium, I'm afraid. I never even saw him in

profile. After about thirty seconds he walked away toward the back of the house, away from me."

"Probably a good thing. What if he'd walked toward you?"

"No problem. I'd have just shut my eyes."

"Uh huh . . . all right. Did you hear anything they were saying? You said they were saying good-bye? What language were they speaking?"

"French, and doing it very well too."

"And what were they talking about?"

"Nothing substantive really, although the probably handsome dark stranger, with the broad back and narrow hips did say, 'If you want to contact me in a hurry don't call my office, call my friend. Just give him a time and we'll meet where we did last week. Okay?' And then Steven just said, 'Okay.'"

"Was the handsome stranger dark?"

"Handsome strangers are always dark, Patrick. Sorry about that. Even in that lousy light I could tell his hair was dark. And his accent—although his French was excellent, native fluency, I'd say—still there was a hint of North Africa running through it. Steven's, by the way, is good but very 'American schoolish,' so to speak."

"So they said good-bye. No other substantive talk but the bit about calling his friend?"

"No, nothing. That was apparently in answer to a question Steven asked before I got there. After that bit, they said good-bye and the dark and undoubtedly handsome stranger walked away into the night."

"By himself?"

"Yes. Steven said good-bye without ever coming out of the library and when the, uh, stranger left he went back in and shut the door."

"Wasn't this unusual?"

"I don't know, Patrick. I'm a virgin as to Steven's clandestine meetings! 'Twas truly my first."

"Look, 'Manda, this is very serious business. There is one hell of a lot riding on it for both sides. I am very worried about you; in fact, I've been thinking about pulling you out before the other side gets rough, and believe me they are capable of it. I think you were right, you saw the end of a clandestine meeting. I can't tell you what Steven's status is, but I'm sure that was a clandestine agent–case officer meeting. Now let's go back to the stranger's departure. Did they shake hands, embrace, pat shoulders, or such?"

"Noooh, they didn't. I see what you mean, Patrick. No, it wasn't a warm parting at all. In retrospect, I guess you could say it was at best neutral—neither friendly nor unfriendly. The stranger just walked out and Steven shut the library door before the guy was ten feet away."

"So we could assume he'd been there before and knew his way out?"

"Yeah. I think so."

"And that if it was an agent–case officer meeting it was not a very friendly one?"

"I guess that's right, but maybe just businesslike."

"And if it was what we think, the stranger was probably the case officer, not the agent?"

"Yeah. Agreed."

"Okay. Let's go back a bit. You said you woke up an hour after you went to sleep. Was it indigestion, or maybe something else?"

She looked at him queryingly.

"Just a thought. I was wondering whether you were *supposed* to wake up and see what you saw!"

"It could be something like that. Hell, I don't know. I did seem to wake up suddenly, but whether it was a noise, I don't know. How could they know I'd see the light and get nosy?" Morley just smiled. "All right, all right! So it could have been a put-on. Why would they want me to do that?"

"I don't know, Amanda. What about this morning, Steven ask any questions? Give any indications he might have seen you on the stairs? Anything out of the ordinary?"

"No. Nothing I can recall. 'Course I've only been there three mornings and he's always nice as pie. I don't think he was any different this morning."

"How about his coming with you to the beauty shop?"

"Unusual? I don't know. Out of character, maybe, maybe not. Was he acting suspicious? Not that I could see. My guess is he was just being Mr. Nice Guy, but I can't say, Patrick."

"And you went back to bed after he closed the library door?"

"Yes. And very quietly too."

"Uh huh. . . . All right. And since you couldn't see him in the library doorway, we can assume he couldn't see you; nor could the stranger."

"We can assume that, yes. And I *was* really quiet."

"Okay. You've convinced me. I came here determined to pull you out if anything odd was happening there, like their cutting off your phone calls or, yes, running clandestine ops out of the house. I find out they've done both, and yet here I am considering letting you go back in, business as usual. Am I making a mistake? Be honest."

"I don't think so, Patrick. God knows, I don't have any death wish, either. I just don't think they have any reason to suspect me of anything."

"S'pose I told you the Sovs had sent a creep out to Leslie Antrim's place to nose around? In England, I mean."

"A Sov leg man? You know that?"

"Yes, so identified by the Brits."

"Uh huh. And what did he find out?"

"Nothing, I hope, but the fact remains that they sent him."

"I see what you mean. Why the Sovs? And why the check?"

"So I ask you, 'Manda, will I make a mistake letting you go back in?"

"Well, I'm in there because you think Steven might be part of a KGB operation; isn't it logical that they'd check out somebody who was getting close to him?"

"Sure. That's to be expected, but we also have to assume they're watching you closely, say, like right now."

She laughed. "Then I guess you'd better let the hairdresser

have at me. If Steven comes back and sees no improvement I'll be in bad trouble."

Morley's head moved slowly from side to side. "All right, love, because I can't see any reason for them wanting to hurt you. If they *do* suspect you're a plant, then you must be an Agency plant—and the 'unwritten law' comes into play. Oh, dammit, what I mean is *don't*, repeat *don't* do anything provocative. Just look and listen, and don't even go out of your way to do that. I want you to run at the first sign of hardball. And you have your signal for Kreeger's people. There will be a car past there twice every hour from now and if your bedroom shade is at half mast—they'll come in and take that place apart till they find you. Got it?"

"Yes, chief!"

"All right. Take care! We'll meet in forty-eight hours, no later, at the university library."

"Got it."

"Good. Take care."

Morley kissed her, authoritatively again, and began his journey to emerge from the back of a shop two doors away.

TWENTY-SIX

RAPID CITY, SOUTH DAKOTA

Joe Shola stood by the large double window looking down at the traffic on busy St. Joe Street. Even in the autumn, long after the summer's tourist flood, it was busy. Although there were not too many similarities between then and now, somehow this view always reminded him of that day thirty-two years ago when he stood by a similar window looking down on a similarly busy street. He was the same—if you can equate an eleven-year-old boy with a forty-three-year-old man—but that's really about all. That was Budapest, not Rapid City; a small walk-up apartment, not a large law office; and most of all those were Russian tanks, trucks, and weapons carriers, not American civilian traffic.

He remembered that last day in Budapest very well. How proud he was, knowing the designations of the tanks and the other vehicles that formed the advance guard for the endless lines of soldiers who marched behind. All with their Red Star markings, the pride of the mighty Red Army. His mother had told him many times about the German soldiers and their cruelty, and how the brave Russians had driven them out.

The boy hadn't minded too much leaving Budapest, knowing

that, as Eva put it, his mother "had gone to join his father." He hadn't realized at that time just what the word "orphan" entailed. He only knew that he'd been terribly lonely since his father died several Christmases ago, and now that his mother was gone too, it would be worse. He had been most anxious to leave. But still.

The next day Eva had brought him to Vienna where Grandfather Shola was waiting to take him to America. They flew to strange and wonderful cities like London, and New York, and Chicago; and then they ended up in South Dakota where Grandfather Shola had a large ranch near the Wyoming border northwest of Rapid City. Grandfather had been a farmer in Hungary, near Szeged his father had told him, before emigrating to America many years ago.

And Joe's own father had grown up on that farm in America. He had met Joe's mother during the war, and they had been married not long afterward, and gone to America to live.

Joe remembered again how he had felt that last day in Budapest. Going to America was kind of like going home—his father's home. His mother had never liked it, he knew. In fact, they had fought about it many times with loud voices. But then his mother hadn't liked Grandfather Shola either. She had told him and his father this several times. So it was no surprise to Joe that shortly after his father died—thrown from a horse on the ranch—he and his mother moved back to Budapest. He knew his mother was a Communist at that time, but he had never understood what it meant. She had always been loving and kind to him. He missed her then, and for many years afterward, but eventually he came to regard Grandfather Shola and his housekeeper, Emily, as his true family.

The buzzer on his intercom snapped him out of this familiar reverie. He pushed a button and answered. A loud and happy voice answered him. "Jose, my amigo, I am calling to synchronize watches with you. I have four twenty-one and, uh, post! Thirty seconds. Mountain Standard. Got it?"

"Post, friend, we are synchronized."

"Good. Now there will be no excuse for your being late to-morrow morning . . . none at all. It's four-thirty at my place. And Joe, on the dot."

"You're on. I'm all packed and I'll be over tonight to transfer to the van. In fact, I think I'll just sleep in it there. The other guys set?"

"Just checked 'em out. You're the last one. They're packing tonight too, and we'll rendezvous at the Mall at four forty-five, usual place, and proceed Injun file."

"I'll be there. I'm really looking forward to it. Don't know when I'll be able to do it again—at least for a couple of years."

"We know, Senator. That's why we want to be in position when the sun rises and the season opens. See you later."

"Will do, my boy, will do."

TWENTY-SEVEN

WASHINGTON, D.C.

He had always claimed that both good things and bad things happened in clumps of threes. God knew they'd had several clumps of bad ones on this case, so when Telchoff identified the Egyptian as a KGB hotshot, Morley figured he had two more to go on the good side before starting to worry again. He did not include his escape from the would-be assassins on G Street or Amanda's spotting of Mattison's midnight visitor as pieces of good luck, confining his definition of the latter to those things, events, that were "entirely out of one's control." And so Morley felt it completely within his due when Kreeger called just as he finished his second cup of coffee the next morning to tell him that they had had a "little kiss from Lady Luck."

"We sure as hell can use it. What's happened?"

"A patrol car brought in a young man last night, an Arab. Gave his name as Samir Aboud, Lebanese, student at American U. Charge, attempted rape. The alleged felony—a bit questionable since there was a time lapse and a big party—involved a female graduate student at A.U. Anyhow, the officers played it seriously, as they should, and booked him, gave him his one call, and put him in a cell.

"His phone call was routinely logged and registered, even though it was unsuccessful—no answer—and here's where we get lucky! The young detective in charge put the number on the computer and it was one that was on my section's watchlist. Guess who?" He laughed.

"Not Farid."

"Close, Patrick. The Egyptian! So the detective called me and I came down to see what kind of fish we'd caught who would waste his one phone call trying to get in touch with the Egyptian.

"So here's this young smart ass, sullen, uncooperative bastard, figures there's no way we're gonna stick him with the rape charge, sittin' there ready to stonewall us. The detective had called and telexed for FBI, CIA, NATO, and Interpol priority checks, so I told him to let the smart ass sit and wait till they came in."

"His local story check out?"

"Yeah, sort of. He was registered as a graduate student at A.U. but he hadn't attended class in four or five weeks. He did have a transcript from a college in Lebanon, and it was in the right name. He lived where he said he did, and he had been an invited guest at the party that preceded the rape attempt, as had the alleged victim. But, you know, the whole background had an odor about it. I can *smell* phonies after all these years.

"So about an hour ago the first checks started to come in— that's one good thing about European checks—those guys' working day started a long time ago. Of course the smart-assed innocent student has a two-page pedigree. His alias and picture gave us a positive ident as a much sought-after Palestinian terrorist, real name Na'im Rasun, member of a PLO splinter group called L'Ange Cinq. Rasun is wanted in Paris for a bombing and an assassination; in Frankfurt for two killings and a bank heist; and in Rome for the big airport shoot-up. These countries are hot for his body, and of course the Israelis would like to fry him for breakfast."

"Jackpot!" Morley rolled his eyes. "A present from heaven. Tell me more, Egil."

"Yup, there's more all right. . . . With this ammo we cracked him in twenty minutes and began to peel off layers. First he admitted his ID, but denied his guilt on the charges—'an Israeli lie,' he said. Then he admitted the charges, giving us a tirade about Palestinian persecution, but said he was here in the U.S. on a legitimate scholarship and 'those days' were behind him. We pushed him a bit and convinced him we were going to frame his murdering ass on the rape charge, and after he served twenty years we'd turn him over to the French. That's when he really wilted—went from cocky to scared, back to proud freedom fighter, and ended up like a nightingale.

"Well, the tale was full of self-justification and some lecturing on Middle East politics, but basically it rang true. He'd been recruited out of a refugee camp in Lebanon when he was fourteen, and his training had included a college education at the American University in Beirut. He'd joined the elite L'Ange Cinq about two years ago after earning his spurs on the West Bank and in Europe. Says L'Ange Cinq is led by Hummous— he doesn't know Hummous's real name, but he is the best, the king of all the freedom fighters. Says the Israelis would give ten of the latest jet fighters to get their hands on Hummous. And now the climax, Patrick.

"This famous terrorist, Hummous, and our Egyptian are one and the same! His picture and alias weren't worth a damn for traces because nobody *had* pictures of him from the past, and the alias is a throwaway. And that's just the beginning."

"Great beginning."

"So young Rasun—he said he's only twenty-two and I believe him—is here to assist Hummous in some kind of 'execution,' he called it. Says he was honored to be selected by Hummous for the job and that the PLO had pulled a lot of strings to get him the student cover on short notice. Anyway, Rasun claims he does not yet know the identity of the execution victim or victims but that they must be very important to bring Hummous over to handle the job. He did know that it would take place at a celebration dinner in Washington, at a big hotel. The timing had to be early November—he figured this from onward planning—and there was a second gun who'd be with him, another Palestinian he knew only as Rajah. I showed him all my pictures but he said Rajah wasn't among them. He did recognize Farid, whom he knew as Otar, but said Otar was not in on the hotel hit as far as he knew. He sort of dismissed Otar as a 'gofer' for Hummous and not a serious fighter."

"He said he didn't know any of the other hoods? The guys from the Virginia hit?"

"Right. Said he doubted they were Palestinians or he'd've known 'em. Thought they were Libyans or some other kind of North Africans."

"How'd Rasun justify blowing all these whistles, Egil? I'd have figured he'd die first."

"He's a scared kid, Patrick. Way over his head in trouble. I asked him the same question. Said, 'What choice do I have?' Then the little bugger laughed and said we'd never catch Hummous anyway. Said nobody ever had!"

"You think he's leveling, Egil?"

"To a large degree, yes. He's scared shitless and we're the closest boogeymen, not the Egyptian. Guess he figures he has nothing to lose telling us all. I don't think he's opened up a hundred percent yet, but he will."

"The Hummous story makes sense to me. If the Egyptian is the KGB deep cover guy, as Telchoff claims, he could sure as hell have become a famous Palestinian terrorist during the last ten years. I haven't heard the name, but I'm sure Jack Milford and his boys have, if Rasun isn't just blowing smoke at us."

"What about the assassination story? This is a new wrinkle, isn't it?"

"Yes, but I'm not surprised. Remember we discussed—and I've talked to Pete about this—we considered the possibility that the KGB had another tasking for the Egyptian. We surmised that even if Telchoff and I hadn't been able to unmask the mole, there was still somebody around who presented a real danger, and that the Egyptian was being kept on to eliminate this person. We also figured there was no cleaner and safer way for them to do it than by a phony Palestinian terrorist attack. Even better if your attackers, assassins, whatever, were provable, bonafide Palestinian terrorists like Rasun. Right?"

"Yeah, I think so. But what if the target—the victim—has no relationship to the Israeli-Palestinian question?"

"I don't think it would matter too much as long as one or both of the assassins were caught, and of course the occasion—and maybe even some additional victims—might have a relevancy."

"Yeah. I see. And I suppose they—the KGB—would have no compunction about throwing the hit men to the wolves."

"Not a bit, Egil, as long as it protected their own asses. Besides, they'd do it in such a way that the Palestinian hit men would never know they'd been had. You see, Hummous is their hero. I'll bet there has never been a KGB taint on the man all these years. You said Rasun told you it was an honor to work with Hummous."

"So we need to identify this dinner that Rasun mentioned, and get a guest list?"

"Exactly. Maybe we can finger the man or men—"

"Or woman."

"Yes—or woman, who is such a danger to the mole that the KGB first team has to run an operation of this scope to get rid of him. I hope so anyway."

Kreeger cracked his knuckles. "Meanwhile there's the problem of the Egyptian. Because of the Rasun story there is now a rather alarming P.D. file on the man, and normal procedure would demand we give him a pretty heavy interview at least. I assume the dinner assassination will be off as soon as he hears we've got his hood on ice, and he'll inevitably have to learn about it—though we can delay it a bit. I can hold off any action for, say, forty-eight or even seventy-two hours as long as Rasun cooperates—and I think he will. So what is your desire, my friend?"

"Hmm. I'd like a shot at identifying the Egyptian's target while he's not yet aware that you've got Rasun, before he has to change plans, I mean. You know, Egil, when he learns about Rasun, the Egyptian may just go out and *hit* the target or targets, to hell with the terrorist cover."

"Agreed. I'll make sure Rasun is securely tucked away, and we'll up the coverage at the Egyptian's office—let's say for forty-eight hours—then we'll have to pull him in, bring the Immigration people in too, I guess."

"Fair enough. I hope the man doesn't bolt before we get ready for him, but I think this approach is the best for everybody concerned."

"I agree. I'll be back—should be within the hour—with whatever dinners and guest lists there are for that time period— I told them to cover November 1 to November 15. Then maybe we can ID the target and do something about it. . . . Don't forget, Patrick, we can pull the Egyptian in anytime! I just won't do it for forty-eight hours without your okay."

"Understood, Egil. And thanks a million. If you ever get tired of cops and robbers, I know some guys at Langley you could teach a few things."

TWENTY-EIGHT

WASHINGTON, D.C.

Kreeger called back an hour later and listed two hotel dinners during the specific time frame that he felt could qualify. There were others, but they were business, local, or club-oriented to an extent that Kreeger judged them out of the running. One of the two probables was a television awards dinner and had an interesting guest list including some major political figures. It was scheduled for November 4th at the Hyatt. The other, at the Washington Hilton on November 15th, was a sports award dinner, and it too had an interesting guest list. Both lists were on their way to Morley by messenger. While he was talking to Kreeger the apartment security desk called to report they had a package for him from Metropolitan P.D. Morley said he'd be down shortly. (He had already decided to change apartments again later in the day, fearing that by now somebody as capable as their Egyptian-Circassian-Palestinian-KGB adversary would have located him again.)

Morley picked up the envelope and headed directly for the Library of Congress. It took him just one hour of research to get the two lists down to two people, both of whom were slated to attend the sports award dinner on the fifteenth. There were lots of political assassination targets on both lists, *if* one were just looking for a terrorist operation; but out of all the names there were only two who seemed to have a possible satellite/East European connection, which, Morley surmised, was a prerequisite. FBI and CIA name traces were in order.

He called Epworth first. "Stanley, may I impose on you for another priority name check; actually there are two. I don't know, but if one or both of them are who I think they are, we may have a life-and-death situation here. I'll explain later so I don't hold you up now. I'm at the Library of Congress, extension forty-two twelve, and I'll be waiting for your call. The names are Joseph Shola, no middle initial, of South Dakota, lawyer in Rapid City; and Kenneth R. Rubeck of Potomac, Maryland, a lawyer with offices on K Street North West. Thanks."

He called Milford and made the same request.

Epworth was back to him within fifteen minutes. "Patrick, you sure as hell do have some interesting requests. Okay, first is Shola, and this will be rough because I'll be reading it from the file for the first time myself. Umm, let's see, you've got basic bio data, I'm sure, so we'll get to the interesting part."

"Bio's pretty sparse here, Stan. I know he's a natural-born citizen on his father's credentials—actually born in Hungary—that he was raised by his grandparents in South Dakota, was an honorable mention All-American football player at Nebraska, a successful attorney, and now—according to a recent footnote addition—is the newly appointed junior senator from South Dakota, completing the unexpired term of the late Merle Blatcher. So anything beyond that is news to me."

"Okay. Good. . . . In nineteen eighty-five, uh, September, Shola was offered an appointment as U.S. District Attorney, so we did a routine 'applicant investigation' on him. First of all, his father, Joseph senior, was a first lieutenant in the U.S. Army. His mother, Lotte Denes, was a Hungarian national working with their government-in-exile out of London. She and Joe met in London in nineteen forty-four and were married in

Germany in May nineteen forty-five. Joseph junior was born in early nineteen forty-six in Budapest, and a year later they moved to South Dakota where Joe senior's parents lived. Then in nineteen fifty-two Joe senior was killed in a riding accident and a year later his widow took Joe junior and returned to Budapest. She died of cancer in nineteen fifty-six and little Joe came home for good to his grandfather in South Dakota shortly after. One interesting point here: two separate interviewees in South Dakota said that Lotte Shola was an outspoken Communist."

"Any records on it?"

"No. In South Dakota during the forties and early fifties nobody was thinking about that. There was no party, no apparatus, nothing out there. The sources said they knew it from talking with her. We didn't make any foreign checks at the time of Joe's investigation since she'd died when he was eleven years old and his own record is spotless. We may want to check with the Agency, but I *don't* think it's pertinent. Okay, to get on with it, the interesting part, I mean. Let's see . . . summer of nineteen sixty-six, Joe Shola had just graduated from the University of Nebraska. He had a feeler or two from pro football, but decided to go to law school at South Dakota U. instead; so he planned to spend the summer visiting Hungary. He told the interviewing Bureau agent that he 'just had' to go back and 'see his roots,' whatever that means; so he took some dough he'd saved and went—with his grandfather's approval."

"By the way," Morley interrupted, "how'd this subject arise?"

"Routine passport check at State. The trip was strictly aboveboard, and the reporting agent said Shola was relaxed about the whole thing. Now comes the most interesting part and *this* Shola *did* volunteer. He said that during that summer of sixty-six he stayed with a cousin, Tomas Gulyas, near Budapest. Tomas was a member of a Communist youth group called the Magyar Patriotic Society, a Soviet front aimed at providing "properly trained" young people for placement in the

Hungarian government. Joe said that Tomas was really apolitical and more interested in getting a good job than becoming a Party member, but nevertheless he was active in the society.

"Anyway, Joe attended 'a few' meetings with his cousin and was well received by the group. He said they seemed to be 'first class' young people, and were eager to learn about the U.S.A. The only apparent clandestine aspect of the society was that everybody used a pseudonym. Jack Milford can probably tell us more about the society. I rang him and asked."

"Were the meetings in Budapest? Open?"

"Yes, in Budapest, and yes, open. That is, they weren't secret. They weren't open to non-members though, unless like Joe, it was an invited guest. Then there was *the* most interesting meeting, in late summer. This was a regional, uh, sort of convention and was held in Prague. Seems there were branches of the society all over Czechoslovakia, as well as in other satellite countries.

"So Joe and Tomas went to Prague for this regional meeting. It was a very well-organized, all-expense-paid affair, with lots of lectures, but also lots of fun, good food, beer, and girls. The lectures were given by real pros, he said, speaking both Hungarian and Czech; but Tomas said they were Russians, 'probably KGB.' Tomas also said that they—the KGB guys—selected certain young people for training in the Soviet Union. Seems he knew a couple who had done the course, and that they got very good government jobs when they returned.

"They mixed the kids up a bit, bunking groups of Hungarians and Czechs together. The accommodations were like army bachelor officers' quarters, quite comfortable, four to a room, strict segregation of boys and girls, no hanky-panky allowed. Joe and Tomas bunked in with two Czech boys, one of whom, phony name Erick, was obviously one of the society leaders. Rumor had it that Erick had been selected for some kind of Russian training course. Joe said he had heard that Erick spoke good English, but it must have been a mistake because when he tried it Erick didn't seem to understand any at all."

"I don't suppose anyone asked him to describe Erick. After all, it was nearly twenty years earlier."

"You're right, they didn't. A Czech kid he'd known slightly for a couple of days so long ago? No way you could trace him—just a throwaway alias."

Morley smiled. "Wishful thinking."

"Last item: Joe had had enough of that society—after the Prague meeting he'd figured out it was just a KGB spy recruiting operation—so he didn't attend any more meetings. He went home a month or so later and began law school. Said he talked Tomas out of the society too."

"Hmmm. Did the society make any effort to get him back?"

"Yeah, but they didn't push very hard. Tomas told him later that after he, Joe, had gone back to the U.S. they came by with some enticements, but he'd decided to be a farmer, so he never did rejoin."

"Incidentally, did Joe Shola ever get that appointment as D.A.?"

"No, but it had nothing to do with the investigative report. A big law firm made him one of those unrefusable offers about that same time and he took it."

"And the report never became a factor when he was appointed to the Senate last month?"

"Hell, no! Who's to bring it up? Not Joe; not us. Why? I doubt it would have raised any hackles anyway. He never covered it up. Hell, Patrick, I'd've voted for the guy myself—if I lived out there."

Morley smiled slightly. "I believe you. Now, Stan, the other prospect, Mr. Rubeck?"

"Kenneth Raymond Rubeck is a pillar of society and an All-American boy, Patrick. Don't think I'll waste much of our time on him. Polish descent, came over with his folks after World War II as D.P.'s. He was two or three months old. Settled D.C. area. Educated Gonzaga High, Georgetown U., and Georgetown Law. Spotless rep, past president of the D.C. Bar, respected husband, and father of six. As I said, not a blemish, not a single question. Oh yes, great sports fan and patron of local Catholic high school teams. Attends the awards dinner every year as he was one of the original sponsors. I think you can scratch Mr. Rubeck."

"Uh huh. I agree. Well, Stan, I won't keep you any longer. I'm very grateful for the quick service. I'll be checking with Jack Milford per your suggestion, but I don't think I'll need any more info. Thanks again. I'll be back to you shortly for more advice, though."

"Any time. Advice I've got plenty of. Call when you feel the urge."

Morley hung up the phone and it rang as soon as it hit the cradle. "Yes."

"Patrick? Jack Milford. Subject is Joe Shola and that Magyar Patriotic Society. You've talked to Stan at the Bureau?"

"Just finished. You guys are really moving today."

"Well, it's the only fun we get, living vicariously. We don't know what you're doing and don't need to, but it sounds important. Anyway to make my report short—since Stan's Bureau files are complete on Joe himself—I'll limit myself to that society front in Hungary and Czechoslovakia. Two items: first, a well-placed source told us in, uh, 1972, that the society was a spawning ground for KGB agents. It ran out of gas in the early nineteen eighties because the kids quit joining. They—the Soviets—started a couple of new groups, but they haven't caught on anything like the societies did in the sixties and seventies.

"Secondly, about those regional meetings like Joe Shola attended in Prague in 1966: the same well-placed source told us they were like the NFL draft, only the draftees, most of them anyway, didn't know they were being inspected, much less drafted, at the time. Seems the KGB officers who ran the meetings looked them over as prospective agents, legal and illegal, all over the world, then went back to Moscow and divided them up for future contact, recruitment, training, whatever. Interesting, eh?"

"Very much so, Jack. Things are finally beginning to make sense. Thanks a lot, my friend. I'll be back to you on the other stuff we talked about. Okay?"

"Any time. I'll be here. Meanwhile I should have a report on that Hummous story in a little while."

Morley gathered his notes into a briefcase, thanked the very helpful librarian, went out front, and got a taxi to his apartment. He did keep alert to any obvious tails but did not change cabs, double back, walk, or do anything else elusive. Something told him that time was more important than security at the moment.

The phone was ringing when he came through the door of his apartment. It was David Byrnes. He too was fast responding. "Patrick, our terrorist desk has definitely heard of Hummous and L'Ange Cinq. Tom Geraghty, the chief, was in the Beirut embassy from seventy-eight to eighty-three—after the Israeli invasion. Tom says the word was around, he'd guess not too long after he got there, about the Cinq, as it was called, and its shadowy leader, Hummous. Unlike the other Palestinian and Moslem groups and splinter groups, they never claimed responsibility for any bombings, killings, whatever; but reliable sources reported that many of the biggest, most successful terrorist actions, the ones where the perpetrators got away, were designed and led by Hummous and his Cinq guys.

"Tom said the guy had already become legendary by the time he left Beirut in eighty-three and that he's continued to operate effectively to date. Tom admits there's a lot of speculation involved in reports about Hummous *and* the Cinq because nobody's ever really *talked* to any of them. Rumor says this Hummous, identified as a Moslem—sect unknown—Palestinian from Ramallah, is the last survivor of a family murdered by Israeli commandos, and is a maniac on the subject. He is also reportedly manic on the subjects of security, discipline, and loyalty.

"One other rumor says that Hummous is an accomplished linguist, speaking good English, French, and German, as well as native Arabic, of course."

"I suppose there are no pictures, descriptions, or the like of this Hummous?"

"Unfortunately, no. He really is a shadowy guy. Nobody

even claims to have seen him, which is always unusual in the case of a celebrity. Oh yes, one other item, fascinating really: Tom said that five or six years ago he was in Damascus talking to one of his old agents, a man who is now quite high in the Syrian government. This guy told Tom, apropos of a long discussion about terrorism, that he had heard from a source of unknown reliability that the famous Hummous was really a Russian Moslem from Yerevan. Tom says he knows this is far-out, but damned if he doesn't believe this guy! Says it would explain a lot of the un-Arabic characteristics of both Hummous *and* the Cinq. This make any sense to you, Patrick?"

Morley frowned and was silent for a long moment. "Yes, it might make good sense, and as your man Geraghty said, it might answer a few questions. Let's keep it in mind. Anything else?"

"Nothing important. I haven't sent you those security questions on the New Delhi embassy, the ones I wanted you to get Telchoff's comments on. They're becoming more serious, and I do think he might be able to help. I'll have them typed up and sent over to you if you think you'll have a chance to ask him. Things seem to point to a long-time local employee in the visa section and his sister who's a clerk in commercial. If it's a Telchoff operation we might be able to clear it up easily, save a lot of time and effort. Okay?"

"Shouldn't be any problem. I'll see that your questions get asked pronto."

"Send them back to the General?"

"Be quicker if you sent them here." He gave his address. "I'll pick them up at the desk."

"That's great, Patrick. I appreciate it."

"Happy to help. And I'm most grateful for your quick response on the terrorist thing. Thanks again."

"No problem. Good hunting."

TWENTY-NINE

WASHINGTON, D.C.

Morley met Kreeger at the Chinese restaurant for dinner. They did not talk much business as they enjoyed the stream of delicious appetizers and entrées, washed down with Tsingtao beer in generous quantity. They drove back to P.D. headquarters in the captain's car; he said jokingly there was less chance of getting mugged that way. Kreeger got them a fresh Thermos of hot coffee, told the desk to hold calls except for an emergency, and they settled back to talk.

Morley had barely finished reporting the latest on Hummous and Shola when the phone rang. Kreeger scowled as he picked it up. "Kreeger," he said, and then listened silently for what seemed a long time, his scowl deepening into rage as he sat perfectly still. Finally, he said, "Thanks," and hung up. He looked at Morley, obviously straining to control himself. "Bad news."

"I guessed."

"Rasun."

"Uh huh."

"He's dead."

Morley nodded slowly. "I see. How'd it happen?"

"Looks like suicide . . . mattress cover slashed in strips,

probably with a razor blade, tied together, hanged himself on the window bars, you know, stood on the bed and jumped off the end. Nobody heard anything. Damn!"

"These things happen, Egil. Nobody's fault. I'd never have suspected the guy as a self-destructor either."

"That's the trouble, Patrick, I still don't."

"Not suicide?"

"Oh shit, I don't know. You see, I had him stashed in maximum with no neighbors, no windows, no mattress covers, no nothing, just in case. Arabs can be funny that way. Depression, things like that. So I wasn't taking any chances. Also, no way anybody could get at him in there—three guard posts to get through."

"He was moved?"

"Yeah. That's why I was so damn mad, although the moves were standard procedure."

"What happened?"

"Murphy's law—the one about anything that can go wrong will. I'd barely gone out the door when a lawyer showed up, asked for a meeting with his client, Rasun. You know I can't put out a written order telling the desk man to lie, but I had told them all orally that I wanted to be notified before Rasun was brought out to see anybody. Well, regular shift desk man is sick, new man tonight. He follows the book—I can't fault him—has Rasun brought up, the lawyer has all the right credentials. Name is Fratten. I've heard of him, but don't know him. They put them in the proper interview room, they're in there fifteen, twenty minutes, some loud talk, the lawyer comes out, leaves, saying he'll be back in the morning."

Kreeger paused to pour more coffee. He offered to fill Morley's, but Patrick refused. "Okay, the desk man called the cell guard in maximum who said it'd be twenty minutes 'fore he could get up to get Rasun, some kind of plumbing emergency flooding the cells and all the inmates were hollering and raising hell. Anyway the desk puts Rasun in a temporary holding cell, a half hour goes by, the cell guard finally comes from maximum, they open the door, and there's Rasun hanging like a side of beef and just as dead. Oh shit, Patrick, what luck."

"You don't suspect he was murdered, do you?"

"No, I guess not. That would be a tough one to figure: you know, why, how, and who. Nooh, I think he was given the idea, pushed, clubbed, or whatever by this little shit lawyer, and then had the opportunity in that low-security holding cell. That's all."

"How'd the lawyer know he was there, and who hired him?"

"Haven't worked that out yet. The lawyer is a frequent caller and knows all the ropes, but who called him? Your guess is as good as mine. I s'pect the Egyptian learned somehow that we had Rasun. Wouldn't be hard, you know, if anyone went looking out at American U. And, of course, he is properly booked here in records. So the Egyptian calls a pro, sends him down to help or scare the poor dumb shit, and that's it. Poof—he's dead. But enough of that—we've got a more immediate problem—Shola!"

"Right. The sports dinner operation is off, I'm sure, but we can damn well assume the Shola operation isn't. In fact, the damn—"

The phone interrupted.

"Kreeger." Again he listened silently. Again he scowled, but this time there was no rage, only resignation in his manner. Finally, "Okay. Can't be helped. No, no, hell, I'd've been standing there just like you. No way you can anticipate something like that."

He listened a bit more, then, "Right, bring him in, book him on attempted murder, hold for Virginia, you know the drill. Right. I'll talk to you later. Yeah, don't worry about it. Okay."

Kreeger hung up and turned to Morley, this time flashing a cynical smile. "What was it you told me about bad things coming in threes? Well, this is sure as hell number two. The Egyptian just left my boys standing in the dining room of a restaurant on M Street in Georgetown. He's long gone, but knowingly or unknowingly he gave us Farid/Otar, whatever, as a present. Shit, all that tells me is that the Egyptian doesn't intend to come back *and* he's sure Farid can't tell us anything we don't know already."

"How'd he lose them?"

"As always, Patrick, the point of attack is at the basics, that is, if it's a good attack; but in my boys' defense we really never pretended we could cover this guy with one team and a foot man, but sometimes that's what you get down to in emergencies. He and Farid took a cab from DuPont Circle to Georgetown, directly to this restaurant, fronting on the south side of M Street. They go in the place, casual as hell, foot man follows them in after a short interval. At this time only one car is in place, others are still in transit. Number-two car man starts around to cover the back, but of course the place is in the middle of the block, shops on either side of the restaurant are closed, so he has to go two hundred feet to the corner to double back and get behind the place. He hurries like hell, but he's too late. He sees nothing. The Egyptian has already gone through the restaurant kitchen—the help objects but doesn't stop him—and down the hill to the next street. Somebody picks him up and they're gone. We don't even know which direction.

"Number-two man comes in through the kitchen—they squawk again but don't stop him either. He checks the john, nobody there, comes into the restaurant where the foot man and Farid, both sitting alone at tables for two, are trying to act like they don't know who the other one is. He's furious, our man, but he's under orders not to arrest anybody without an okay, so he goes to the restaurant's office, badges his way in, and calls. I told them to tell him to arrest the bastard! I assume he's done it and is bringing him in now."

"Uh huh. Understandable. Simple proof of that old saying that a knowledgeable subject can always beat a routine surveillance. I'm not surprised he bolted. I'm surprised it was so soon, though. I thought he might hang on longer. . . . Damn, Egil, you don't suppose he's gone after Shola himself, do you?"

"Don't think so, though I'd be afraid to bet on it. But I do think he has, or will very shortly, put a couple of his stable of hoods on it. My guess is he'd be very surprised to learn we'd identified his target so quickly."

"So we'd better get in touch with Shola. I'd like to bring him here, if he's willing, and talk to him, show him some pictures."

"You could do that out there."

"But we can take better care of him here, Egil."

"Yeah, you're right." He called South Dakota information and got Shola's office and home phone numbers. Neither answered. He looked at Morley and shook his head. "I'll have to work through the P.D., I guess. Let's see what we can do."

Kreeger picked up the phone again, dialed two digits. "Captain Kreeger. This Molly? Listen, I need a quick favor. You still got that Bureau book with all the police chiefs' names and numbers in it? Good. Look up Rapid City, South Dakota. I need the chief's name and the P.D. number. Okay? No, I'll hang on." He sat, pen poised over his notebook for about a minute.

"Yeah, eight months old? Yeah, I'm sure too. No problem. Let me have it."

He wrote a name and a number on the page. "Thanks, Molly."

He got an outside line, then dialed the South Dakota code and number. "Hello. This is Captain Kreeger of the . . . yeah, that's K,R,E,E,G,E,R of the Metropolitan Police Department in Washington, D.C. I'd . . ." He stopped to listen.

For the first time since their conversation began, Kreeger grinned at Patrick. "Oh, that's great. You've been here. Then you know what Washington's all about. Good. Now, Sergeant Moore, I'd like to speak to Chief Dixon. Does he happen to be in? Uh huh, it is a bit late. Say, would he chop our heads off if I called him at home? Oh sure, no problem. Here's my number. . . . Right." He hung up, looked at Morley, and smiled again.

"Good P.D. out there. Desk sergeant wants to verify who I am before he lets me talk to the chief." The phone rang.

"Captain Kreeger here. Sure, I understand, no problem. Okay, patch him in. Chief Dixon, Egil Kreeger in Washington. Yes, sir, glad to talk to you too. Got what could be an emergency, Chief, and I need to talk to a lawyer in your town. No answer at either his office or home. Man's name is Joseph Shola, office on St. Joseph, home. . . . Oh, you know Joe.

Good. No, I didn't know about it. . . . I'd really appreciate it, Chief. Call me back as soon as you find out. I'll be waiting. Thanks a million, Chief."

Kreeger was smiling as he turned to Morley. "Those people out there have gotta be great. Chief said today was the first day of deer hunting season and he reckoned Joe Shola was out somewhere tryin' to get his limit. Loves venison, Joe does, according to the chief. He's gonna call around and find out who he went with, where they went, and when they plan to be back. Then he'll call back and you and I will take it from there. Oh yeah, he said Joe was one of the best shots in the state."

"Maybe we should let Joe take on the Egyptian or his hoods, fully warned of course." Morley smiled.

Kreeger said seriously, "Poor Joe isn't expecting the deer to shoot first. Unfair game I guess you'd call it." They both laughed.

"You're right. We should even up the odds a bit."

"You weren't thinking about maybe putting yourself on Shola's team, were you, Patrick?"

"Something like that. I was thinking about you and me both maybe getting in a little deer hunting; but let's hear what the chief has to say first."

The phone rang right on cue. Kreeger picked it up. "Kreeger. Yes, sir." He listened again for a long time, but his face registered no emotion. Finally he said, "Thanks, Chief. I'll look forward to meeting you. . . . Right. Back to you soon as we get the details worked out. No, no, I won't be bringing anyone from my department. No, but a federal officer will be with me. . . . Right. Yes, I think it would be a good idea to bring the Bureau into it. Tell the man I'll clear it all with Assistant Director Epworth at the Bureau here before we come. . . . Great, Chief, look forward to it. 'Bye and thanks."

He leaned back in his chair looking at Morley, then smiled. "Whew! You want action, call Chief Dixon."

"What gives, Egil? I only heard one side of the conversation."

"Shola is a bachelor and his housekeeper/cook is off while he's away hunting, but since there's a weekend involved she doesn't rightly know when he'll be back to Rapid. (They call Rapid City 'Rapid,' Patrick. Remember that when you get out there)."

"I'm going on a trip?"

"Yup. You and I are goin' on a deer and asshole hunt in South Dakota, and we better get out there because the deer are running and the assholes are right behind them!"

"Hoods there already?"

"I think so. But let me fill you in from the top. The housekeeper was a dud, so Chief Dixon called Shola's secretary. She had the whole drill. There are four guys—Shola and three friends—in a four-wheel, big tire van, and they're in the Badlands for three days. Today was the first. Now it gets interesting. Just before she closed the office this afternoon, says the secretary, two men came in to see Shola—'urgent business' but no appointment—Murphy and O'Brien, nature of business unknown. They were obviously disappointed to find Shola gone, and not too subtle in their efforts to learn where they might find him. However, they were well dressed and polite men, spoke good English, and smiled a lot. She told them he was hunting in the Badlands and would be back in two more days. They asked a few 'tourist type' questions and left. She didn't see their car, just assumes they had one."

Kreeger made his usual pit stop for coffee. Then, "The secretary said the two men did not look like a Murphy or an O'Brien (although her name was McCarthy, she didn't claim expertise). They were dark complected, dark haired, more Latin types, and really quite good looking. She pegged them at five ten or eleven and a hundred and seventy-five pounds, and she was definite on this aspect. Seems she's a health club devotee and knows weights and heights. Lastly she said they looked like brothers."

"Very interesting. Any more?"

"Only one item, coincidence or connected, who knows. At

8:15 P.M., 'Rapid' (see, I'm getting prepared) time tonight a broken rear window in Shola's house set off the burglar alarm. The police came and searched. No evidence of entry or burglary, so they concluded it was probably kids or amateurs who were scared away by the noise. Who knows how old the kids were?"

"So you think we should go?"

"Absolutely. This is a D.C. and federal case, and we should see it through. We can't jump ship in midstream and expect some new or local guys to come in and pick up our marbles. I see no alternative."

"You talked me into it, Egil."

"Didn't take much."

"I guess not. I called the General and laid on a plane for us just in case. What time shall we make it?"

"Earlier the better! Remember, those thugs are already there and lookin'."

"Six A.M. all right? That'll get us to Ellsworth Air Force Base before eight A.M. 'Rapid' time."

"You rascal, you've done a bit of exploration yourself."

"I kinda thought we'd end up going out there to save Shola's skin. Anyway, we'll have a van waiting at Ellsworth and we'll be into the Badlands by nine-thirty or ten. And the best part, I think we'll be knowing where to look but the opposition won't."

"The odds aren't bad either, Patrick."

"No, six to two isn't bad in a shootout; but in a sniper operation like I suspect this is, I think the real odds are even, just you and me against those Blues Brothers."

"I s'pose you're right. Okay, my boy, get some sleep and I'll see you at five-thirty at Andrews Operations, right?"

"You got it, Captain. See you then."

Though neither man said anything more, each had a strong sense that he was at last on the brink of breaking this frustrating case wide open.

THIRTY

WASHINGTON, D.C.

There was a message under Morley's door when he got home. It said simply "Call A at M after 10:30 and before 11." He assumed it meant 11:00 P.M., and it was just after 10:30 so he called Amanda at Mattison's number. She sounded normal and bouncy. "Hello, hello!"

"Leslie! It's John. You said I should call some night."

"John . . . John . . . Umm, I'm sorry, but my memory's terrible, and really, there are so many Johns!"

"John Piper. Georgetown. Wednesday. Energy Economics class."

"Oh, that John!"

"Yes, Leslie, that John. Next time I'll have to dunk your pigtails in the inkwell so you'll remember me!"

"Oh, John, I'm afraid you have the wrong Leslie. Oh dear, I'm sorry, but I don't have any pigtails."

"Yes you do, Leslie, take another look."

"Oh, you're right! I do have pigtails, and they're blue on the tips! What kind of ink do you have at school, John?"

"Oh lordy, Leslie, my ink is red. I use it to do my bookkeeping.

"So, have you seen anything? Heard anything?"

"Yes and no. Voices woke me, not quiet like last time, much louder. I went back to the stairs—very carefully—and this time I saw them in profile, Steven and the visitor. There was no talk. The visitor turned and left—I recognized his back; then Steven turned and went into the library again. Never made a move to see the stranger out. Same as before."

"Get any new impressions, like they were angry with each other, more friendly, whatever?"

"No. Hard to do in that light and distance, with no conversation."

"But you heard angry voices at first, didn't you?"

"You've got a point, but when I got in position to observe, I felt that they had already said good-bye, although I didn't hear them do it, and were just turning away."

"Was this last night?"

"Yes, about twelve-thirty, thirty-five."

"And Steven, did you know he was up?"

"Yes, he was supposedly reading in the library. He's more of a night person than I am."

"You're obviously incompatible. Say no when he pops the question."

"Maybe. Maybe not."

"Where is he right now? Does he often leave you home alone at night while he's out on the town?"

She giggled. "Out on the town? Steven? Not too likely. No, John dear—say, are you the John dear who makes those big tractors and stuff?"

"No, my mother loved Bambi."

"I see—anyway, John dear, Steven has, at my request, gone to the ice cream store for a couple of shakes. First to the post office, then to the store. I figured we'd have a half hour."

"You cut it pretty close. What about recorders?"

"What about them? I had every audio class they taught, and I go over these phones every day."

"Good. Now let's review our plans just in case the innocent

Steven and the dark, handsome stranger. . . ! Damn! Did the stranger have a mustache?"

"No, clean-shaven. Good macho profile though. Lots of jaw."

"I've got to show you some pictures. If I sent a package, say, by messenger, would you get it?"

"I don't see why not."

"This one would be very bad if it were to fall into the wrong hands. Suppose I had it delivered in a specific time frame, say eleven-thirty to twelve noon. You do have only afternoon classes tomorrow?"

"Yes. From two on, so do it, have it delivered between eleven-thirty and noon here. I'll be here and I'll damn well answer the door. If need be I'll tell them I'm expecting a package. *I* can be mysterious too."

"Not too mysterious, love. All I want you to do is look at four pictures and then tell me if any of them are the midnight visitor. They will be numbered from one to four. Your answer will be either 'no' or the number. Got it?"

"I think so. What number follows two?"

"I'm really afraid you are the wrong Leslie! Now, love, let's do that review; just in case Steven and the stranger raised their voices *in hopes* of getting you up to view their parting, I want to stress once more that at the first sign of trouble you *will* signal the boys outside. Secondly, you *will* call your friend Beth tomorrow evening to confirm a study session at one, two, three, or four o'clock, or you will say no, you can't come. Lastly, you will be there when the messenger arrives because he won't leave the pictures with anyone but you, and if he leaves without seeing you the boys in blue will move in with warrants and sidearms. Got it?"

"Got it. But I'd better hang up 'cuz I see headlights in the driveway—my milk shake has arrived. Ta ta."

THIRTY-ONE

MOSCOW, U.S.S.R.

Yuri Aleksandrovich Globitsyn sat in silent fury while his favorite secretary, Nadi Malinova, put the coffee mug on his desk, centering it on the black hot pad with the red hammer and sickle crocheted on it. She went to the refrigerator and got the cream, filled the small ceramic pitcher, and placed it beside the coffee next to the matching sugar bowl. "Will there be anything else, Chairman?"

Globitsyn dismissed her with an uncustomary flutter of his hand. Nadi Malinova knew from this that the Chairman was angry and wanted to be alone. He *was* angry, but he did *not* want to be alone. As Nadi reached for the door latch she heard his voice and turned around. "Nadi, send Colonel Asimov in."

"Yes, Chairman." That made him feel better. He mused as she shut the door behind her. At least he could count on Nadi! She says, "Yes, Chairman," not "I'll try" or "I'll see if he's here," like that substitute cow the pool sent him. He almost smiled, then took a sip of coffee.

There was a light rap and Asimov entered. "Good evening, Chairman." Globitsyn nodded, got up, and walked to the refrigerator. He brought the familiar bottle of iced vodka and two glasses, filled them, gave one to Asimov, drank half the other, and sat on the edge of the desk, glass still in hand. "V.V., our friend Pierre has had more bad luck, and he's trying to bail himself out too quickly. I am worried."

Asimov raised those dark and shaggy eyebrows. "What has happened, Chairman?"

"They had the two plans, you remember, to 'clear the agent Kotch forever.' The one, the deception, is ready and imminent. As we agreed it is dangerous, but if it works it solves many problems. I think we have to stay with this one. But the second has turned to shit, V.V., and I don't even know who to blame!"

Asimov continued to stare silently. Globitsyn shrugged and went on. "It was one of Pierre's damn Arabs! The police picked him up on a phony charge, beat and threaten him and he tells all. Pierre got to him through some lawyer and the Arab took himself out, but it was too late—the 'terrorist' operation to get rid of agent Kotch's last danger is a failure, but here is the trouble, V.V. Pierre has sent three of his gun-happy Arabs out to, uh, South Dakota, in the western U.S.A., with orders to kill this man, the one who can identify Kotch. He doesn't put any limits on these Arabs, just turns them loose. He is waiting now to hear the results. The Arabs are overdue reporting and he has no idea what happened. Meanwhile the other operation, as I said, has started. It's too late to call it off even if we wanted to. Some mess, eh?"

"Chairman, it does indeed look like a mess, but I think we would be premature to say all is lost. The Washington operation, which I have agreed from the start was worth the risk, has not failed, and I don't think it will. Now, this Arab's arrest was one of those things, Chairman. Unfortunately, we all have to deal with and use human beings, and so we are often foiled by their stupidity. Poor Pierre! He can plan for them, discipline them, and train them, but he cannot instill courage or common sense. His reaction to go after this target out in Dakota immediately is basically sound. I don't see any chance of the Amis putting all of this together so quickly. Whether it was Pierre's idea, or Kotch's, or joint, I think it is good and in keeping with the whole idea of flagging the Arabs with this whole operation. It also may distract the Amis from what is happening in Washington, *if* they ever connect it, which I doubt."

"You make me feel better, V.V. I'm not sure I share your optimism, but I respect your judgment so it makes me feel better. I am persuaded that it might be better—in the final analysis—to have this other man killed out in Dakota. I understand shootings of this sort are very common out there. My last worry, V.V., is Pierre. How long to leave him there in the U.S.A.?"

"That, from my plateau of knowledge, Chairman, which I realize is far short of yours, would appear to be an easy decision. I would pull him out immediately. He *is* already underground, isn't he?"

"Yes, he is in hiding and we do have a good plan for getting him to Cuba; but I can't take a chance on leaving Kotch there alone if there is still any danger."

"I see. So you would leave Pierre in place till we're sure the decoy ploy worked and the Dakota man is dead."

"Right. I think I must."

"Agreed, Chairman. That is the way it should be handled. In my humble opinion."

Globitsyn filled their glasses again. They touched them and drank silently.

THIRTY-TWO

BADLANDS, SOUTH DAKOTA

It seemed like just a long glide from where their jet crossed the muddy and not so wide Missouri to the southeast end of the runway at Ellsworth Air Force Base outside Rapid City. FBI Special Agent Jim Nance was waiting with a fully equipped van: camping provisions and hunting equipment, armaments far exceeding those necessary for hunting deer. Nance suggested they start driving for the Badlands, stopping to get any other items, such as clothing or shoes, in Wall on the way.

They had discussed with Epworth and Nance the night before the possibility of using a helicopter to locate the suspected assassins and "taking" them before anything happened. But they had decided against it because they would have no cause to arrest them; they would have to let them go, and give them, or some other hoods, a later opportunity to kill Shola somewhere else. In the end, they concluded that it would be better to let the hoods attack and catch them in the act, hoping this would discourage the Egyptian once and for all.

Nance briefed them as they drove east on I-90 toward Wall. "I talked to a guy who hunted with Shola and Pepper the last couple years, but couldn't get away this time. Andy Toke, this guy, says they always open the season in the Badlands rather than in the Black Hills. The Hills have more deer and are easier to hunt, but they're more crowded. Andy says they always come in on two-forty from Wall, down to Interior, and then strike out from there. He said that Shola always checks in the first night by radio with Alf Norgaard in Pine Ridge. Alf's a ham and an old friend; in fact, Alf used to hunt with them years ago.

"I called Alf this morning. He said they'd checked in last night. They were on the southeast side of Snake Butte, but weren't having much luck and intended to work west today, toward Kyle, and see how things went."

"Will they call him tonight?"

"He doesn't think so. Not unless they need some kind of help."

"So we'll just go looking and hoping?"

"Yeah, but it shouldn't be too bad though. They won't take their van very far off the road, even if they might be hunting some distance away. I think we'll spot 'em eventually—today, I mean."

Kreeger chimed in. "If it's too easy to find them maybe we'll be too late. We don't know what time the hoods got started, last night or this morning. Hope to God they don't get to Shola and his guys first!"

Nance smiled. "I figure we've got a lot going for us, Egil. We know where Shola was last night and where he was heading early this morning. We also know that the assassins are here but they don't know we are!"

"You don't figure they could have overheard Shola's call to the ham in Pine Ridge?"

"That's a real long shot. Would have taken a lot of luck, a hell of a lot. At five o'clock last evening the hoods got the first indication that they might not be able to take Shola out in Rapid. They'd've had to gear up a lot faster than I think they could. Shola called Alf about six P.M. last night, and it was dark early because of the cloud cover. No, I think they're maybe a couple of hours ahead of us at the most. And I think also there's no way they'd risk a daytime operation."

"Why not?"

"They're city dudes, Egil, and they're paid killers. City dudes won't risk a big noisy shoot-out in daylight with the chance of immediate discovery, and then a getaway with no cover through strange territory. And paid killers—hell, I'm sure you guys know a hell of a lot more about that than I—but my experience is that they don't like short odds, and since it'd be four to two against them, they'll want the added advantage of darkness."

Morley said, "Incidentally, Jim, Egil, and I feel you should take charge of this operation as soon as we make contact with the Shola group. They sure as hell will be more apt to side with a known and respected law enforcement officer than with two Eastern dudes with badges and a strange story. Besides, as we have agreed, we're going to have to shoot to kill if the hoods do attack—it's too risky any other way—and this is a pretty heady assignment for some amateur hunters. We'll need your status and prestige."

Nance agreed fully.

When they stopped in Wall, Nance called his office while Morley and Kreeger bought hunting-type jackets at the famous Wall Drug Store. Nance said he'd lucked out. "Two guys stopped in a small store on I-Ninety east of Rapid last night and bought some jackets, shirts, and boots. My men drew blanks at all the gun stores, so I figure they must've had 'em before they came to Rapid. Also, they, or I assume it was one of them, called a neighbor of Shola's last night. Said he was an old friend from college in town for the day or two. The neighbor told him Shola was hunting in the Badlands, so we now can assume that the hoods know."

"And we don't have any idea what kind of fire power they have or will use."

"Right, Egil, but whatever it is we'll be able to match it."

It was getting on toward noon when they left Wall and got

into the Badlands. They drove the same route Shola's group had taken the day before, and then continued west to the area near Kyle. Here they stopped every few minutes to climb the crumbly hills and look around. No luck. They went past Kyle to the next wide spot, Sharp's Corner, where Nance talked an Indian into letting him use his phone to call Norgaard in Pine Ridge. Norgaard had not heard from Shola but said his guess would be that if they weren't having any luck, the hunters would go north back toward the Badlands, and probably along the gully of Medicine Root Creek. Norgaard also said nobody else had been in touch with him in regard to Shola's party.

They doubled back almost to Kyle and then turned north along the dry gully that in wetter years was Medicine Root. In the distance they could see the ridges and rising hills of the gray-blue clay of the Badlands. They went north all the way to Highway 44 on the east side of the gully, then turned and came back on the west side, detouring numerous times to inspect divergent little washes and valleys that led off farther to the west and into the beautifully variegated hills.

It was almost dusk, and they had come back south to the small paved road that connected Kyle and Sharp's Corner, when, upon mounting a long and fairly steep ridge, they could see a parked van where the ridge peaked and then quickly petered out to the south. The vehicle was in a draw that looped between two hills, one being the ridge, and sheltered on both sides from wind and view. Had they looked earlier or later by just a few hundred feet they might have missed it; however, had they come up the gully from the road on the west side, they'd have seen it hours earlier.

At Nance's suggestion they drove down the west side of the ridge and then turned and approached the van openly from the south. As he pointed out, they didn't know *whose* van it was. They were lucky. It was the Shola party and three of them were beginning to pitch camp. The other was a hundred yards up the draw dressing what looked like a large deer. The hunters introduced themselves, then Nance called them all over in the

shadow of their tent, beckoning for the deer-skinner to join
them. "Mr. Shola, gentlemen, I'm Jim Nance of the Rapid City
FBI; Mr. Pepper will vouch for me, but here are my credentials." He passed his credential case around.

"I hope we can keep this very short because it's possible
we're under observation right now. I don't want to scare you
but this is the deal. We have very solid information that two
assassins have been sent to kill you, Mr. Shola. It's a long story
and Mr. Morley and Mr. Kreeger have been dispatched from
Washington, so you know damn well it's a serious fear we have.
I'll brief you later, but I want to skip it now so it will appear we
just stopped, had a coffee with you, and went on."

Shola sputtered. "Wait a minute. Who the hell wants to kill
me? Why? You can't just brush this off."

Kreeger answered "The KGB wants to kill you, my friend,
and they are bad and determined enemies to have. They think
you can 'finger' a very important spy they have in Washington
and they don't want you to get the opportunity."

"A spy? Who? I don't know any KGB spies. Do I?"

"We don't know, Mr. Shola; important thing is that the KGB
thinks you do, and they're willing to kill to avoid your meeting
with this one."

Nance broke in. "Please, Joe, we can give you all the details
you want later. We'd like to keep it short now in case the killers
are watching. Now here's what we propose. We will pretend to
camp up along this ridge, east side, a mile or so north, then
come back after dark and set up here to be ready when and if
the assassins come."

"You sure they'll wait 'til dark?" This was Pepper.

"No, sir, can't ever be sure; but I think it's a very good bet
they will. Any way you look at it the odds are still four armed
men to two, and I think these hoods will want the advantage of
night *and* surprise. We plan to take both away from them."

Kreeger had backed their van so the rear end was sheltered
from a west or north view by the tent. He and Morley un-
loaded three large cartons and a fourth wooden box. Nance

continued. "We want to protect *you* and to capture the assassins, and we figure the best way to do it is to sit here and be ready. We could start for Rapid, and maybe we'd make it without attack, but I doubt it; and even if we did, how do we handle the future? Joe is still a target. It'll be dark in an hour and we don't know what kind of equipment these hoods have. If we stay here we can set the rules and have the odds. But if you fellas want to take off for Rapid we'll go with you ridin' shotgun. Your choice."

The men whispered among themselves. It was over quickly and it was Pepper who spoke. "If we make a run for it, even if we make it, Joe here has to keep lookin' over his shoulder, right? Is that the way it is?"

Nance nodded.

"Okay," said Pepper. "We're in, and if you guys want us, we'd like to be in on the reception, not hiding in our tent. Okay?"

Nance smiled as he nodded again. Pepper smiled back, and then there were handshakes all around. Nance broke it up. "Okay, fellas, we should move on and set up our own camp. It'll be dark in less than an hour." He looked at his watch. "In exactly one hour and thirty minutes we will come around the end of the ridge"—he pointed—"from east to west and then turn north toward your camp. I suggest strongly that you set up watch as soon as it's dark, with one two-man team at the rear of the tent covering the north approaches, I guess you'd say north *and* west, and the other team covering the south and east from down near the end of the ridge. Don't set up too near the tent, which could possibly be the focal point of any attack. Okay?"

The four hunters nodded. "Okay. Your south east team will see us approach. When you see us, say, 'Stop.' We'll stop and say, 'Nance.' If we don't, shoot." He smiled. "Make sure we hear the stop, though! We'd better move off now. I assure you we'll have time for questions and answers later."

"Fine, Mr. Nance. I'll be at the end of the ridge from ten

minutes before the hour is up. We'll be ready." It was Shola taking over as natural leader. Morley smiled to himself. The man had stayed in the background—after all, it was his neck they were all trying to save—until his friends voted to stay and fight, then he moved.

As they drove away Nance mentioned that Shola had told him they'd seen only two other hunting vans all day. One was three men from Rapid, two of whom he'd known; and the second, just an hour or so ago, was a dark green Chevy with two men in it. This one didn't stop—in fact, it hadn't come close enough for Shola to see the occupants—but they *had* waved. This latter van had been heading north-northwest along the west side of the ridge. "Bet that was our boys. I've got a feeling," said Morley.

Kreeger had a more immediate problem. "Hey, Jim, don't let's go too far away. Remember we gotta make this trek back in the dark with a good bit of equipment."

Nance laughed. "I'll keep that in mind, Egil. I think we should go another mile or so, get out, look around, decide we don't like that place, turn around, and come back to that draw with the trees we just passed."

"You think somebody's watching?"

"Might be. Remember how far we could see around us from some of those hills we climbed today?"

It seemed to be a lot longer walk than it was, and they were glad when Nance, who was leading the way, motioned them to a stop by a clump of brush. They had developed good night vision by this time and could see that they were almost at the end of the ridge. A coyote bawled in the distance and Kreeger grunted. "Holy shit, Jim, are you sure that's not a little kid crying?" Both "city dudes" had winced the first time they'd heard the unique sound, and only a bit less with each succeeding repetition.

Nance was laughing as he whispered. "Soon as we turn the

corner up ahead—'bout thirty feet—they should see us and give the signal. I'd suggest that if we see somebody and they *don't* signal after a couple seconds that we flatten down with our pieces at the ready. Okay?" Both dudes grunted assent and followed Nance.

They rounded the corner and heard a low, barked "Stop." They stopped, and Nance said his name. Shola and one of his group, a man named Ben Eilers, approached. "Been very quiet, Jim. We're set up as you suggested. Pepper and Smitty are on the other side of the tent."

They walked to the east side of the tent where they were joined by Pepper and Smith. The dark night seemed to get even darker as a thick cloud cover moved in. The men gathered around Nance, who spoke in a low but very audible whisper. "We don't think anything will happen for a while, but we do anticipate that they will come sooner rather than later so they can do their dirty mission and still get back to Rapid before first light. So if you fellas don't mind I'll earn some of that tax money you pay me and take charge here."

Everybody nodded. "We're gonna set up a buddy perimeter watch, three teams looking north, east and west; each team with one of the big infrared lanterns; each man with his rifle, a handgun, an infrared flashlight and infrared goggles on. Pat Morley, you and Ben Eilers take the west perimeter, Egil Kreeger and Nels Smith the north, and Joe Shola and Jack Pepper the east. I'll cover the south myself from a position where I can signal all teams and see signals from any team.

"Any team sees or hears an indication of an approach they'll signal south toward me, with their flashlight, two longs, a short, a long. Got it? That's just an *alert:* you've heard or seen something. Okay? Now, when you're sure we're being approached, holler your team direction—'west,' 'east,' or 'north'—as loud as you can, turn your lantern on, and point it toward what you heard or saw! Okay?"

Nods all around again. "All right. The other two teams, when they hear a 'direction call' should put on their goggles and point their lanterns in that direction. Hopefully we'll have a couple startled gunmen, and we can wrap them up; if they still want to fight, then we'll just have to oblige them. Okay? Any suggestions?"

"What if they come from the south?" This was Shola.

"Same deal. I hear something, I follow the same procedures, except I've got a big flashlight instead of a lantern. I plan to be moving back and forth but I'll be watching the mouth of the draw all the time—and you guys for signals. I don't think they'll come from the south because it's by far the longest exposed approach, but people do strange things and we can't be certain. Anybody else?"

Pepper's smile was in his voice. "Do we shoot to kill?"

"If you shoot, shoot to kill. If these guys are sneaking up you can bet their objective is to *kill you*! Don't even give it a thought. A wounded man can kill you; a dead man can't."

There were no more questions. "Okay, gentlemen, I think we should get into position." Nance chuckled. "It'd be damn embarrassing for all of us to be sitting here with all this firepower and equipment and be taken by surprise before we set up."

"Yeah, maybe even lethally embarrassing."

"Without a doubt. Oh, Jim." It was Pepper. "Why don't we have the lanterns on all the time? Couldn't we see them approaching better and sooner?"

Nance smiled. "Reason is, we figure that if we thought of infrared they might have too! In fact, they might do us one better and use infrared 'scopes' on their weapons as well as goggles and lanterns. If possible, we want to surprise them with our preparations and hope they'll give up without a shot; we'd have trouble doing this if they could see our lantern's beams. Okay, let's get posted."

Time did move faster than they'd expected, but it still dragged. There was a false alarm flashlight signal from the east team—something had moved, but it was not human—and then shortly after eleven, about when they had figured it might happen, Morley and Eilers heard a sound that was definitely not part of the Badlands night scene.

Morley signaled toward Nance and saw him relay it. The sound came again: clay and pebbles rolling softly as someone made his way slowly and carefully down the thirty-degree pitch of the west ridge. He placed the sound about fifty feet up and the same to the right. Morley smiled to himself. The hoods were coming *where* as well as *when* they had expected them: from the west, over the steepest part of the ridge, and in a line with the hunters' tent.

Morley made an instant decision. He pushed Eilers into a prone position, pointed the infrared lantern at the noise, flicked the switch on, and hollered "West" at the top of his voice.

There was a hiatus of seconds while Morley looked along the tunnel of infrared light at two men in black, crouched about twenty feet up the hill and holding some kind of automatic weapons. Morley's mind registered the fact that the intruders had goggles too and one of them was trying to focus what must be an infrared flashlight on him.

Kreeger's lantern swung around from the north, adding its light to the eerie scene as Nance's voice started its bullhorn warning. "You on the hill, lay down your wea—"

A single shot rang out from the south. The men on the slope started to raise their guns, but they were fatally late. Morley's Uzi cut them in half in two quick bursts, and their weapons preceded their broken bodies rolling down those last yards of the ridge.

Morley patted Eilers. "Keep your rifle on those two. If they move an eyelash, shoot!" He was gone in a fast crouch toward Nance, who lay in a heap, blocking the light from his fallen flashlight. The third man or team—that was what it had to be—did not shoot again nor did he seem to have any infrared light, so Morley let his goggles hang loose as he took a quick look at Nance. It appeared that he'd taken a hit in the right temple but there was so much blood. He tried a quick pulse check, but couldn't find any.

There was a sudden quiet again, and Morley could hear a faint padding and scraping of running feet to the south. His fury rose with his adrenaline as he set out at full speed toward the noise. After about a hundred yards, he stopped, lay prone behind a small bush, and flipped his goggles on. Oh God, he was in the middle of an infrared light tunnel! He began a spin to one side as two bullets skimmed into the ground he'd just vacated. Almost simultaneously there was a loud bang from behind and left, and then kind of an animal yelp of pain from the area of the muzzle fire ahead. Morley smiled to himself as he came up in a crouch to the right of the beam. Never underestimate your friendly local policeman, he thought.

Kreeger arrived, whispering, "You okay, Pat?"

"Yeah, thanks to you."

"Got your Uzi?"

"Yeah. Let's go get the fucker. He killed Nance."

They separated about twenty yards and then began to move south in parallel lines. There was still a lane of infrared light emanating from the third man's flashlight. It didn't move, but continued to hug the ground. Not knowing where the man was or even if he was alive, Morley and Kreeger moved past the flashlight and then pinched together carefully behind it. The man was nowhere to be seen.

They flipped their goggles down and waited for natural night vision to come back as they moved cautiously to the south. They had hooked their flashlights back onto their belts, since if the third man had retained *his* goggles, there would be only disadvantage to them in using the light and giving him a beam to shoot down.

Morley and Kreeger started running again, but more slowly and closer together. Ahead of them the sounds of running grew as their quarry seemed to give up any attempt at stealth. Suddenly his steps seemed to turn sharply west. Kreeger edged closer to Morley, whispering, "I'll bet he's getting closer to his van."

Morley nodded. "Let's speed up. In, say, ten seconds you

stop, lay flat, and aim your infrared beam at his noise. I'll be wide right and if he so much as twitches his gun in your direction I'll blow him away."

"Gotcha. Start counting."

"One, one thousand, two, one th . . ."

At ten, Morley stopped in a crouch, goggles on, Uzi up. The beam came on from behind and left, wavered, then focused on a goggled, kneeling man, not more than fifty feet away, who was looking down the beam and bringing a rifle to bear on it. Morley's finger tightened, the Uzi erupted in a staccato, the kneeling man pitched forward onto the ground.

THIRTY-THREE

WASHINGTON, D.C.

Kreeger had a P.D. cruiser waiting at Andrews when they landed, so Morley rode back to headquarters with him. They began to use the two phone lines in Kreeger's office.

Morley's first call was to Amanda's classmate, Beth. She had heard from Amanda, who had made a date with her for four o'clock, ostensibly for a study session. Morley was both satisfied and scared. Number four was Hummous. It had been he who was Mattison's midnight visitor. Beth said she and Amanda were actually meeting at the University library at four P.M. Morley ordered Beth, who was one of Milford's people, to gather up Amanda and go immediately and directly to a previously selected safehouse, and to remain there till he came for them; no answering calls, no answering the door, nothing. He warned her against being swayed by Amanda's blandishments; she was not even to *think* about going back to Steven's. No way! He emphasized that these were orders, and there was no judgment factor involved—just go to the safehouse; don't let Amanda go pick up jewelry, clothes, or anything else; and call him when the two of them have arrived there safely. Beth said she understood and would comply fully.

Morley turned to Kreeger as he hung up from Beth. "You know, I sent Amanda four pictures to see if any of them could be recognized as Mattison's midnight visitor. The ident was quick and certain—the Egyptian. No mustache but no question either. I wish I knew what those bastards are up to now. Damn, we can't wait and see. Amanda will be out this afternoon. I don't think they'll *do* anything today. I just hope to God, I'm right! I know I interrupted you, Egil. What's your news?"

"I briefed Stan Epworth on our little hunting trip in the Badlands, but he'd heard most of it from Jim Nance. As you know, Jim's head wound was not serious, just a bloody damn furrow along the side. They are still keeping him in the hospital at Rapid because there was a concussion along with the wound, but that rascal is running the show from his bed. Stan had the initial tracer on the hoods. They were all out of Denver, uh, one Bobby Salem, the leader, and the Adams boys, Joe and Sam. They are native born, but have some connections, according to Denver P.D. files, to a suspected terrorist group of mixed nationalities, which operate out of Mexico. I'm sure, and Denver agrees, that Hummous has Mexican terrorist contacts that set the deal up. By the way, I'm having my chief send a letter to the FBI director. You know, a 'praising' thank you."

"I'll have the General weigh in too. Jim sure as hell deserves it. Head wound and all, he got those hunters squared away and so scared to talk I bet they haven't told their wives yet."

"Stan says they'll be keeping Joe Shola under cover till we tell 'em it's safe to surface him again." Kreeger looked at Morley, a sly grin beginning to transform his serious face. "And you, Patrick, did you finish your private business with Shola? And was it successful?"

"Yes and no. I finished, but the results are not all in yet by a long shot. Shola is a very careful, very honest witness, and he was far from sure on his ident. However, he said our Kotch and Erick from Prague *could be* the same person, but he certainly couldn't condemn a man on his identification. He simply was not certain. He did give me a couple of other checkable facts about Erick—Shola is one of those people with fantastic memories—which, if they check out, should help pin things down. . . . I know you'll understand, Egil, but I'll keep this thing to myself till I'm sure. Okay?"

"Certainly. No problem. I know you have to be, uh, without any reasonable doubt."

"Thanks. Now with—" The phone interrupted and Kreeger answered. Morley had a feeling of déjà vu as Kreeger listened silently, then the big man smiled and said, "He's right here," and handed Morley the phone. It was Pansy.

"I was telling the captain that our friend Pete has been kinda low the last couple days. I figure he thinks he hasn't been much use to you fellows, hasn't seen you, hasn't contributed, you know. He's a doer, Mr. Godfrey, and if he isn't doing, I notice he tends to get down. Anyway, that's neither here nor there. He read something in the morning paper and now he's happy; in fact, he's excited! Says it's a surprise and he'd like to spring it on you because it's good news for a change. He's giggling and being mysterious like a little kid. Couldn't wait for me to get in touch with you. I know how you feel about the security, but could you come? Soon? He'd be so pleased!"

"Fifteen minutes suit him?"

"Oh yes, Mr. Godfrey. I'll tell him right away. And thanks."

"You've got that turned around, Pansy. It's I who should be thanking you. See you soon."

Kreeger laughed. "I'm glad you're going, Patrick. Pansy sounded as down as she said Pete was. Y'know, I think she's soft for the guy."

Morley shook his head slowly. "Wouldn't be the first safe house romance I'd ever heard of, but somehow I think it's more empathy than romance. Anyway, I've got a feeling that it's something worthwhile that's titillating old Pete."

* * *

Telchoff was waiting near the door, smiling widely, when Pansy let Morley in. "Godfrey, my friend, good news! I think we solve whole question that Circassian Moslem, okay? We find many things, solve many questions, too. You see, Godfrey, Ivanova she is coming to U.S.A. Florida!" He waved the front section of the morning paper. "See, is here in the paper. Ivanova arrives two days, Florida. I must see her, Godfrey! Ivanova will have much news, KGB/Globitsyn news, solve many questions."

Telchoff held the paper while Morley read the article. Three Soviet cosmonauts, including one Mikhail Koransky, were coming to the U.S. as the first step in an exchange program to witness the lift-off of number one in the new series of space shots. They would arrive the day after tomorrow and the launch was set for the next day. The last sentence of the article said the cosmonauts would be accompanied by their wives. Koranskaya and Ivanova were one and the same.

Telchoff could hardly contain his excitement. "Ah, Godfrey, is lifetime chance. Ivanova knows everything going on in Globitsyn's office. She will tell us."

"Maybe she won't even talk to us, Pete. Remember, in the eyes of the Soviet government you are a traitor. I doubt she would even see you."

"No, Godfrey, you do not know Ivanova as old Pete does. Ivanova hates Globitsyn, hates the new fascists who have taken over the Party, loves old Pete. I tell the truth. She is not problem, I promise. Can we go?"

Morley smiled. "Yes, of course. This could be a chance of a lifetime and we have to take it. I'll need to make a few arrangements, and then I'll be back to you with a solid plan. Okay? Shouldn't be more than late afternoon."

Telchoff was beaming. "Good, friend Godfrey, good. This will be good thing we do, much worth doing. You will see! Ivanova is something else. Knows many secrets. Tells old Pete all, for sure."

"Great, Pete. I'll be phoning soon."

Back at his old apartment (he simply hadn't had time to change, and now there wasn't going to be time again) Morley got on the phone: to the General to make arrangements for Florida; to Kreeger to tell him about the revised plans; to Jack Milford to ask him for file checks on the members of the Soviet cosmonauts' party; to the General's NASA contact at the Kennedy Space Center for data on the Russian visitors' program and arrangements; and then to a number in Chicago.

It rang five times and Morley was about to give up when a breathless voice he knew very well answered. "Yes.'

"Yes, yourself, darling. Did I wake you?"

"I should be so lucky. Haven't had time for a nap since I got here."

"Then maybe I shouldn't've called. I thought you might be bored and I was going to offer you a job."

"Oh. Permanent?"

"No. You have one of those; you're just on, uh, security leave right now."

"Oh, that's what this is. Do you know it snowed here last night? Snowed, dammit!"

"How quickly we forget. You used to live there and like it."

"Live, yes; like, not much. What do you have in mind, Patrick, my love?"

"Like to do me a favor?"

"Yes."

"No questions?"

"Ummm, no . . yes. When do I start?"

"Immediately."

"Fine. Where?"

"Florida."

"You devil, you've been leading me on! You've finished, and—"

"Not quite. I'm still on the job. I need you to help; and the locale is Cape Canaveral."

"I see. You need *my* help? What can I say? I accept."

"Okay. Fly to Orlando, rent a car, drive to Cocoa Beach—all tomorrow."

"My own name?"

"Yes. No problem that far. But I'll have a room reserved for you at the Holiday Inn in Cocoa under the name Ann Chesley. Got it?"

"Yes, Holiday, Cocoa, Ann Chesley, tomorrow."

"Right. Check in and wait. I'll come or call before seven P.M. We'll have dinner and I'll brief you on the caper, as they say in the movies."

"Give me an idea, Patrick. Have a heart!"

"Okay. Ann Chesley is a staff writer for *Women in Action*, the big New York monthly and she's gonna interview some Russian ladies, wives of cosmonauts. Okay?"

"Sounds fun. Will I need any ID?"

"I'll have it there for you."

"Disguise?"

"No, don't think it's necessary."

"Is Ann Chesley real?"

"No, but everything else will be."

"You mean the Russians call the magazine, they'll backstop me?"

"You got it."

"And you'll tell me what to ask, how to handle the interview?"

"Yes, as far as you'll need. It'll be short."

"I see. You want me to isolate somebody by faking an interview, then you'll take over. Right?"

"Essentially, yes, that's it; but you do have to look and act the part. There'll be others to fool in order to accomplish the isolation of the, uh, target. Suffice it to say, darling, your job is important, essential, and you will require professional level skills; I believe you can do it better than anyone else, and besides I trust you more. That do it?"

"Of course. One last question, though. Do I get a round trip to Orlando or will we be going home from there?"

"Round trip, sweetheart, but it won't be much longer, I'm sure."

"Foolish question, but I had to ask it. Another foolish one—the last, I promise—should I wear my bulletproof bra?"

"I don't think anybody will be shooting feature writers. I said it was an important job, not a dangerous one. See you mañana."

"Ta."

THIRTY-FOUR

WASHINGTON, D.C.

Morley had postponed a couple of interviews to assure that he would be home by the phone before four o'clock. He had even called Beth again to assure her of that. When she hadn't phoned by 4:30 he had a premonition of bad news, and strong feelings of guilt. They should have been at the safe house by 4:20 at the latest. Maybe Amanda had just been late. But somehow he knew it wasn't so. At 4:40 Beth called. She was still at the library and Amanda hadn't shown. Morley took the number of the pay phone, told her to wait and that he'd be back to her in fifteen minutes.

As usual, Kreeger answered his own phone. "Egil, Amanda didn't show at the library. I think the boys better go in soonest."

"They're in, Patrick. Your line's been busy. The patrol at four twenty-five saw the shade down, called me, and I sent a team of six in there. I'm waiting for a call now. Should hear any minute. Hold it, the other line's buzzing. Hang on."

Half a minute passed, then Kreeger came on again. "Patrick, the place is deserted. They went through it completely. All seems normal—clothes in closets, food in fridge, booze in bar, all that. There just isn't anybody there. Hang on a minute. Brown wanted to tell me something else."

Another thirty seconds, then Kreeger came back on Morley's line. "This may help explain a few things, including some of those secret comings and goings. My man Brown who led the, uh, inspection party, tells me that there is a section of wall in the pantry that opens into a hallway of the house next door. I'm checking, but I'm sure we'll find it belongs to Jeb Mattison or some stooge of his. I'll bet also that we'll find it's seldom occupied. Has its own connecting garage and all. Nice facility. Can't figure why or how Mattison used it. Only thing I can think of that makes sense would be a guest house. Well, I'll leave that one with you.

"Back to Amanda. I have a class X APB out on her—that's one where the leaker of information gets shot at dawn, but it has all the search and urgency requirements of a class A one. Okay?"

Morley's voice sounded dull. "That I leave up to you, Egil. You know how I—and a lot of other people—feel about Amanda, and you know best what to do."

"Don't give up, my good friend, we're going into high gear on this one. We'll find her."

"I hope so, Egil. I know if it's possible you will. Keep me posted. I'll be leaving for Florida with Pete midafternoon tomorrow. I'll stay in close touch till then."

"Fine. Oh, I can give you a spot of good news. Jim Nance called me. He's out of the hospital, feeling great and tying up loose ends. He found the lair of those three killers, a motel suite and it was, like their van, a gold mine for gun collectors. He's also got a lead on where they came from—the guns I mean. The bastards were prepared for whatever kind of killing they had to do. Never will understand why the third guy came from the south with a rifle."

"I'm glad he wasn't a better shot, Egil. Nance must have been a sitting duck in that light."

"Yeah. We'll never know, I guess. Nobody's come to ID the

corpses yet, and my guess is they never will. The hunters have all held the line." He laughed. "Don't think our friend the Egyptian—I assume he's figured out by now that his assassins failed—will come forth to ID them. We'll let Nance bury them out on the lone prairie and forget 'em."

"But it disturbs hell out of me—when I realize Amanda's in their hands—that those hoods were ready to kill four innocent hunters in cold blood because somebody gave them some dough and told them to do it. I mean, the guy who's running this show is the son-of-a-bitch who's got Amanda!"

"We do our best and hope, Patrick."

Morley called Stan Epworth at the Bureau. "Stan, I'm sorry to be so late, but we've had a bit of a flap and I've been tied up. Are we still on for early morning at the lab? Fine. No, that's great. I'll be there at 8:30. Two other things, Stan: one, your man Nance out in Rapid City is first class. Can't say enough good about him. Pass it on, if you will. Good. And second, the flap I mentioned is a kidnapping, an Agency officer, female, one of the best. Kreeger will be briefing you, I'm sure, as soon as I get off the phone. Okay? Nothing else. See you in the morning."

He dialed Milford at the Agency. "Jack? Bad news. We were pulling Amanda out of the Mattison place this afternoon but she didn't show for her contact with Beth. I assume Beth has called you. . . . No, it gets worse instead of better. Kreeger's M.P.D. guys went in about five P.M. and the place is deserted, not a soul. Her clothes are still in the closet, no sign of a struggle. Oh, they did find a kind of semisecret doorway to the house next door which may or may not mean anything. Damn, I'm sorry as hell. We should've pulled her after she saw that first meeting. But you know Amanda. I'll bet she never backed down in her whole life."

By the time he'd finished with his call to the General giving him the bad news about Amanda, and confirming his plans for

Cape Canaveral the next afternoon, Morley had barely ten minutes to shower and be ready for Milford's man. The latter was on the dot and he buzzed him up. His name was Jack Daniel, which had undoubtedly intrigued people over the years; and he was in his mid-twenties, small, slender, bespectacled, but with a mischievous, rather than a scholarly look about him. Morley liked the young man's appearance and demeanor.

"Mr. Morley, we have a lot of material on Hummous and L'Ange Cinq, as you can well imagine. They've been operating in the Middle East—Jordan and Lebanon at first, and then lots of other places—before moving into Europe occasionally, starting, say, about six years ago. Anyway, I'm fairly up on the files, so for tonight I've made some notes to give you just a general rundown. We've already started a full, formal review and should have it ready late tomorrow."

"Fine, Jack. Brief me as you suggest. I have any questions, I'll ask."

"Good. We had a penetration of the Cinq up till three years ago. Problem was always where and how to meet him. I mean those guys were really under tough control and discipline. First reason we ever began to suspect that Hummous, whose real name is supposed to be Salim Naheri, and who's supposed to be from Ramallah, is not an Arab at all. I mean he ran the Cinq with an iron fist."

"Uh huh. Your man still inside?"

"No, sir. Hummous suspected him and had him shot."

"He's not an Arab, what is he?"

"We've had lots of theories on that. Our best guess, and that is all it is, a guess, is that he is a Southwest Asian Soviet. It follows from that—if he's a Russian masquerading as an Arab and killing people—he's got to be KGB. Still we do *not* have any first-person info on that, and we cannot be certain."

"Is he the number-one elite of the Palestinian terrorists, as Rasun claimed?"

"No question of that, Mr. Morley. He is indeed number one: the best, and he's lasted the longest. Even his people are top choice. In fact, one of the reasons Hummous himself is so shadowy is the high degree of discipline and loyalty he instills in his men. Rasun, I gather, was an exception at first, but his suicide was in line with past performances of his men."

"Well, Jack, I won't keep you any longer. This has been very useful and I appreciate your coming by after hours like this."

"My pleasure, sir."

"Well, thanks anyway. And by the way, hold off on that formal file review for a couple days. I'll be back to you or Mr. Milford on it shortly. Okay?"

"Sure thing."

"And, Jack, I hate to ask the question—I'm sure you're tired of it—but are you?"

"The real McCoy? No. Related? Yes. My paternal great-granduncle established the still, legally, in 1866 in Lynchburg, Tennessee. Each generation has had a boy or two named after old Uncle Jack."

THIRTY-FIVE

WASHINGTON, D.C.

The J. Edgar Hoover Building was busy and well-populated at
8:20 when Morley arrived, although office hours actually began
at 9:00. The guard called Epworth, and his assistant came
down to escort Morley to the lab where Special Agent Sam
Moretta and Epworth were waiting. Morley outlined his problem and Moretta nodded affirmatively at each point. He was
smiling at the end. Morley returned his smile. "I take it from
your good spirits, Sam, that you can do it. Right?"

"Sure can. Only variables are what you'd expect: we'll have a
range of eight to ten miles under favorable terrain conditions."

"How about from a 'copter?"

"Double it, at least."

"What interferes the most?"

"The usual: distance, big buildings, hills, and so on."

"So a 'copter or other high ground is best."

"Yeah, generally speaking."

"Any other variables?"

"Lots, but the important one—and one we can *do* something
about—is the 'melt time' for the gelatin."

"Uh huh. And what controls that?"

"Body heat, stomach contents, acidity, thickness of gelatin cover. But not to worry, we can, as I said, control these factors with clothing, diet, and antacids to the point where we can predict when the gelatin will be melted and the transmission will begin—within a minute or ninety seconds at most. It will beep every three seconds for the next twenty-four hours once it starts."

"Fine. And a metal detector will not pick it up?"

"No way; no metal."

"Stan says you've got three of the receivers."

"We've got four, but I don't trust one of 'em so you'll only have three, yes."

At this point Kreeger arrived, also escorted by Stan's assistant. He apologized for being late. Looked at Pat as he explained they'd had what they thought was a hot lead on their current number one crime, but it hadn't panned out. Moretta briefed him quickly on the tiny transmitter that, ensconced in its gelatin covering, was still no bigger or heavier than an M & M.

When Moretta began to explain the care and use of those custom-built receivers Kreeger watched and listened carefully. That was to be his province.

After Moretta had finished the briefing and promised to have the "pill" and the receivers, complete with full instructions, ready that afternoon, Epworth and Morley escorted Kreeger to the front door, then went to see the Bureau armaments expert, Special Agent Mac Johnston, down at the range. Johnston was as careful and slow as Moretta had been hyper, but it was apparent immediately that he knew his business extremely well. Morley explained the situation he expected to be in and why he expected to be unarmed at that time. His problem was that unless there was a malfunction of the gun or the ammunition he would be dead.

They finally agreed on the desired result and Johnston prepared a test bullet with a potent mixture. They tested it on a robot-held revolver and the results were quite catastrophic for both the revolver and the robot; then Morley asked for ten more grains of explosive in the mixture. Johnston saw no problem in having the bullets ready for him late that afternoon.

THIRTY-SIX

CAPE CANAVERAL, FLORIDA

The Soviet cosmonauts' party, eleven in all, were settled in penthouse suites of the newest hotel in the Canaveral area, just a few minutes drive from the launch pads at Kennedy Space Center. "Dead City," as the Center had been called for those two-plus years of forced inactivity after the Challenger tragedy, was alive again.

The Russians had been through the ceremonies of a welcome luncheon, met their American counterparts, made toasts, and were enjoying a couple hours' rest before embarking on a "golden tour" of the Center and then moving into the evening's festivities. The countdown had begun and the launch was only thirty-eight hours away.

Mariya Koranskaya, wife of the designated pilot of the Soviet launch six months hence, seemed to be a very pleasant, intelligent woman. She had responded carefully at first to Ann Chesley's contact and request for an interview, the contact arranged by Ann's publisher and approved by Dr. Warlinsky, the head of the cosmonaut party. Koranskaya became more enthused after she met Chesley in person; the reporter's warm and interested woman-to-woman approach appealed to the Russian. Koranskaya had a fair command of English, and while they could have managed without an interpreter, both agreed that such a facility would be useful. Chesley's publisher had furnished one from Columbia University just in case.

Koranskaya had reported the fact, time, and place of the interview to the political officer who was, of course, an integral part of the Soviet delegation; and he, introduced as Mr. Drobin, was present when Chesley and the interpreter arrived, and accompanied them to the small private dining room on the hotel's main floor where the interview was to be conducted. The two Russians seemed surprised to find TV cameras and technicians in the room, but were obviously pleased when Chesley told them she hoped the interview would get a spot on national TV. This ploy worked exactly the way Morley and Telchoff thought it would: after the tea was served and the cameras got ready to roll, Mr. Drobin excused himself, saying he would return later.

As Drobin left from one door Morley in disguise and Telchoff in ecstasy came in the other. Mariya, initially startled and afraid, recognized Telchoff and, laughing happily, rushed to embrace him, hanging on as if he were the last man in the world. The phony TV men and the Bureau interpreter left. The two Russians sat down on the couch and the flood of words became more ordered.

After a couple minutes Morley was able to catch Telchoff's eye and point to his watch, and the well-briefed Pete patted the woman's knee. The words stopped and for the first time she noticed Morley. She smiled radiantly. "Ah, you are Godfrey, yes? I see. You help good Ivan Petrovich, friend, hah? I am happy meeting you."

Morley bowed and took the proffered hand. "I am very pleased to meet you, Mariya."

Telchoff came in impatiently. "Vonsha does not know how much time we have. Drobin come back here?"

"Da, don't know."

"Okay, Vonsha. We speak Russian. Many words, small time.

I inter-pur-et, huh, for Godfrey." He looked to Morley for an okay and for the first time saw Angela, who had taken a seat by the kitchen hallway door. "Aha, you are news lady, Miss, ah?"

"Chesley. Ann Chesley. Nice to meet you, Mr. Telchoff."

The dark eyebrows raised. "Ah! You know Pete! Is good. You are Godfrey's friend? Is okay we talk with, uh, Miss Ann Chesley, news lady here?"

Morley laughed. "Miss Chesley is a friend. No problem. Go right ahead."

Telchoff winked at Morley, then turned to Ivanova. He unleashed a few short bursts of Russian, to which Ivanova replied at some length, and with a rapidity that nullified Morley's college and army Russian. She stopped and Telchoff turned toward Morley. "She say Globitsyn like man crazy for last month. Is because old Pete escapes him, but mostly because Borodin and this Kotch—"

Morley interrupted. "She knows about Borodin and Kotch? Is this common knowledge in KGB headquarters?"

Telchoff laughed with loud delight. "Oh no, friend Godfrey! Is Ivanova good friend—I tell you—Nadi Malinova! Nadi she, you say?, con-fee-den-shul secretary to Globitsyn. She know ever'thing. She type ever'thing. She tell ever'thing to Vonsha, uh, Ivanova. Very good friend, schoolgirls, you say? Gymnasium same, hometown same. You see?"

Morley smiled. "Does she know who Kotch is?" Telchoff turned and asked her in Russian.

"Oh no, Godfrey, say not talk much about Kotch. Name on file but Nadi not read. Is in safe used only by Globitsyn. Yes, Nadi know Kotch in trouble, 'cause Borodin, but that is all!"

Morley nodded. "I see. Please go ahead."

"She say Globitsyn full much vodka tell Nadi Malinova he scared because General Secretary—is friend Globitsyn—say must take care of Kotch problem or Party will say all Globitsyn fault. You see, Godfrey, if Globitsyn lose Kotch, he lose his head maybe. Go to Siberia for sure, yes. Nadi say Globitsyn call it 'make snowball along Lena'! Ha! Funny; but Yuri Aleksandrovich not really think funny."

Ivanova, who seemed to be following Telchoff's interpretation with great interest, laughed. "Is right, Ivan Petrovich. He is worried."

"Aha yes, Vonsha. . . . So Globitsyn sends crazy Sadimoff to U.S., to kill old Pete and kill, uh, Godfrey." He looked slyly at Morley as if to say, "I know your real name," but Morley just smiled knowingly and motioned for him to proceed. ". . . and anybody who is trouble for Kotch. Now he is, you say?, con-fear-enz-ing with V.V. Asimov, longtime KGB madman. V.V. used to run wet operations, now senior consult-er, huh?"

Telchoff stopped for breath and Morley cut in. "I assume Sadimoff is your Circassian Moslem friend, the man we called the Egyptian?"

"Is right, Godfrey." He held his right palm toward Morley and turned to Ivanova, speaking questioningly, and then listening as she replied in some length. "Yes, is Nadim Sadimoff from Tblisi, senior KGB colonel, she say. Has been illegal Lebanon, Syria, Libya, many places, for ten, twelve year, she say. Is called Salim Naheri, supposed to be Palestinian. Arabs call Hummous. Famous terrorist. Very secret man. Very hot operation for Globitsyn.

"Ivanova say this Sadimoff is crazy killer, very bad man. Kill babies, women, ever'thing. But say Asimov worse bad man, and Globitsyn listens to him! Says Asimov is, you say?, umm, Indian say?, guru, for Sadimoff. Is maybe relative. Says he comes from Moskva. Nadi Malinova say no true. Is from Tiblisi too or maybe Yerevan. Not Great Russian; probably Circassian too."

Morley handed Telchoff Maksud's picture with the others. Ivanova idented it quickly as Sadimoff and then spouted Russian for thirty seconds. Pete listened and then smiled. "Yes, Godfrey, is Sadimoff. She say same man. Say Globitsyn not like use this man. He is, you say?, bloodthirsty mad man. Too

much kill, kill, kill. But he is successful and, anyway, Globitsyn listens to Asimov."

Ivanova cut in. "He is speak, uh, so . . . um. . . ."

"Good?"

"Yes, so good Engless, yes, good." She spoke more in Russian.

Telchoff kissed her cheek. "Nadi say this Sadimoff, uh, when
child, live with uncle in Beirut, learn much good Arabic, English, French. One, maybe best, KGB language man, yes."

"And Asimov is his guru and pushed him for good jobs?"

Telchoff looked puzzled, then nodded and smiled. "Ah, yes,
Godfrey, is Sadimoff guru, uh, push, yes, and Globitsyn listen, many years, many good jobs for Sadimoff."

Ivanova interrupted with a burst of Russian, obviously emotional. Telchoff laughed and patted her knee again. She looked
embarrassed. "She say Asimov very bad person, is peder-ast,
you know, molest small boys. Say is man no heart and be dead
long before without friend Globitsyn. Say too bad—Russia
much better without Asimov. Even is maybe Azerbaidzhani
masking as Great Russian! How you say, hundred p'cent
phony. Eh?"

"And this all affects Sadimoff? He acts like Asimov taught
him?"

Telchoff nodded rapidly. "Yes, Godfrey, is true. This is why
Nadi an' Vonsha do not like. Say Sadimoff not great man. Is,
uh, you say?, creature of Asimov. Globitsyn gives carte
blanche to Sadimoff, he makes big mess! Say bad for Russia.
Say Russia and U.S.A. must have peace with other. Say bad
men Globitsyn, Asimov, Sadimoff not want peace! Want to
make troubles.

"Nadi says Globitsyn tell Nadi he must okay bad things.
There is no choice: he must save this Kotch! He say okay big
killing, much U.S.A. people and blame Arabs. Sadimoff like
this. He is sadist. Likes to carve victims with knife. Some
things, Globitsyn tell Nadi, he say okay because too late not to

say okay. Must do to get, uh, Godfrey and Amis off Kotch back."

"Does she know any details on these bad things, Pete?"

Telchoff spoke quickly and Ivanova answered just as rapidly. He turned to Morley. "Nadi told her Globitsyn say one thing very bad, cause revenge, okay?, problem for KGB, but must take chance. He okay this thing, he say."

Morley's heart sank. "She has no idea what this thing, this operation is?"

"No, Godfrey, I ask same question. Say no, he not say more to Nadi, but he is afraid, she is sure."

Ivanova opened her mouth to speak, but stopped suddenly, face blanching, eyes wide in terror as they focused over Telchoff's shoulder and past Morley toward the open kitchen-hallway door. Telchoff turned slowly as did Morley, who edged to his right as he did so, assuring that whoever had scared Ivanova would have at least two separated targets. There was a big Slavic-featured man in a shapeless gray suit standing inside the open door and moving slowly forward. He was pointing a very large and lethal-looking handgun at Telchoff's chest and angrily muttering in Russian, "You! You! You!"

The next ten seconds were kaleidoscopically confusing. The big man kept coming forward, moving the barrel of his gun from Telchoff to Ivanova to Morley and back. He stopped. The gun centered once again on Telchoff, although he continued to glance at Morley.

Out of the corner of his eye Morley could see Angela, who had been shielded from the big man's view by the open door where he had come in, moving slowly and carefully toward the gunman, something in her hand. The gunman's fingers seemed to tighten on the trigger. Angela began to raise her arm, the object in her hand going higher and higher. There was a faint, then rising, crescendo of an airplane coming from the south. The noise increased as the tableau seemed frozen in time. Then Angela's arm flashed downward. There was a flat plopping sound and the big man's body seemed to collapse from the knees upward; his fingers tightening in reflex pulled the trigger just as the plane's noise was at its height. Telchoff and Ivanova ducked reflexively but unnecessarily as the bullet whined harmlessly over their heads embedding itself in the corner of the ceiling on the far side of the room.

Morley moved quickly to pick up the pistol, check both doors, and then to Angela who stood over the gunman's body with a metal statuette still in her hand. He led her back to the chair, whispered a few soothing phrases in her ear, and then went back to the gunman, kneeling down and checking his pulse. The man was alive, so he smiled and nodded at Angela. "He's all right, darling. You didn't kill him." Then he looked at Pete, raising his eyebrows. Telchoff understood fully and immediately.

"Why don't we let the ladies continue the interview in the coffee shop, Pete, while we get this man some attention."

Ivanova started to speak, but Telchoff interrupted with a quiet flood of Russian, patting her back seemingly to emphasize points. Finally the troubled look on Ivanova's face gave way to a smile. Nodding to Angela, he walked Ivanova to the door with his arm around her. Angela waited while Pete kissed the woman long and tenderly, then the two ladies went down the hall toward the lobby.

"What was that all about, Pete?"

Telchoff pointed toward the prone gunman. "Is Aleksei Feodorovich Drobin, KGB officer, Godfrey. He know me for long time. Ivanova say Drobin cannot go back Russia! She finished, husband finished, all finished! I say Godfrey and Pete we take care Drobin. Not to worry. She understand." He smiled. "So how we take care, friend Godfrey? Putting Drobin in cement mixer, huh? Okay?"

Morley smiled grimly. "I wish it were that easy, Pete. S'pose he might want to defect?"

Telchoff shook his head forcefully. "No way, Godfrey. Drobin is stupid Chekist type. Not political, just does what boss says, no questions asked. No, he would not defect."

"So he *would* turn Ivanova in to KGB."

"Oh yes, Godfrey. Is what Ivanova say. She say you just 'take care' this man, yes!"

"And we can't—I mean we don't want Ivanova to stay here. We don't want her to defect while she's here as NASA's guest." Morley looked at Telchoff searchingly. "Besides, Pete, I want you to see Ivanova once more and set up a communications link to start her reporting to you again! Okay? Will she do this?"

The Russian nodded. "Yes, I think yes."

"Good. Okay, let's haul this man over to that closet. I don't know who's gonna walk in here next. Is it possible there were *two* KGB officers with the cosmonaut party?"

"Oh no, Godfrey." He smiled, self-satisfiedly. "I ask Ivanova this same question. No. Drobin is only one."

The man on the floor groaned, and Telchoff picked the statuette off the floor and hit him on the back of the head. He lay still as they pulled him across the floor, then into a closet that housed extra china, table linens, and such. There was a knock on the door. The FBI interpreter who had been acting as lookout near the lobby entrance while the big KGB man came in unexpectedly by way of the kitchen had seen the ladies come out and wanted to know if the show was over. They assured him it was, thanked him, and he went away. Morley looked at Telchoff and winked. "Better he doesn't know, Pete. Now you watch Drobin—here's his gun—while I make a couple phone calls, okay?"

"Oh, yes, Godfrey, I watch this fucker good." As Morley exited toward the lobby and its bank of pay phones, Telchoff put the revolver in his waistband, picked up the statuette, and went into the linen closet. There was another dull thud, a pause, a second one, then Telchoff emerged from the closet, wiped the bottom of the statuette with a hand towel, and replaced it on the table where it had been when they first entered the room.

THIRTY-SEVEN

FLORIDA TO WASHINGTON, D.C.

"Godfrey, you hard-working son-of-a-gun. All the time business—you must have some holiday, vacation! Maybe go on holiday with Miss Ann Chesley, news lady, huh? Some lady, friend Godfrey." He laughed. "Old Pete think she maybe more friend, not so much news lady! Huh?"

"Pete, I should stop trying to fool you. I lose every time. For sure. Yes, she is much more friend, but also for one day she was a very good news lady. She liked Ivanova, by the way. Very much."

"Is good, Godfrey. Ivanova liked very much this Ann Chesley. Ask Ann to come to Moscow for visit. Have fun, see sights, all that stuff, huh. Ann Chesley say she like to do this thing. Yes. Ivanova say any time come!"

"And there was no trouble with our communications arrangement?"

"No problem. She say this good way. She is happy help Russia and U.S.A. have peace together. She say present KGB leadership bad, no want peace, want trouble. She help, though only on some things."

"One thing troubles me, Pete. Ivanova's motivation. This is a big step she's taking, you know. There is a great difference between keeping her boyfriend up to date on the happenings that affect him and passing secret KGB information to the U.S. government. I hope she won't get cold feet or get herself 'doubled' after she gets back."

Telchoff laughed. "No problem. Ivanova has never been Party member, never accepted Party bullshit. She say Party exploits Russian people, ruins our country, only hope is be like America. Says we strong, rich, and free, and Russia be same too if get rid of one-party state. Says KGB keeps Party in power, so get rid of KGB, get rid of Party."

Telchoff's smile was fleeting and cynical. "I am sure, Godfrey, Ivanova can be trusted and will do good job for us. You know she is grateful too we keep her and husband pilot out of trouble with Drobin."

He smiled cynically again. "Maybe she did not think how Pete and Godfrey got her *in* trouble in first place! Say, Godfrey, can you tell me how 'we' take care of Drobin?"

"Sure. Our military friends faked an accident, an auto hit and run, on Cape Canaveral. They put Drobin in the base hospital, notified Dr. Warlinsky, but Drobin 'died' before the doctor could get to the hospital. In fact, they said he was dead when they took him out of the hotel. Military police and county police are 'looking' for the hit-and-run car or truck but no luck yet. Dr. Warlinsky signed a release for the body, which was cremated, and the ashes were given back to him long before he received KGB's request for sending the corpse back to Russia."

Telchoff was grinning and nodding his head. "No KGB autopsy, you say?"

"Unfortunately, no, poor fellow! And the police have no leads on the hit-and-run car. Much like the one which murdered our dear friend Jack Glover. KGB will worry, but there is nothing they can do."

"Aha! I like that, Godfrey, that hit-and-run car just like Jack Glover. Those fuckers understand this thing; it is, you say?, their own language, huh?"

"Exactly. Only in this case they will always wonder *why* it happened to Drobin. I don't think they can or will ever connect it to Ivanova. She told Warlinsky that Drobin had said he was going to take a walk down to the ocean."

"And he is killed on this walk, eh?"

"That's what happened, Pete. . . . One other item, as long as we're talking business—before our holiday, of course." Morley looked at Telchoff, who was rolling his eyes upward in mock supplication. "What will happen to Globitsyn when we catch Kotch? And how will this affect Ivanova's position?"

Telchoff turned on his self-satisfied smile again. "I was asking same question to Ivanova, Godfrey! She say Globitsyn scared but not really too much. He is good friend General Secretary and you know, Godfrey, same as U.S.A.: boss can't fire a friend without enemy saying, 'Why you hire him in first place, huh?' Ivanova say Globitsyn will put blame on some other man just like with this Delta operation in India. . . ."

Telchoff stopped and stared out the window of the jet into the dark night over the Atlantic. Then he turned toward Morley. He looked excited. "Godfrey! I just think of something, maybe important, that I did not remember before!"

Morley waited silently, some instinct telling him this was indeed important, and that Telchoff would think it out.

The Russian began nodding slowly, then smiled. "I did not remember this, Godfrey. Is about Globitsyn and India, but I did not put it together before. Yes, it is important, I think!"

He looked very thoughtful. "It was two years, maybe some more, maybe some less; but you can figure out. You said before, 'Tell about times you meet Globitsyn' but I did not think about this time. You see, I did not meet Globitsyn, but only *saw* him in India! Yes, two years ago. You find."

Morley nodded silently.

"Was the time when U.S.A., uh, delegates come to Delhi to discuss Sikh problem, other South Asia problems, Sri Lanka, Bangladesh, you know. Meeting is secret, some say maybe Pakistani delegates come in secret too! India asked U.S.A. for help in stability in South Asia. Okay? KGB, Politburo, very much interested this, a hot item, so KGB sent priority one intelligence requirement for Residentura. You know, Godfrey, say, 'Make big push, use agents, get all results of this conference.'

"Remember, I tell you about this shithead operation Delta run by Globitsyn and his shithead deputy, Megov? This was already in planning stage so Globitsyn was pushing hard for Residentura get ever'thing about this meeting. Okay? They want to know anything if it concerns Delta."

Morley smiled and slowly nodded.

"Okay. This time Zavadze was chief and Pete number two at Residentura. I am on holiday in the mountains, up near Mussoorie, hunting, fishing, drinking vodka, but mostly getting away from shithead work Zavadze piled on! So, Godfrey, Pete come back one Sunday evening, go past embassy which is near home, and there I see Globitsyn! He is in front of embassy talking to Ambassador, maybe saying good-bye, while Ambassador's car waits. I was driving by quick, so he did not see me.

"I think this is suspicious, Pete not knowing Globitsyn is coming, but I had not been to office for week, so did not worry about it. Went home, slept, came to office next day. Busy, busy, much shitwork Zavadze save from holiday, you know. Days go by, busy, busy. Say Thursday, Friday, Zavadze come my office, sit down to have nice little chat.

"This much unusual, Godfrey. Zavadze's father is big Party man, and Zavadze much stuck up. If Zavadze want see old Pete, have chat, he would phone, say come to his office. Also he is not much for chats, you know. So Zavadze he chat about mountains, about weather, about hunting, an' then say, 'Hey, Pete, you see old friend Yuri Aleksandrovich last week?' I say no, was he up in mountains? Zavadze ignore, says no, he is in Delhi. Now old Pete interested. I smell, you say?, the rat! Ask Zavadze what Globitsyn come for India? What do? How long? Why come?

"Zavadze get very angry at not knowing answers why

Globitsyn come to India at all. I decide to push Zavadze and see what happens. Zavadze says there were two signals from Center while Pete in mountains. He says signals come Monday; first one say cancel agent assignments for getting results of big U.S.A./India conference. Second say Chairman Globitsyn coming Delhi Wednesday for a routine inspection of Residentura. Okay."

He stopped to pour a drink from the vodka bottle that stood on the table between their lounge chairs. They were alone, except for the pilot and navigator/engineer on the sleek military jet as it streaked through the night toward Washington. Then Telchoff continued. "Yes, Zavadze is really pissed off! He says Globitsyn stay ambassador's residence, but did not visit office, not inspect Residentura, not even phone Zavadze. By Sunday Zavadze was really shook up. Scared."

Telchoff was laughing as he recalled the scene, shaking his head from side to side, roaring and wiping away tears. "Oh, Godfrey, you should see this arrogant shit, Zavadze. He was terrified. He is afraid Globitsyn is angry and will send him to Siberia; or worse, leave him in Delhi forever. He thinks I am old friend of Globitsyn, so he asks please, please find out why Globitsyn treat him like so? Find out what goes on in Moscow. I say will see what I can do. Not tell Zavadze Globitsyn hate me much more than he hates him.

"So say to Zavadze, forget whole thing. Globitsyn is funny man, I say. He had some reason come Delhi, maybe have Indian woman, hot memsahib, who knows? Say has other reason, not Zavadze. If Zavadze is reason, I say, Zavadze would be long gone by now. I say not to worry—be good to old Pete, stay out of trouble. Zavadze, he thank me and says Pete is good friend, with good advice. So Zavadze he sick one, maybe two, months later. Go back to Moscow, die. Cancer, I think. Nobody say. Globitsyn leaves Pete in charge of Residentura, but never says anything about why he came to visit Delhi. I ask Ivanova. She did not know. Even Nadi Malinova not know. Maybe Globitsyn he say, 'Nadi no tell or I kill you or some such.' Anyway, it was big mystery and so I forget till now. Old Pete's memory is for shit."

Morley laughed. "No, Pete, your memory is excellent. I don't know what we'd do without it. You've remembered many, many useful things. So I assume Globitsyn just went along, thinking nothing more about it?"

"Yes, Godfrey. I think he is much like old Pete, with too much else to think about. Besides, I'm sure he did not know I saw him." He paused. "But now, Godfrey, do you think the same way old Pete does on this thing? This Globitsyn come to Delhi for reason, huh? Same reason Center say call off agents from big U.S.A. conference?"

"Exactly, Pete! The KGB never lost interest in the conference results; in fact, they wanted them so badly they sent the head man to get them—"

Telchoff broke in excitedly. "The KGB finds out after sending their signal for requirement, 'all agents signal.' They find out have agent in the delegation. With this agent at the meeting they do not want local Residentura agents to get in way!"

Morley was excited too. "And this agent could well be American, probably Kotch, or Globitsyn would have sent somebody else to handle him. He came to Delhi as Kotch's case officer, nothing else."

"I think yes, Godfrey. Globitsyn wants glory! Kotch has KGB case officer in Washington, but it is easy for Globitsyn to say bad security for this man follow Kotch to Delhi. Is true. So Globitsyn comes to inspect Delhi Residentura. Routine. Secure. Right?"

"Right. Any other answer smacks too much of coincidence. It has to be that way! Also Kotch must have been added to the delegation at the last minute."

"You can find records, Godfrey? You can tell who this Kotch is?"

Morley looked strange. His eyes clouded and seemed to look far away. Then he refocused on Telchoff. "I think so. I guess I should say confirm my suspicions." He patted Telchoff on the back. "Yes, friend Pete, I have the feeling that with your help, we are going to unearth our mole." He looked at the Russian seriously, his hand on his shoulder. "Remember, Pete, when I told you that we would avenge Jack Glover's death and fuck Yuri Globitsyn at the same time? Well, my friend, I think we *are* about to do just that."

Morley had called Kreeger from Florida and again soon after they had landed at Andrews. The news on Amanda was good only if one considered no news that way. Pansy and her two-man "family" had picked Pete up at the airport and taken him back to the safe house. Morley had left his car in the official parking area. He drove straight to his apartment. It was after midnight and it had been a long hard day. He called Angela in Chicago and all was well. Finally, teeth brushed, he crawled into bed. The phone rang. "Stan Epworth, Pat. Sorry to be calling so late. I tried to get you earlier."

"No problem, Stan. What's up?"

"Got some interesting investigative reports out of Chicago. I think we may just have uncovered the tip of a pretty big iceberg."

"Sounds interesting."

"It is, believe me. Remember, you asked us to go back and do another neighborhood check on the West side on the Czech boy?"

"Yeah. Get something?"

"I think you should read it yourself. How about getting together first thing in the morning? Eight-thirty okay?"

"Fine, see you then. 'Night." Patrick Morley drifted off into the best sleep he had had in weeks.

THIRTY-EIGHT

WASHINGTON, D.C.

Morley was in Epworth's office before eight-thirty, reading an investigative report while Epworth attacked the pile of papers on his desk. Morley finished and sat back in his chair, a sad look on his face. Epworth pushed his reading pile aside and looked at Morley inquiringly.

"It's always the little things, Stan; the one loose string that you never saw, or you saw and disregarded. I have to take off my hat to the bastards, a very well-thought-out operation."

"Yeah, except for the time bomb they left behind. But I guess you're right. Hell, we missed it twice—no, three times if you count that applicant go'round twenty years ago. And we might've done it forever if you hadn't raised the point." He smiled. "Though I must say that our man in Chicago got the willies about the same time you did, so we *may* have ended up the same."

"I'm sure he would have, Stan. It just took a new look at the record—like he and I did—and it stood out that nobody had ever questioned that neighbor! I s'pose this was the first time it was really important."

"No, I can't hide behind that, Pat. We teach our boys that *every* investigation is important!"

"Well, it was amazing. Think of the odds of that crazy old man seeing the mole after what—a fifteen-year lapse, I guess— and recognizing him as the little kid he'd known under a different name!"

"You told me you never trust coincidences, but it has to be a pretty big one—maybe an all-time winner—that old man Konig would then move into the exact same damn neighborhood that the mole was using! Fantastic."

"And then the old guy's in a nursing home 'cuz he's got about ten percent of his marbles left; but that ten percent involves remembering details from the old days though he couldn't tell you if he had breakfast today. . . . Incidentally, your agent, Finneran, did a hell of a job getting that much out of the old guy."

"Thanks, I'll tell his boss you said that. He's a good young man, I knew his dad; the kid is second-generation Bureau. Comes by it naturally."

"Figures." He laughed softly to himself, then still smiling, turned toward Epworth. "I can just see that bloody bastard Globitsyn. Here he's got this natural—a Czech kid raised in Chicago for seven years but maturing back in Prague and loving all their Communist horseshit. He's got a P.O.W. in Hanoi from that same neighborhood in Chicago who's an orphan, joined the army as a 'child,' no close friends either Chicago or Vietnam. He comes back in an exchange and the KGB keeps tabs on him. Kid never gets past San Francisco on his way home, never had much desire anyway, nothing to go home to. Anyway he dies in San Francisco, maybe the KGB helped him, maybe they didn't; but they were there and they knew—that he'd died, that he was an unidentified derelict, and that he was a person no more. Enter the mole. He shows up in Chicago. He knows Chicago, he speaks 'Chicago,' he *is* Chicago. He's got the right papers, he knows the right history, he's even got the right prints because the whole thing is a fraud! But who's to question?

"He doesn't come back to the old neighborhood. He's got the G.I. bill and he goes to school, gets his degree, and goes to Washington. The rest we know and the whole thing is damn scary. As I said, here's the sonofabitch Globitsyn: fat, dumb, and happy with his super mole upwardly mobile toward the top levels of the USG. Everybody's happy in the U.S.S.R., and Globitsyn's looking great.

"But back in this nursing home sits old Konig, like you said, a time bomb. They didn't even suspect him; hell, they don't even know he exists! Think of the irony, Stan. They try to kill Telchoff, try to kill me, kill poor Jack Glover, try to kill Joe Shola who saw the mole in Prague but can't ident him positively today, blow their best 'Arab' agent, and they still lose the mole!"

"Couldn't happen to a nicer bunch of guys. But don't be so modest. The old guy in Chicago was just confirmation. You already had your suspicions."

"Yeah, I did. The thing is that now it's no longer a deniable case, it's open and shut, thanks to your guys."

"Tickled it worked out that way, Pat. What happens now? We make the arrest?"

"Not while they've got Amanda, Stan. I'd like to leave everything just as it is—no waves, not even a ripple. Nobody but us knows about Chicago. The KGB and the mole think they've got us by the balls. Let 'em think so for a little longer."

"How much longer, Pat? You know we'll have a real problem if Sadimoff and the mole turn up in Moscow at a press conference or something."

Morley laughed. "Stan, *they* think they've won. They think their mole is safe. No way they're gonna panic and pull him out. He's getting more valuable every day where he is."

"Okay. I agree . . . but what happens next?"

"Me, Stan! They want to take me out of the game—for good. I think that's why they snatched Amanda—bait to get me on the hook."

"So? They knock you off, then what? The rest of us roll over and die?"

"Two things they don't know: one, how much we know; and two, how much I've shared with others. Maybe they think I'm a loner on this case, and that lots of knowledge will die with me, then the mole goes back to work, Sadimoff goes to Cuba. Happy ending, Communist style."

"So that's why you want the bug and the bullets?"

"Exactly. Those assholes won't take any chances. I'm never gonna get near them unless they're convinced I can't hurt 'em."

Before returning to his apartment Morley stopped by the General's office and looked at the records of the New Delhi peace conference of two years previous. Just as he and Pete had figured—the final piece.

He spent much of the afternoon writing a long and precisely detailed account of everything that had happened in the Kotch case with innumerable footnotes and references. He called the General's office and had his messenger come and pick it up. It was marked for General Ashley's attention first thing next morning.

Lastly, Morley called his various contacts to check their late news. Milford said there was nothing worthwhile; though he was still optimistic about Amanda. Byrnes had no new items; said he was going to New York later tonight on some U.N. business. Kreeger repeated that no news was good, and said he had the "receiver teams" briefed and ready, and a man in place to get Morley's signal if and when the Egyptian called him.

Next he called the General, whose first words were, "Anything new on Amanda?"

Morley's voice was bitter. "No, dammit, and the longer it goes the more I worry."

"You still think this is a ploy to get us off the Kotch chase?"

"Yes, sir. That's what scares me. I think they'd use drastic measures to convince us that Kotch is dead and I'm afraid they might include Amanda. In fact, I suspect they include me too."

The General did not seem convinced. "That's pretty drastic all right. Do you have any evidence to back up your theory?"

Morley sighed audibly. "To me it makes all kinds of sense; but, no I don't have any real evidence as to their plans. I guess I figure it's what I might do if our roles were reversed."

Ashley laughed. "No, I can't see you proposing any action that drastic, Pat. Not your style at all."

"No, I guess not; but if anything's happened to Amanda, it might damn well become my style."

The General's voice remained light. "You don't seem to have your usual optimism."

"No, I just can't be optimistic. In fact, I sent over to you just a while ago a write-up of all my thoughts on the Kotch case in the event that. . . ." Morley's voice trailed away.

Ashley's voice now showed the first signs of serious concern. "That sounds ominous, Pat. Do you really believe it's that bad?"

"Yes, I do. I hope not, but I'm prepared for the worst."

"I see. I'll be here till about nine-thirty, then straight home. Let me know if anything comes up."

"Will do, General."

"And good luck."

Morley had the sandwich and milk that Special Agent Moretta told him to use as preparation for swallowing the gelatin bug. He was watching the dusk turn into dark when the phone rang. It was Kreeger, who said he'd pick him up in ten minutes and brief him en route. Morley had a sinking feeling and a premonition of disaster.

They had crossed the Roosevelt Bridge and headed west on I-66 before Kreeger turned and said, "Bad news, Pat, in case you haven't figured it yet."

Morley just waited silently.

"Amanda's dead. An apparent murder-suicide thing. . . . I say 'apparent' because I don't believe it, and I know you won't."

"Who's the suicide?"

"Mattison."

"Of course, who else? Where is it?"

"Not far. Oakton area, just off this interstate. House owned by a friend of Mattison who's in Europe for a month."

"How'd you find it? I guess I mean who knows so far?"

"We were lucky to find it. It could easily have been several days from now. The weekly maid had cleaned two days ago. Thought she'd left her wallet, been looking everywhere else for two days, went back about forty-five minutes ago to look. Found the bodies in an upstairs bedroom and called Fairfax police. They were on the ball, sent an unmarked car with two detectives and when they called the identifications in, it matched Amanda's name with our class X APB and they called me. The detectives are there, and no one else. They haven't even called the medics. I figured we wanted this tight as hell till we decide how we go."

"Absolutely, Egil. Those bastards will call tonight, I'm sure, as long as they don't know we've discovered the murders—I'm sure it's plural. And, Egil, I can't tell you how badly I want those bastards to call!"

They turned off the interstate and then doubled back about a mile to a very quiet rural neighborhood. The house was set back from the road and had only a minimum of lights on. They could not see the police car till they turned behind the house where the driveway broadened to a parking area in front of a two-car garage. Detective Sergeant Carlen met them at the back door and led them through a long hallway and up a curving flight of stairs to a front bedroom.

Amanda lay on the floor near the bed as if she'd been sitting on the edge of the bed and fallen off. There was a wound in her left temple and lots of blood on her head, her dress, and the rug; just a little was on the bed. The blood argued that they were looking at the actual murder scene.

Steven Mattison was ten feet away, still sitting in a heavy desk chair but slumped forward onto the flat surface of a large rolltop desk. He too had a single wound, in the right temple, and with very visible powder burns. There was blood all over the right side of the desk and the man, and the rug was splattered. His left arm was folded under his head and upper torso on the desk, and his right arm hung limply toward the floor between the desk and the chair. An S&W .38 caliber revolver lay on the rug next to the desk leg.

Both bodies were fully clothed. On the desktop, pushed back to the edge of the first layer of pigeonholes, was a sheet of writing paper. It had four lines of typing on it and the initials *SM* at the bottom. Morley bent to read it. "I am sorry—about my life and my death. The life made the death inevitable, although neither was my idea in the beginning. I am sorry too about Leslie's family but now we can be together. There was no other way. I had no choice." The initials were written with a ball-point pen. There was one the same color near the paper on the desk.

Morley had not said a word since they'd entered the house. Kreeger came up behind and put his arm over the younger man's shoulders. "We'll get these sons-of-bitches, Patrick. That's a promise."

Morley turned, nodding slowly and sadly. "Yes, we will, Egil. Thanks. It may be tonight. Guess I'd better get on home." He was almost like a sleepwalker. Kreeger turned toward Detective Carlen. "We're gonna leave now. It's very important that no one knows tonight that these bodies have been found. We'd greatly appreciate it if you could keep the activity around here to a minimum till tomorrow. Bring in your medical and forensic people to be sure, but ask them to come in unmarked cars and no sirens."

Carlen nodded. "Will do, Captain. We understand."

"Good. Thanks a lot, fella."

Kreeger dropped Morley off at his front door, reminding him of the signal arrangements for this evening and night. Morley managed a weak smile. "I'm all right now, Egil. Just a little bout of self-pity. It's over. I'll be ready when they call and I know you will too! Wish us both luck and see you later, my friend." Kreeger felt better as he drove away, noting his man in place across the street.

Upstairs, Morley had another sandwich and glass of milk. Then he sat near the phone and waited. His eyes were as cold as the crispy night.

THIRTY-NINE

WASHINGTON, D.C.

The phone rang at 10:05 P.M. Morley answered after two more rings. "Mr. Morley?" A very strange accent.

"Yes."

"You do not know me. I—"

"Don't be too sure of that, Colonel!"

There was a slight pause, then a soft chuckle. "Ah, Mr. Morley, you *are* quick! You know who I am, eh? You know *why* I am here maybe?"

"I don't know. I don't even know *where* you are."

"Please, Mr. Morley, no games. I have serious business."

"Really? Tell me about it."

"Mr. Morley, we must talk."

"About what, Colonel?"

"This mole, this CIA girl. I think you have a big problem."

"Problem, Colonel? I think not. I know who the mole is. We can pick him up anytime. His usefulness to you is at an end. And you? You may get out of the U.S. or you may not; but you harm that girl and I'll come after you, friend, and that's a promise!"

"Mr. Morley, we must talk about, uh, cutting losses. You

have the illegal agent, I admit. But you do not have the girl. That is what I want to talk about: an exchange, as you say, me for the girl."

"Why should we do that, Colonel Sadimoff? Why should we bargain with a terrorist? It's against our principles, always has been."

"Because, Mr. Morley, no bargain, and we will make Miss Amanda Wickersham disappear . . . for good!"

"I suppose I must humor you. Sentiment for government employees who are paid well to take risks is not one of my failings; but you've got my curiosity up, friend. When and where do you propose we talk?"

"I will call within an hour and give instructions, Mr. Morley. You have made the right decision." He hung up.

Five minutes later Kreeger called. "We almost had him, Pat. The call was from the lobby of the Hyatt in Bethesda. I'm sure he slipped out the front door and down the stairs to the Metro. No way of knowing. Well, I s'pose he had a damn good idea of how long he could talk safely. So when and where is the meeting?"

"Don't know yet. Said he'd call back within the hour."

"D'you think he knows we found the bodies?"

"Hard to say. He's probably a hell of an actor after all these years under cover. But I don't know, it could be he thinks he's clean. Could be he thinks we bought the murder-suicide story or maybe he doesn't give a damn. After all, what've they got to lose? The die was cast when they killed Jack Glover. Mattison had become a pain in the ass. You know."

"So why the meeting? Isn't he wasting getaway time?"

"Very simple, my friend. He wants to kill me."

"But why? Why take the risk?"

"Hard to say. Maybe I bought Mattison as Kotch; if I did, great. If I didn't then maybe I'd be mad enough to meet just to get my hands on them. . . . You know, that kind of 'spy thinking.'"

"Yeah, but why this big effort to kill you?"

"Well, if I didn't buy Mattison then they might figure I've got the real Kotch pegged. But they also figure I don't have real proof yet or I'd have picked him up. So knock me off. Maybe I've been doing a solo and haven't told anyone—at least told them all. Maybe just revenge. Maybe they're just nuts. Oh shit, Egil, I don't know. All I'm sure of is that they want to get me isolated and that playing along is probably the only way I'll get to see either of them."

"I'd feel a lot better if you'd let me go with you."

Morley smiled. "That makes two of us; but I've known all along that this thing was gonna come down to me and that Circassian Moslem one-on-one. But I'm counting on your getting there in the nick of time, so to speak."

"All right. We'll be in place and we'll play it your way."

"It'll work out, Egil. Maretta tested the bug on me, on my stomach. He gives me a spread of about five minutes—thirty to thirty-five—depending on time lapsed after eating the prescribed meal."

"Uh huh . . . and in thirty-five minutes that asshole Egyptian could have you halfway to Richmond and leave our receivers sucking air!"

"I've got a feeling they won't even leave the District, though I expect they'll try to convince me that they have."

"You're betting your life on that feeling, Pat, you know that."

"Yeah, I guess so, although I've got a couple of aces to play that they don't know about."

"Remember, they're pretty good at this game too."

Morley laughed. "Don't remind me. No, I'm not underestimating these assholes, Egil. I just think they're underestimating *us*."

Kreeger shook his head. "Patrick, you continue to amaze me. In fact, your confidence seems to be catching. Damned if I'm not getting that feeling too. You know, like the assholes have had their share, and now luck's on our side!"

"Attaboy. I don't think they're any loopholes in the coverage."

"Well, we'll do our best."

"Keep your fingers crossed. See you later."

"Good luck!"

It was a few minutes before 11:00 P.M. when Sadimoff called back. He told Morley to leave immediately—"No calls, no signals, just go!"—and proceed to the Rosslyn Metro station. He said that a man in a tan raincoat and a tan hat with a red feather in the band would contact him there. He was to follow this man's orders.

His preset signal to Kreeger's watchers was simply to turn out the lights when he left. A foot man and a car would follow him because Sadimoff would expect it; but they were not to close in and not to be upset when Morley's escorts lost them.

Morley came out of the Rosslyn station and moved to the side, allowing the people behind to go past. He had palmed the gelatin "bug" and was holding it carefully in his left hand. A man in the described outfit approached with his hand out. "Mr. Morley?"

Morley accepted the handshake. He had never seen the man before but he'd examined a number of Kreeger's pictures that looked like him: young, dark hair and complexion, very Mediterranean looking. The man motioned him back into the station and down the escalator. As they reached the bottom the man pulled him around and they ducked under the rail and into the sparse group on the up escalator. The man turned to be sure that nobody else pulled the same trick. Satisfied, he guided Morley outside and to the curb where a dark-colored, medium-sized car waited. They got in the backseat and the car pulled away quickly and headed across Key Bridge toward Georgetown. Under cover of scratching his nose, Morley swallowed the "bug." He looked at his watch: 11:27 P.M.

The car crossed the bridge, turning left and then staying in the left lane of Canal Road. Traffic was not heavy but it was steady, so Morley was surprised when the driver made an unsignaled and illegal U-turn in the middle of the block, sneaking in between two oncoming cars and forcing a third into a screeching, horn-blowing stop. He went back over the bridge to Rosslyn and pulled into the Marriott parking area. Morley and the tan raincoat man got out and entered the back door of the hotel with a key. The car drove away. They took the elevator to the fifth floor and knocked on the door of Room 510.

When it opened, his companion shoved Morley inside. There were two men there and they too looked Mediterranean. One said, "We must search you. Take off all your clothes."

Morley stripped naked and stood there while the number-one man watched by the door, and the two new ones went through his clothes on the bed. They checked them by hand and eye, and then by a metal detector and some kind of a flat tool that had to be an electronic receiver. They paid particular attention to buttons, belt loops, shoes, and lapels; it was inevitable they would find the tiny bug in the belt buckle, although the metal made it a problem. When they dug it out they put it aside wordlessly and went on with their search.

They went over every inch of his body and body orifices by hand, finger, and eye; and then they used the metal detector and receiver. Morley held his breath for fear the gelatin covering might have melted too quickly. It hadn't.

The men took his wallet, watch, coins, and keys, putting them in a plastic bag and placing it on the dresser. They left the mutilated belt buckle and the bug sitting beside the bag and left. Number-one man told Morley to get dressed, and they sat there for a long time, until the phone rang, after which they left.

A different car was waiting in the back parking lot, with the two men from the room in the front seat. The car had not yet cleared the parking lot when Morley sensed a sudden movement on his left. He twisted his head to the left and started to raise his arm to defend but he was too late. The blunt object had descended and he was unconscious.

Morley's brain came back into action slowly, but he had been instinctively careful from the first stirrings of consciousness to give no sign of it. His head hurt and his right arm was sore, but as his senses came more into focus, he could determine that neither was seriously damaged. He could sense further that he was in a room with people in it, but he decided they weren't going to talk in front of him until he was able to participate in the conversation. So he opened his eyes, stirred, groaned, lifted his head, and looked around.

He was lying on a thick and comfortable rug in a dimly lit, but obviously large room. It was well and comfortably furnished, and the two walls of heavily draped windows told him it was a corner room. He turned his head as he came up to a sitting position, viewing the other half of the room. About ten or twelve feet away, sitting in a big lounge chair, was a man, an amused look on his face as he watched Morley's movements.

The man looked like his pictures, although without the mustache his face seemed thinner and more drawn—or maybe it was the strain. There was no doubt, however, that Morley was at last in the presence of the infamous Colonel Sadimoff. The watcher smiled pleasantly. "Ah, Mr. Morley. I hope I have not inconvenienced you too much, but please understand we had to determine if you were wired." He shook his index finger. "We were disappointed, but not surprised that you were." He shrugged. "That bug will only lead your friends to the empty hotel room. And the, uh, temporary unconsciousness was a necessary part of security."

Sadimoff smiled smugly. "And I can say I am certain you were not followed here. So, Mr. Morley, you and I are here alone—except for my sentries, of course—and we can have that little chat."

Morley just continued to look at the man with a puzzled expression on his face. Sadimoff shrugged again. "Maybe a drink will clear your head, Mr. Morley. Scotch perhaps, or maybe vodka. . . . Yes, I think vodka would be more appropriate." He laughed, and took a bottle from an ice bucket at the side of his chair and filled the two large ponies that had been icing in the bucket.

Morley rose, shaking his head to clear it, and moved to another lounge chair, facing Sadimoff's on the other side of a small table. Sadimoff put the glass on the table in front of Morley, touched it with his own, and drank deeply. Morley sipped his slowly. Sadimoff licked his lips. His face became serious. "Now let us talk."

Morley still sat silently.

Sadimoff's face stiffened. "All right, Mr. Morley." His dark eyes seemed shiny black, almost reptilian in their unblinking coldness, as he stared at Morley. He hissed, "Arrogant Western bastard! You think anybody darker skinned is a fool, especially Asiatics and Africans! You have made a serious mistake, my silly friend. You really think I do not know that stupid Kotch has panicked and killed himself and the girl? You really believe I would let you trap me, capture me, by pretending to trade for a girl we both know is dead? You fool, you won a battle. You have killed Kotch, yes; but you lost the war, Mr. Morley, you, personally, have lost it!"

Sadimoff seemed to have worked himself into a rage. He stood up, his body stiff with anger, and began to pace the floor. Then, as quickly as it had surfaced, his anger appeared to subside. His face softened and he smiled sadly. "No, Mr. Morley, I cannot bargain or negotiate with you—but I think you know that. Correct?"

Morley continued to stare at him silently.

"It does not matter. You are here and alone. Motivation is not important. The fact is I cannot let you go. But no matter, I cannot take your word anyway."

Morley smiled, shaking his head in amused disbelief. "What a performance—righteous indignation from a terrorist! A killer of women and children. A KGB colonel with piles of bodies behind him, who has lived a murderous lie for the last ten years, has the temerity to lecture me on morality. And on arrogance! Of course I know who you are, and why your masters Globitsyn and Asimov sent you. Of course I knew you knew about Mattison and the girl, you stupid fucking son-of-a-bitch.

You killed them. Or did you have one of your hired scum do it for you?"

Morley's scornful tirade had stopped Sadimoff in midstride and he'd turned toward him, mouth partly open, a look of puzzled disbelief on his face. Morley went on before he could speak. "And you stand here talking to me just as if you belonged to the human race, you miserable bastard." His voice took on a sad note. "Hell, you can't even equate yourself with the real Arab terrorists. At least they have *some* selfless or understandable motivation. But you, you are just a KGB fraud. And most sadly, it's all been for nothing! You are finished, Colonel."

Sadimoff's face had run the gamut of expression, from disbelief and amazement, through hot anger and cold fury, to grudging but still puzzled amusement. He smiled but it fell short of his cold, cold eyes. "Very good, Mr. Morley, you have a vicious and, uh, much practiced tongue. I frankly do not know *why* you want to make me angry, but you have succeeded. Do you have, as you say, a death wish?" He shook his head slowly. "You are a professional, Mr. Morley. You must know we can't leave you behind when I go. You knew when you agreed to meet that the girl was dead, that there could be no negotiations. I think you staked your life on the assumption you could lead your people to me. But you lost, Mr. Morley, though I *am* puzzled by your attempt to provoke me into killing you *sooner*! Was it not one of yours who said, 'While there is life, there is hope'?" This time the smile—triumphant—*did* reach his eyes.

Morley imitated the Russian's slow head shake in mock sadness. "How have you stayed alive so long, Colonel? You mention the phrase 'death wish'; do you really think I have one? Do you believe I would come into your trap alone? With no assets? Ah, you are an even bigger fool than I thought."

Sadimoff stood, hands on hips, smirk on face, watching. Morley decided the man was still too confident, so he went on. "You still don't understand, do you? I'll spell it out for you. I have known who Kotch is for some time now, and you much longer, I might add! But I didn't get the final piece of, uh, 'courtroom proof' till yesterday. No matter, it was inevitable. You KGB clowns have botched this operation up from the start—you and Kotch, and your masters, Globitsyn and Asimov."

Sadimoff could not quite conceal his surprise. Morley continued quickly, pressing his advantage—he had the Russian's undivided attention.

"You killed Jack Glover. What for? Stupid, stupid, stupid! You tried for Telchoff and me. Botched again. You sent your stupid punk assassins after Joe Shola. In case you haven't figured it out, those three are in unmarked graves and Shola didn't even remember Jerry Cerni's face! He wasn't any danger to you at all. Then you kill poor Mattison trying to pass him off as Kotch. Who dreamed that one up? Fools! We already knew. . . . But you weren't through yet, no, you had to kill Amanda. Now *you're* dead, my friend—you and Kotch. Hell, I'd've never let you *go* once you killed Glover; but now I can't even let you *live*."

Sadimoff stared in silence, evidently giving himself a mental pep talk. Finally he managed a smile, but again it never reached his eyes. "Morley, you are an amazing man, but it is you who are a fool." He shook his head slowly. "You are alone, yet you will not accept this fact." His smile became more of an unpleasant smirk as he continued. "You were unconscious for"—he looked at his watch (as Morley had noted when he first came to, there was no clock in the room)—"almost twenty-four hours." He chuckled. "Oh yes, you are a *very* long way from your friend Captain Kreeger. Your sore shoulder—where you had these injections—it tells you this is true, no? And so we see who wins and who is dead. . . . Yes, you are the good gambler, Morley, but you see it is Sadimoff holding all the cards."

Morley gave him his best "more in sadness than anger" look. "Colonel bloody Sadimoff, I know where I am; I know how long I've been here, and by now so does Kreeger. I was unconscious for less than three hours and I was awake when the needle went in. Nothing happened. There was no injection; it just made the arm sore—that's the first thing you've been right about. Believe it, your game is over. Time is running out for you two."

The Russian was starting to crack. He was puzzled and nervous. He'd never had a "victim" gnaw at his confidence like this before. He was very uncertain as he asked, "Why do you keep saying 'you two'? There is only myself and two guards outside. How many do you think, huh?"

"Come off it, Sadimoff. Kotch wouldn't miss my demise for anything. I've given him too much trouble . . . beginning in Brussels four years ago, eh, David?"

David Byrnes was his usual well-groomed self as he entered from the adjoining room. Even his face had its usual friendly smile. "Well, Patrick, you *are* right; I really couldn't miss this last scene. But, you know, it *was* a scene and you *were* acting!"

He smiled widely. "Such a line of bullshit you've been giving to my friend Nadim. I decided it's a waste of time to let the play go on any longer. If it makes you feel better, I confess I wasn't too optimistic about fooling you with the Mattison ploy. But it was worth a try. In fact, it still might fool the others with you not around. And of course, my friend, it was good enough to get you here, wasn't it?" He laughed. "Oh yes, that's why we sent the cleaning woman in. Besides, Patrick, you *are* a loner—always have been—I'm sure you haven't shared all your brilliant thoughts with the others yet."

Morley sat and stared, lines of amusement starting to show on his face. "Poor David—or should I call you Jerry, or would you prefer Erick? Anyway, you two amateurs have been out of your league. And you've gone sloppy in futile efforts to stave off the inevitable. You know, I respect patriots of any country, even spies, as long as they play by the rules, but you two went crazy. You killed Glover for nothing, Amanda for less, and even innocent Mattison, whose only crime was wanting to be left alone. Yes, we figured out the KGB has been trying to recruit him for years, trying to convince him that his mother is still alive and in their hands." Morley laughed. "Not bad really. You *might* have convinced him eventually, but I doubt it."

"Come on, Patrick, bullshit is bullshit, but that's a bit much. You want me to believe that Mattison *and* your girl were a setup . . . just to fool us?"

"You got it, pal. I wish to God I hadn't done it. I never thought you'd be so stupid as to kill them. Which one of you sold that crazy scheme to the other?"

It was Byrnes's turn to be angry. "Your biggest mistake, Morley, is talking like you're in charge here." His right arm came out from behind his back. His hand was holding a revolver. Morley prayed silently that it was the same one he'd seen that day in the desk drawer.

Byrnes was not through yet. He was smiling, pleasantly, as always. "Patrick, you must be one hell of a poker player. You're bluffing all the way. You were brought here clean, we know. The area is still clean. You talk like you're holding four aces and we know you don't even have a pair of deuces!"

Morley laughed. "Have it your way, Jerry, but everybody knows: the General, Milford, Epworth, Kreeger, and—oh, yes, let's not forget Telchoff. He really helped us pin it down. Remember your trip to New Delhi two years ago? The South Asia Political Stability Conference? Ah, yes, Jerry, I thought you might."

Byrnes was thinking. "You mentioned Brussels; you didn't like the solution to our problem?" He smiled.

"Not really, Jerry; but the General did, and I didn't think it was worth any more of our time. However, the convenient suicide of our main suspect was a bit suspicious."

"What made you change your mind—if you did?"

"Oh, I did, Jerry. Guess I've never accepted coincidences at face value. My God, man, and you had the temerity to try the same ploy again with Mattison and Amanda, just like in Brussels. You are a fool, Jerry, a stupid, bloodthirsty fool."

Byrnes was frankly curious. "But that was just yesterday;

what put you on to me earlier?" He laughed to cover his seriousness. "Not that it matters . . . now."

"Of course it matters, Jerry. I'm telling you *everybody* knows! We were just waiting for all the pieces to fit in. I s'pose it doesn't matter; you're right—for the wrong reason. Anyway, right off the bat, I should have known, but it was one of those things your brain recognizes and then stores away, and it doesn't click into your thinking till later. I talked to many people about the KGB mole but only one of them"—he smiled— "the mole himself, refused to call the mole a mole! Only you, Jerry, insisted on calling him an illegal. Think about it. So like you, really. Titles were always important to you, weren't they?"

Byrnes looked scornful. "Rather weak, Patrick, you must admit."

"Perhaps. But the other slip wasn't. It was you who put me on to the San Francisco operation, featuring the three U.S. officials with East European backgrounds. It was a legitimate lead, despite your motives; but what you forgot was that nobody but me and a few selected Agency officials in Washington knew that it was in his *last* signal that Borodin had given that clue. I was convinced that none of the Agency officials had leaked it, and after worrying a while, I had to conclude that the only place you could have learned this fact was from KGB Moscow. So it had to be you. At this point I quit speculating and began looking for evidence."

Sarcastically, "And did you find it?"

"Doesn't matter, Jerry."

"Why not?"

"When you assholes killed Amanda it became a new game with new rules. Your silent friend there"—he nodded toward Sadimoff—"he knows what I'm talking about."

"But what do you mean?"

"Oh, Jerry, you're being very obtuse. All right: you don't need evidence if there isn't going to be any trial!"

"I see." Byrnes laughed. "You're right, Patrick, but as you

said earlier, for all the wrong reasons. There isn't going to be any trial because the accused is leaving for Cuba in a few minutes and the chief prosecution witness is going to be dead."

Morley continued to smile. "Cuba, eh? Well, lots of luck, Jerry."

"Why do you keep calling me Jerry?"

"It's your name, isn't it?"

"It was." He smiled. "And I guess it will be again. Shouldn't worry about it, should I?"

"Jerry, my boy. I couldn't care less about what you worry about; but you damn well ought to start worrying about your own ass. You guys don't have much time."

"Patrick, you are indeed something else." He turned toward Sadimoff, at the same time raising his revolver, pointing it at the left side of Morley's chest. "Nadim, would you check the guards and tell them we'll be out in five minutes."

Byrnes stood there pointing the gun, silent, until Sadimoff returned and nodded to him. Byrnes's finger began to tighten on the trigger. Morley, still smiling, watched the trigger carefully. Byrnes had not cocked the gun so there had to be the first click of double action. It came. The finger tightened and Morley, anticipating the second click, dropped to the floor. The explosion came a millisecond later, just as Special Agent Johnston had said it would. It blew back into the shooter's face, also as he said it would.

Sadimoff just stood for a moment staring down at Byrnes's mutilated torso. He hadn't been close enough to catch any serious blowback, but there was a very odd look on his face. He turned toward Morley, taking his own revolver out of the shoulder holster. Morley had a few bad seconds until the Russian turned the gun butt first and offered it to him.

Sadimoff smiled. "I think maybe it was wrong to call your bluff, Mr. Morley. I do not wish to make the same mistake. You have won the game, as you call it. I have lost."

"And you will stand trial for murder, Colonel. Does that not concern you?"

Sadimoff continued to smile and then he answered as Morley had expected him to—almost word for word. "I don't worry too much, Mr. Morley. You see, my government will make your government an exchange offer; your newspapers will not let them refuse."

"You're very current on your news and your vernacular, Colonel. One would never know you'd spent the last ten years in the desert." Morley raised the revolver to point at Sadimoff's chest and began to edge closer.

The first signs of alarm appeared. Sadimoff stopped smiling. Morley came closer, gun barrel steady, finger tightening perceptibly within the trigger guard. Sadimoff said in a cracking voice, "You cannot do this thing!"

"Of course I can."

"But it's murder!"

"Of course it is."

"But—"

"But what? It was you who changed the rules, friend."

Sadimoff's move was quick and good but not quick enough or good enough. The magnum slug entered his body just below his left nipple, ploughed through his heart, and exited, leaving a large and gory hole in his back.

It was only a moment later that Egil Kreeger entered the room, embraced Morley in a bear hug, then looked down curiously at the two bodies. He smiled. "They shoot each other? I guess two to one—should say five to one—we picked up the three guards right after this one"—he pointed his toe at Sadimoff—"came out to talk to them. Anyway, I figured those odds wouldn't scare you, Pat, so I waited as we agreed—till we heard the second shot. . . . Hey! That first one was a doozy!"

Morley was kneeling, examining the remains of Byrnes's torn and misshapen pistol. "Wonder if he had a warranty on it?"

"It's possible, but dynamite probably voids it. Lucky he didn't switch guns on you!"

"No way, Egil. He was always a very orderly son of a bitch. I knew I could count on him using his own gun."

"You must be a hell of a poker player."

"Dammit, Egil. If people keep saying that to me, I'm gonna have to learn the game."

"Sure you are." He smiled and looked back at Sadimoff. "Self-defense?"

"All the way! He went for me after the other gun, uh, mis-fired. Gun went off . . . lucky it was pointed at him when it did."

"Yeah, real lucky. Guess we'd better let the boys in and clear up this mess. You want Byrnes to be an accident victim with our tame mortician in charge?"

"Right. There will be some publicity on it. The man wasn't a nonentity. Let's do it in your friend's town in southern Maryland. Okay?"

"No problem. And the other one?"

"Burn him and dump the ashes in a garbage can."

"You got it, but it won't bring Amanda back."

"I know. I wish, but it won't."

"Or poor Mattison."

"No, it won't, will it? Hey, by the way, where the hell are we and what time is it?"

"We're in Maryland, just past the Potomac area. Quiet little farm. Nice setup." He held his watch toward Morley. "It's six-fifteen A.M."

"Hmm. Well, Egil, I'm leaving for Florida this afternoon be-fore the General thinks up another one. Angela'd be tickled if I brought you with me."

"Give me a few days—a week—to clear up all the loose ends. I'll be in touch as soon as I can get away."

"Do it, and the sooner the better."

The two men walked outside. There was a line of pink-orange on the eastern horizon. Best to get busy before the local citizenry got up. They shook hands and parted.

EPILOGUE

MOSCOW, U.S.S.R.

Yuri Aleksandrovich Globitsyn watched with apparent pleasure as the trim derriere of his favorite secretary disappeared through the office door. A moment later a knock, and then she peered around the corner as she opened the door partway. "It is Sergei Mikhailovich, Chairman. He wishes to see you."

Globitsyn smiled and waved to her. "Let him in, Nadi."

The handsome young captain entered. He too was smiling. "Good morning, Chairman."

"You will have some coffee with me?"

"Delighted, sir."

The older man looked around his visitor to the secretary, who was still half in, half out of the door. "Some coffee for our guest, Nadi." He winked at her. The visitor did not notice.

The captain waited until the secretary returned with the tray, mixed his coffee, and placed it on the small table next to his chair. "You asked me to stop by this morning, sir."

"Ah yes, my young friend. I wish to bring you up to date on this affair in Odessa. I want you to go down there and help Comrade Belgrin."

"Whatever you wish, sir."

"Well, Sergei Mikhailovich, as you know, Belgrin's people picked up these two Turkish sailors about a week ago. They had been arrested for drunkenness, missed their ship, and were about to be turned over to their consulate for deportation when one of them began to tell a very strange story.

"Since I last talked to you about it, things have developed a bit more. I think that what we have here is a piece of first-rate intelligence, Mishka, and I suspect that left to his own devices Belgrin will miss an important opportunity. I want you to interrogate this Turk and follow up on his story. He says his ship delivered two loads of secret electronic equipment to Rize, a small port near Trabzon, west. We have some independent confirmation from a Kurd source that there is heavy construction going on in a valley of the Tatos Mountains about fifteen, twenty kilometers from Rize. This source said there was a new and well-camouflaged road into the valley from Rize. We have had satellite photos confirming the construction although it looked old and abandoned, but the road doesn't show up.

"Anyway, Mishka, you will understand better when you talk to this Turk. Belgrin is expecting you. I have signaled him by telex."

"And Comrade Belgrin, sir, is he pleased to have my help?"

"Sergei Mikhailovich, if you were not my good friend, I do not know how you would survive your own impetuousness. I do not give one gram of shit whether Belgrin likes it or not. As I said, left to his own devices, he would fuck up the whole operation! Do you understand?"

The younger man nodded. "Yes, sir."

"Good. Now, just do your job. Do not worry about what Belgrin thinks, what he likes or doesn't like. For your ears only, Mishka, Comrade Belgrin is being recalled. I have decided to dismiss all the henchmen of the traitor, Asimov."

"Very good, sir. I think that is a good move."

"Oh you do, do you?"

The younger man chose to ignore the sarcasm. "Yes, sir, I

think that the traitor, Asimov, had created a personality cult. One need look no farther than the incident of the other traitor, Sadimoff, in the U.S.A., who chose to obey Asimov's stupid directives in defiance of you, his Chairman! Indeed, sir, I think that prudence dictates we clear out Asimov's whole gang!"

Globitsyn looked amused; he was not displeased. "You make a good point, Mishka; in fact, it is similar to one I made to the General Secretary. He agreed we should cut out the cancer wherever it might be. He felt that we must have a smashed operation every so often as a 'cleansing and learning process.'"

"He said that, sir?"

"Yes, I think that was an exact quote."

"The Secretary General is a very wise man."

"I'll tell him you said so."

"Please, sir. I did not mean it that way."

"I know, Mishka. I couldn't resist the comment."

"If I may ask, sir, was the Secretary General angry with Asimov about losing Kotch?"

"Livid, Mishka, livid!" Globitsyn smiled widely. "He said something like 'I hope someday we can finally rid our forces of the insidious Andropov group.' Then he said he backed my efforts fully, and wished me luck!"

"Very good, sir. And may I ask also, sir, if you have decided on a punishment for this Ami, Morley?"

Globitsyn looked angry for a moment, and the younger man feared he'd overstepped the bounds of proper questions again. But no, Globitsyn's eyes were cold; it was evident that his fury was for the American. "I assure you, Sergei Mikhailovich, that I have not forgotten this man, Morley, but he is just a bad dream at the moment; when we have attended to our high priority tasks, we will then take up the matter of his, as you say, punishment. Meanwhile, back to this Odessa operation. I want you to. . . ."